Stripped

Stripped

Blue HEAT

TARA WYATT

AVONIMPULSE
An imprint of HarperCollinsPublishers

Excerpt from *Schooled* copyright © 2019 by Tara Wyatt.

STRIPPED. Copyright © 2018 by Tara Wyatt. All rights reserved. Printed in the United States of America. No part of this book may be used or reproduced in any manner whatsoever without written permission except in the case of brief quotations embodied in critical articles and reviews. For information, address HarperCollins Publishers, 195 Broadway, New York, NY 10007.

Digital Edition MAY 2018 ISBN: 978-0-06-279247-1
Print Edition ISBN: 978-0-06-279258-7

Cover design by Nadine Badalaty
Cover photographs ©anetta/Shutterstock (man); ©RDaniel/Shutterstock (badge); ©CHAIN FOTO24/Shutterstock (background)

Avon Impulse and the Avon Impulse logo are registered trademarks of HarperCollins Publishers in the United States of America.

Avon and HarperCollins are registered trademarks of HarperCollins Publishers in the United States of America and other countries.

FIRST EDITION

18 19 20 21 22   HDC   10 9 8 7 6 5 4 3 2 1

For Shannon Richard, my fellow romance author, wine lover, dog obsessive, and Chris Hemsworth enthusiast. There are a million reasons why we're friends and I couldn't have made it through this book without you. I love your face!

Acknowledgments

THE ORIGINAL IDEA for this book came to me a long time ago, and I've been dying to write this book for some time. A huge thank you to my agent extraordinaire, Sarah Younger, for all of your hard work, encouragement, patience, and support. This project wouldn't have found a home without you. Thank you, also, to my amazingly talented editor, Nicole Fischer, for your enthusiasm for this project and insightful feedback that made my idea shine. I'm so thrilled to be working with you. And thank you to the entire hardworking Avon team for everything you do.

Thank you to my family—especially my husband, Graham—for your tireless support and encouragement over the past few years. Knowing that you're all behind me means the world to me.

Shout out to my crew, my squad, my girls: Amanda,

Robin, and Sarah. The past year has been a tough one for all of us, and I'm so glad we all made it through together. I love you guys.

A special thank you to my amazing community of writer friends, especially Harper St. George, my critique partner; Nicki Pau Preto, my BAE; Eve Silver, who kicks my ass when I need it; Kelly Siskind, who is beyond kind; Brighton Walsh, who encouraged me in the San Antonio airport after RWA 2014 to "write that fucking book, girl!"; and the wonderful members of the Toronto Romance Writers, who inspire, teach, and motivate me each and every month.

Special shout out to Shannon Richard, who was there for me when I needed her most, who cheered me on, who gave me a shoulder to cry on, and who loved this book from the very beginning. Tough times often show us who we can count on; Shannon, with you I ran out of numbers.

Bonus shout outs: Channing Tatum, pinot grigio, fuzzy unicorn slippers, Chris Hemsworth, and Schroeder, the world's cutest dachshund and furriest muse.

Prologue

DETECTIVE SAWYER MATTHEWS stood stiffly at attention as sweat trickled between his shoulder blades. Thunder rumbled in the distance, pulsing through the still, thick Atlanta air. On either side of him, Detectives Jack Ward and Amelia Perez stood, unmoving. How Amelia was even standing upright, Sawyer had no idea. He'd spent the past week numbing himself with alcohol and punishing workouts, trying to forget the fact that his best friend was gone.

Murdered, in cold blood.

Behind him, row after row of uniformed police officers, all in dress blues identical to his own, filed in silently, filling up the cemetery lawn. Black-clad and heat-wilted civilians filed in too, lining the far-right side of the roped-off area, dropping into the white plastic seats. From somewhere off to the side, harp music began playing. Fucking harp music. God, Ryan would've hated that. A surge of anger pushed through Sawyer, and he flexed his sweaty hands in his white cotton gloves. A bead of sweat rolled down over his temple, and he knew his short hair was soaked beneath his hat. He clenched his jaw, just needing to get through this, and then he could shower and go get good and drunk with Jack and Amelia.

Another rumble of thunder blended with the harp, giving the music an ominous feel, and Sawyer swallowed thickly. No way was he going to cry. That was for later, when he was alone. Only ever when he was alone. Like yesterday morning, in the shower, when the tiniest memory of Ryan had snuck up on him: the two of them eating pizza, drinking beer and watching football. They'd been roommates at the Academy over ten years ago, and had been best friends ever since. Knowing he'd never talk to Ryan again, never hear him laugh or get a stupid text from him, he'd completely lost it. Sitting on the tile floor of his shower, he'd sobbed and sobbed as water pelted him. As he'd wished harder than he'd ever wished for anything in his life that it wasn't true. But for seven mornings in a row now, he'd woken up in a world where Ryan was gone.

Sawyer had gone through a shitty divorce two years ago. Before he and his wife split up, he thought he'd had his entire life figured out, but it turned out he'd been grasping at smoke, trying to hold something insubstantial in his hand. He'd wanted it to be something it wasn't. With the end of his marriage, he'd been forced to call everything he'd thought he'd known about himself, about life, about women and relationships, into question. But as hard as that had been—hell, still was sometimes—losing Ryan was, without hyperbole, a million times worse. He felt like a robot just going through the motions every day, trying to pass as human. Eat food. Drink water. Respond when people talked to him. Exercise. Watch TV. Sleep. Exist, somehow, despite the haze of grief shrouding him.

The honor guard assigned to Ryan's flag-draped casket began escorting it up the makeshift aisle between the uniformed officers and the civilians, leading it toward the open grave at the front. The harp music changed to "Ave Maria," and Amelia let out a tiny, shuddering gasp. She'd dated Ryan for over a year and she'd loved him just as much as Sawyer had, and he wished he could break formation and pull her into his arms. Not that she'd want that. She'd probably shove him away and tell him to get his fucking hands off her.

The casket came to a stop beside the grave where it would forever lie. A breeze kicked up around them, ruffling the red and white stripes of the flag, the leaves of the trees above them rustling softly. Amelia quietly cleared her throat, and when Sawyer glanced over at her, she blinked, sending two tears cascading down her cheeks. He forced himself to take a deep breath, fighting back the crushing wave of angry despair threatening to swallow him.

From his seat at the front, their team's leader, Captain

DeMarcus Hill, stood and made his way to the wooden podium. Back at the church, both the chief of police and Ryan's father had given eulogies in between the seemingly endless prayers and hymns.

"A hero. A son. A friend. A brother, to his family, and to his Atlanta Police family," he said, his deep voice booming over the lawn. "Detective Ryan Walker was all of those things and more. His bravery in the face of danger is a shining example of the courage, dedication and sacrifice required of police officers, every single day. Today, we honor Detective Walker, not only because of how he died, but because of how he lived."

Amelia wobbled slightly beside him and he glanced over, meeting her eyes. She gave him the tiniest of nods, assuring him she was okay. DeMarcus continued, listing Ryan's accomplishments, telling a funny story about his first day as a HEAT detective, praising him as an outstanding community member and police officer. After a moment of silence, he stepped away from the podium, and the chirp of a police radio echoed through the air.

"Whiskey-nine-twenty?" The dispatcher's voice came through the speakers, using Ryan's on-duty call sign. "Whiskey-nine-twenty, are you by the radio?" Silence filled the air, and a sharp ache radiated through Sawyer's chest. "Dispatch to whiskey-nine-twenty. Please come in." Lightning flickered in the sky, and Sawyer had to remind himself to breathe. It felt like shards of glass were digging into his lungs, but he needed oxygen if he didn't want to pass out. His chest constricted and he clamped his teeth together, refusing to let that wave of pain crest over him, knowing he'd drown in it.

The radio chirped again. "Mark whiskey-nine-twenty out of service." A final chirp. "Whiskey-nine-twenty, Detective Ryan Walker, badge number nine-nine-six-one, is out of service. End of watch. Rest in peace."

Amelia's face crumpled, but she kept her rigid stance, not flinching at the first volley of gunfire from the twenty-one-gun salute. Sawyer glanced at Jack beside him, and he could practically see the anger vibrating off him, his jaw and shoulders tight, his expression grim. The honor guard began folding the flag.

The four of them had been a team. But now one of them was being lowered into the ground as "Taps" played and Ryan's mother cried silently in the front row, shoulders shaking as she clutched the folded flag from Ryan's casket. Thunder rumbled through the air and a light rain began to fall, dripping off the brim of Sawyer's police cap. As he watched the casket disappear into the soft earth, anger beat hotly through his veins.

He would get the bastard responsible for Ryan's death. He would bring Ernesto Hernandez down, if it was the last thing he did.

Chapter One

Unbe-fucking-lievable.

Brooke Simmons stomped into the lobby bar of the St. Regis Atlanta, humiliation and anger simmering through her. Ignoring the confused stares of the handful of patrons sitting scattered at tables, she headed to the long wooden bar at the back of the room, her heels clicking sharply against the faux-wood tiles. She rubbed at the scrape on her cheek, blood rushing to her already heated face. Squaring her shoulders, she focused on her destination, refusing to hang her head in shame. After all, she hadn't done anything wrong, except date the wrong guy.

Again. For like the eleventy-billionth time.

Forever alone. Might as well get it tattooed across her forehead. Save everyone the goddamn trouble.

She slammed her clutch down on the bar as she

came to a halt, peering at the bottles of liquor lining the backlit shelves. *Bingo.* A small smile tugged at her lips. Nothing like a little payback.

The bartender saw her and ambled over, shooting her a smile. "What can I getcha?"

"I'll take a double of the Macallan there," she said, tipping her chin at the bottle on the top shelf.

He nodded and started to reach for the twelve-year-old malt.

"No. Not that one. The thirty."

The bartender's arm paused midair. His eyes roved over her, taking in her disheveled hair, the scrape on her cheek, the torn strap of her lavender dress. Thankfully he couldn't see the drops of blood on her skirt since she was visible only from the waist up.

"This is a hundred dollars an ounce. You sure?" he asked, studying her warily.

"Yep. Just charge it to my room. 614, last name is Karlsson." Let that fucker Peter pay for her drink. Asshole.

He studied her for another second before shrugging and grabbing the bottle. As he poured her drink, she settled herself in one of the red leather chairs lining the bar, toying with her clutch as she looked around. She could still feel the adrenaline pumping through her veins, her heart galloping in her chest.

Only one other person sat at the bar, a man in his early-to-midthirties a few seats down from her. He didn't look at her, his attention on one of the flat-screen TVs above the bar. She only meant to give him a quick glance, taking stock of her surroundings, but her eyes lingered on him. Short, light brown hair, stubble coating his strong jaw. He was muscular and broad, his black T-shirt stretched tight across his shoulders. His big hand was curled around his glass.

It was a nice hand. Strong and masculine.

She huffed out a breath and rolled her eyes at herself. She never learned, obviously. The bartender set her drink down in front of her and she took a healthy sip. The scotch was velvety on her tongue, earthy and smooth with hints of fruit and oak. She swallowed and it warmed her from the inside out. She wasn't an expert scotch drinker by any means, but she could tell this was quality shit. She took another sip, rolling her shoulders and trying to shake off the horrible night she'd had.

With a flick of her wrist, she checked her watch. Just after eleven thirty.

"Hey, can you turn it to the Braves?" she asked the bartender, pointing at the TVs. "They're in San Diego. Game should still be on."

"Don't bother. They're down by four." The deep voice had come from the man sitting a few seats away. He glanced at her and then returned his attention to the TV.

"And how would you know?" she shot back, her temper frayed at the edges thanks to the night she'd had.

He held up his phone and wiggled it at her without actually looking at her.

She frowned. "They could come back. This is September baseball," she said, and that time he did look at her. His eyes were blue, almost startlingly so. Little lines fanned out around his eyes. His skin was tanned, but he didn't look like the tanning bed, waxed balls type. There was something rugged about him. The slightly weathered skin, the jaw scruff, the big hands. The simple T-shirt, jeans and boots. Like a dude in a truck commercial or something. Normally she went for the preppy types with lean bodies and expensive suits. This guy was completely the opposite, but she had to admit that he was attractive. There was something appealingly simple in his ruggedness. As though he was a man, and she was a woman, and things didn't need to be more complicated than that.

She met his eyes again, and he quirked an eyebrow. He'd caught her checking him out, and while she might've blushed in other circumstances, getting caught checking out a good-looking man in a bar was *far* from the worst thing that had happened to her tonight. After a second, he looked away and didn't say anything, returning his attention to his drink, frowning slightly as he looked at it.

Fine. Whatever. Broody McSexypants clearly wanted to be left alone.

The bartender flipped one of the TVs to the Braves game and she settled in, sipping her drink as she tried to shut her brain off with liquor and the soothing rhythm of a baseball game. She felt her clutch vibrate and she fished her phone out.

Dani: Are you ok?? I will stab whoever you need.

She sighed and finished the rest of her very expensive drink. It was a simple question on the surface, but complicated the further you peeled it back. An onion of a question, her grandpa would've called it, if he were still here.

Was she okay? In a lot of ways, yeah. She was okay. She was healthy. Had a job she enjoyed, and was up for a promotion. She had a nice apartment and lots of friends. But beneath all that, she was lonely. And although she was trying to do something about that—God, she was trying—nothing ever worked out. On top of that, things had only been getting worse lately. Bad date after bad date after bad date, until her love life felt like some terrible sitcom. And if this was how things went when she was still relatively young—thirty was far from over the hill—attractive, with a good job, she didn't want to think about what the future held.

But underneath all of that, even below the loneliness, was the fear that she was going to end up alone. Her parents were dead, and so was her grandfather. Nan was her only remaining family, and she was ninety. Once Nan was gone, Brooke would be completely and totally alone on the planet. She had friends, but having friends wasn't the same as having someone to come home to every day. Having someone who cared *if* she came home each day.

So, given all of that, why did she keep picking these losers? What was it about her that seemed to make her a magnet for these guys? Guys who lied, who didn't have their shit together, who were just plain weird?

Mentally, trying to shore up her battered confidence, Brooke ticked through her attributes. Pretty. Fit. Smart. Funny. Good job. All-around decent person. She gave a tiny nod, trying to convince herself that the fault was definitely with the men, and *not* with her. And screw them for making her doubt herself.

She texted Dani back.

I'm fine. Please enjoy the rest of the wedding.
Sorry about causing a scene.

The man a few seats away got up and headed for the bathroom. Jesus, he was tall. At least six-foot-four, maybe even bigger, and his T-shirt strained against his muscles as he reached into his pocket for his phone. She found herself appreciating the hell out of his ass as he walked past, the way his jeans clung to the muscles. Very nice.

Granted, given her dating instincts lately, he was probably obsessed with his mother. Or he was a pervert. Or an overgrown man-child. Or married.

The word *married* bounced around her skull, and a fresh wave of humiliation crashed into her. She signaled to the bartender for another drink, again charging it to that asshole Peter's room. Pushing it all away, she returned her attention to the game. The Braves hit a two-run homer, closing the deficit in the score to two.

"What happened to your dress?" The man had returned and was now standing a few feet away from her, his bright blue eyes narrowed with concern. "Are you okay? Do you need help?" His deep voice was quiet, yet intense.

Something softened in her chest at his sincerity. "No, I don't need help. I'm fine."

He didn't answer, his gaze sweeping slowly up and down her body. Heat flushed over her skin under that icy hot stare. "You sure?"

"Yeah. Long story." She glanced at his left hand. No ring. No ring tan. At least that was something.

He squinted at her for a second, and then sat down closer to her than before, so that only one seat was separating them. The bartender set another drink in front of him, and he leaned back, one arm thrown over the back of his seat. His eyes did another slow sweep up and down her body.

"There's blood on your skirt."

His deep voice sent a little shiver through her. "Don't worry, it's not mine."

"Whose is it?"

"Doesn't matter. He deserved it."

At that, he frowned, his brow furrowing. "Did someone try to hurt you?" There was an edge to his voice, an intensity that had her toes curling in her stilettos. It did nothing to dissipate the adrenaline still floating through her system.

"No. It's . . ." She shook her head slowly. "Just a bad night."

"Mmm." He nodded and sipped his drink. Just then, the Braves scored another run, bringing the score within one.

"Told you they'd come back."

He sighed and glanced up at the TV, and something shifted in his eyes. He looked almost . . . sad. As though he were remembering something. She blinked, and the sadness was gone, replaced with that impassive, masculine confidence that seemed to pour off him.

She watched his hand as he lifted his drink to his mouth and took a sip, his Adam's apple bobbing as he swallowed. The cords in his forearm bunched and flexed as he moved, and her stomach did a slow turn.

"So, what happened?" he asked, his eyes still on the TV.

"You're nosy." She wasn't sure if she found it appealing or annoying. Maybe a little of both.

"Sometimes." He turned to face her, one eyebrow quirked. His blue eyes held hers, and just for a second, she felt pinned under the weight of his gaze. A sensation she couldn't even name exploded through her. It was lust, and need, and desire, and an appealing kind of vulnerability, all rolled into one. As though he wasn't just looking at her, but seeing her in some fundamental way.

Holy shit, he was hot. Sexy and quietly confident and . . . a *man*. He just kept watching her, and her stomach tightened and pulled. She found herself wanting to connect with him, to open up. To share the burden of her humiliating night. For some reason, even though he was a stranger, she wanted to tell him what had happened.

"I'm here for a wedding." She pointed in the direction of the hotel's ballroom. "I brought my boyfriend as my date." She knocked back the rest of her scotch. "We haven't been dating long. Anyway, it turns out that he's married."

The man's eyebrows shot up. "Damn."

"Yeah. You wanna know how I found out?" He didn't say anything, so she continued. "His wife found out about *me*, and showed up at the wedding. Confronted me in front of everyone, and then tried to fight me. Her *husband* tried to get in between us, and she caught him in the face with her elbow. Probably broke his nose." She glanced down at her skirt, her heart picking up speed as she remembered the humiliating scene. "It's his blood."

He let out a low whistle. "That's a shit-tastic night, hands down. Another drink?"

She nodded. "Yeah." Her phone buzzed again, but she ignored it. There was no one she wanted to talk to right now. "So obviously, I'm done with him."

"Obviously."

She wasn't upset about the breakup, not really. She'd only been dating Peter for a couple of months. She wasn't shattered or on the verge of falling apart. The fresh blow to her ego was hard to take, though, and she laughed sadly, trying to suppress the niggling fear that she'd never find someone, that there was no one out there for her. "Pretty much par for the course lately."

Once again, his eyes swept slowly up her body, lingering on her legs, on her hips, on her breasts. Her skin tingled and warmed, and she knew it wasn't from the scotch. No, it was from the way this man—this stranger—was feasting on her with his eyes. She let her gaze wander from his ruggedly handsome face and down his body, taking in the hard muscles, the broad shoulders, the thick thighs.

After all, fair was fair.

When her eyes met his again, something in the air around them shifted, and the tiniest hint of a smile turned up the corner of his mouth.

Oh. Her entire body responded to that twitch of his mouth. She could feel her pulse throbbing in her throat. In her chest. Between her legs. Jesus. Picking up a guy should've been the last thing on her mind after the night she'd had, and yet something about him had her thinking with her lady parts. Her very turned-on lady parts.

"I find that hard to believe," he said, his deep voice rasping over her suddenly sensitive skin.

"What?" What the hell had they been talking about?

"That shitty dates are par for the course."

"Oh. Yeah, no, it's true. Let's see," she said, holding up her hand to tick the horrible experiences off on her fingers. "There was the guy who thought vampires are real. Or the guy who showed up to my place to pick me up when he was completely wasted. He passed out on my couch, woke up in the middle of the night, then ate an entire box of cereal and peed all over my floor."

"Get out." He shook his head sadly, but amusement shone in his eyes.

She smiled, surprised how good it felt to share all of this. "There was also the guy who showed up to our movie date in a Batman onesie complete with cape."

He shook his head again. "That's pathetic."

"Oh, let me tell you about pathetic." She regaled him with tales from her disastrous dating life, including the date who'd taken her to Hooters and spent the entire time rating the waitresses, the date who'd had a surprise KKK tattoo, and the date who'd demanded a blow job because he'd bought her dinner. He listened, an unreadable expression on his face. More than once, his gaze dropped to her mouth.

"I don't know why I'm telling you all this."

"Because we're strangers. After tonight, we'll never see each other again."

She nodded slowly. He was right. There was something cathartic about talking to him, as though she could somehow purge her recent string of bad dates by sharing them with this ridiculously hot man. It felt . . . damn, it felt good to talk to him.

Their eyes met and the air between them seemed to thicken, almost shimmering.

The Braves' star slugger stepped up to the plate and Brooke reached over to nudge the man's arm. He glanced down at where she'd touched him. "He's gonna tie it up."

He frowned. "We'll see."

"You wanna bet on it?"

Any trace of happiness vanished from his face. "No."

"Anyone ever tell you you're kinda grumpy?"

"Yep." He sipped his drink, his face completely unreadable.

She opened and closed her mouth, not sure what to say to that.

"You're staying at the hotel?" he asked, his attention on the TV.

She frowned, unsure at this sudden change in topic. "Yeah." After the disaster at the wedding, she'd gone and booked herself a separate room, and retrieved her things from Peter's. She could've just driven home—she hadn't had much to drink at the wedding—but that would've made her feel even worse, somehow. Besides, she'd promised to meet up with Dani at their favorite Buckhead breakfast spot tomorrow morning.

The man finished his drink. "I'm Sawyer." He turned to her and held out his hand.

She shook it, pleasure rippling through her at the feel of his big, warm, slightly rough hand around hers. "Brooke."

He moved into the seat next to her. "I'm sorry you're having a shitty night, Brooke." Something hot and needy pulsed through her at the sound of her name spoken in his deep voice. He leaned a bit closer. "I'm gonna level with you. I'm having a shitty night too. Shitty month, really."

"I'm sorry to hear that. I'd ask if you want to talk about it, but I'm guessing that's a big fat no."

He nodded slowly. "Mmm. You would be right." He paused for a second and then turned to face her. "You wanna get out of here?"

She opened her mouth to say yes—because hell yes, she did—but then slammed it shut when she realized that wasn't a good idea. After her recent string of less-than-awesome decisions when it came to men, it was probably for the best if she kept her dress on tonight.

She tried to feign indignation, more for herself and her own willpower than for him. "What? No. I don't even know you." She pushed out of her seat, grabbing her clutch, feeling both disappointed and aroused. "Sorry if we got our signals crossed, or whatever." She spun on her heel, the tattered fabric of her skirt swirling around her knees.

"You don't actually want to walk away."

His voice hit her right between the shoulder blades, sending a shiver down her spine.

"I don't?" She turned to face him and their eyes locked.

He gestured at the empty chair beside him. "No."

"And you know that how?" she challenged him, taking a step closer but not sitting back down. She felt slightly unnerved at how well he could read her. Unnerved, and turned on.

He smiled and his entire face changed. It lit up like a Christmas tree, his blue eyes sparkling as the skin around them crinkled. With that smile, he wasn't just sexy. He was devastatingly handsome.

Oh. Oh, oh, oh.

"Sit down and I'll tell you."

With her heart pounding in her chest, she sat down in the seat beside him, close enough that she could feel the warmth from his skin. He was right. She didn't want to walk away. Everything she wanted was tied up in this man.

"I'm listening," she said, setting her clutch back down on the bar.

He leaned a bit closer, and she caught a whiff of something faintly spicy. She wasn't sure if it was his aftershave, or just his skin. She licked her lips and swallowed, breathing him in. He smelled good. Better than good. Like man and sex.

He closed a hand around her forearm and an electric current shot through her. Her entire body was vibrating at the feel of that big hand wrapped around her, his skin against hers.

His voice was low when he spoke, and she felt every single syllable deep in her belly. "You noticed me the second you walked in here, and I felt you notice me." His thumb rubbed a slow circle against her wrist, sparks emanating outward from his touch. "Your pulse is racing. Your pupils are dilated. You like what you see. You like my hand on you. Every time you make eye contact, I feel it, like a kick in the gut. I bet you do too." He reached up and tucked a strand of hair behind her ear. "You're fucking gorgeous," he said, his voice a little rough. His fingertips were coarse but gentle against her skin, and goose bumps erupted everywhere. She inhaled sharply, and it wasn't butterflies flapping in her stomach.

It was a whole damn menagerie.

He leaned in closer and his breath tickled her skin in an immensely appealing way. "I swear on my life that I'm not married, or a secret weirdo of some kind. I don't have any tattoos, and I definitely don't own any onesies." He dipped his head and inhaled, and her entire body pulsed with awareness.

"Did you just smell me?" she asked, her voice barely above a whisper.

"Mmm." The sound came out low and gruff, and she felt an answering tug in her stomach. Never in a million years would she have thought she'd find the whole caveman thing appealing. But right here, right now, it was really working for her.

Insanity. That's what this was. She'd endured one too many bad dates, and she was finally losing her damn mind. Because what she wanted, more than anything, was to kiss this man. She didn't even know his last name, didn't know where he was from, but she knew she wanted his mouth on hers. After the horror of her evening, she wanted to feel desirable. Wanted to feel needed. Wanted to feel good.

Wanted him.

"You're thinking about kissing me," he said, staring at her intently as though he could read her mind. Hell, maybe he could. He met her eyes. "Let me tell you something, Brooke. Life is real fucking short, and you should go after the things you want while you've got the chance." The sadness she'd seen in his eyes earlier returned, and her chest constricted in sympathy.

"You're practically a stranger," she whispered, but it didn't feel like an argument against taking him up to her room. The fact that she didn't know him was hot, and slightly taboo, and turning her on more by the second.

His lips brushed against her ear as he spoke. "Doesn't mean I can't give you exactly what you need."

She pulled back to meet his eyes. So blue. So guarded, as though he were fighting back those flashes of pain. As though he wanted this as much as she did. "And what is it I need, Sawyer?"

"To forget about the string of losers you've been dating."

"And you think you're the man for the job?"

"You tell me." He cupped her cheek and kissed her, his lips firm and warm against hers. He kissed exactly the way she expected him to, with confidence and a rough edge, taking what he wanted. There was nothing tentative or uncertain in the way his mouth moved against hers. He nipped at her bottom lip and she swayed, her body melting into his. He soothed his bite with a swipe of his tongue, and she opened for him with a soft moan. He let out a low, approving rumble and claimed her mouth with slow, hot strokes of his tongue. Fire licked over her skin, and she forgot everything—her name, where she was, her horrible night—it was all obliterated by the feel of Sawyer's mouth on hers, of his tongue sliding against hers in a dirty, promising rhythm. He made a gruff sound and deepened the kiss, the taste of his scotch mingling with hers. His stubble rasped against her skin, intensifying the friction of their mouths. His hand moved from her cheek to the back of her head, and with his fingers tangled in her hair, he tugged her closer.

Holy hell, the man could kiss. She wanted to drown in it, the rough, demanding way he owned her mouth with his. Never would she have thought that she'd like to be kissed like this, but now she wasn't sure how she'd ever go back to uncertain, limp, tentative kisses.

And if this was how he kissed, she was about ready to dissolve into a puddle of lust imagining how he did other things. Her entire body felt like one giant throb, with her clit at the epicenter. He groaned against her mouth, the sound vibrating through her, winding her tighter. She'd never felt so achingly empty, so wet, so desperate for more from a kiss before, and she knew her mind was already made up.

He was right. This was exactly what she needed. What they both needed, if she had to guess.

She managed to break the kiss, tearing her mouth away from his. "Yes. Upstairs. Now."

THE ELEVATOR DOORS slid closed and Sawyer tugged Brooke against him, wanting to drown in her mouth, in her body. To feel something good. To forget about the near constant ache in his chest, just for a few hours. Drinking, punishing workouts, burying himself in cases, nothing worked. So it was time for a new plan. He was going to fuck this woman's brains out and make her lose her damn mind in the hopes of shutting his off. A night of distraction and relief. Exactly what he'd been hoping to find.

As he crushed his mouth to hers again, she moaned, her tongue stroking against his, sending more blood rushing to his already hard cock. He trailed his hands down her back and to her ass, giving her cheeks a firm squeeze. With a soft chime, the elevator doors opened onto her floor, and she broke the kiss. Threading her long, slender fingers through his, she led him down the hall. Her blond hair fell in styled waves around her shoulders, and when she glanced back at him over her shoulder, her warm brown eyes sparkled at him as she smiled. God, she was pretty. High cheekbones, delicate features, killer smile. She was tall, at least five-foot-ten, with slender arms and long, toned legs. Clearly fit, she moved with an athletic grace that he'd found appealing the second he'd laid eyes on her. Small, perky breasts, and what had felt like an equally perky ass, but he wouldn't know for sure until he got her out of that dress.

As far as distractions went, he could've done far, far worse. She'd come across as funny and confident despite her string of bad dates. She'd exuded a warmth that he'd found immensely appealing. He'd tried so hard to stay numb in the week since Ryan's funeral, but she'd melted that hard knot in his chest so easily, reminding him of what it was like to feel good.

The ripped strap of her dress slid down her shoulder, and he reached forward and pushed it back into place, letting his fingers linger on her soft, warm skin. She turned suddenly and fisted her hands in his shirt, pulling his mouth back to hers, kissing him hungrily, catching him off guard. A low, gruff moan rumbled from somewhere deep in his chest and he slid his arms around her, pulling her tight against him. Her body fit perfectly against his. A surge of something hot and sweet curled through him, and he knew he'd made the right decision to try to pick her up. Vaguely he wondered where she was from, what her last name was, what she did for a living, but none of that mattered for tonight. This wasn't a date. This was sex.

Not that he dated, in the traditional sense. Hadn't since the divorce. No, it was always just sex, and he liked it that way. Simple. Easy. Painless.

He deepened the kiss, claiming her mouth as images flashed through his mind. Everything he wanted to do with Brooke. To her. Have her do to him. Given the deliciously greedy way she was kissing him, she seemed to be up for what he liked, what he needed, but he had to be sure. Something was coiling tight inside him, and he knew it was only a matter of time—minutes, probably, with how damn good her mouth felt—before it snapped free and he gave in to the hot oblivion that came with hard, dirty fucking. He broke the kiss and spoke low, urgent words against her throat. "Tell me if I get too rough with you."

Heat flared in her eyes and she rocked her hips against him, letting out a shuddery breath when his erection slid against her hip. She bit at his bottom lip, tugging and then releasing him with a slow smile. "I like rough."

Halle-fucking-lujah.

She scraped her nails down his chest, just enough to sting even through the cotton of his T-shirt, and he smiled. For the first time in weeks, luck was on his side. He kissed her again, deep and bruising, and she sighed against his mouth. Blood rushed through his veins, and his cock throbbed against his zipper. The temptation to back her up against the wall and fuck her in the hallway was strong, despite the likely indecent exposure charge they'd both get when caught. Something was building between them, an explosive need, with each kiss, every touch fueling the fire. He needed this woman with an intensity that ripped through him like nothing he'd ever felt before.

With a growl, he broke the kiss. "Which room?"

Her hands trembled a little as she fumbled for her

key card in her bag, and a sense of pure, masculine satisfaction cascaded over him. He'd done that to her, with his mouth, his hands, the few words he'd said. And he couldn't wait to do more. She led him two doors down from where they'd stopped and slipped the card into the slot. The lock released with a click, the little green light flashing.

Green light. Go.

As though she'd read his mind, she pushed her hands up under his shirt as they stumbled into her room, a mess of hungry mouths and tangled limbs. In a swift series of movements, he yanked his shirt off over his head, dropped it to the floor and kissed her again, slow and deep. Her hands traced over his biceps, across his pecs and down his abs. She let out a low, appreciative moan and broke the kiss.

She took a half step back, her eyes devouring his naked chest in the semidarkness. "I need to see you." She stepped away, kicking off her shoes, and the bedside lamp flicked on. Brooke crawled across the bed toward where he stood at its foot. "Oh, hell yes," she breathed, coming to a stop in front of him, her fingers tracing over the ridges of his abs. "Even better than I hoped. Almost perfect."

He started to smile, but then stopped. "Almost?"

"I'm not done checking you out yet. Final verdict isn't in." She kissed a path over his chest, her teeth nipping at his skin. Then, her eyes holding his, she skimmed a hand lower, down to the bulge in his jeans.

She rubbed her palm up the length of him and her mouth fell open. "I take back the 'almost,'" she whispered, stroking him through his jeans. He rocked his hips into her hand, wanting more of her touch, and for a second, he closed his eyes. Just letting himself feel good. And sure, part of it was the fact that Brooke was stroking his cock, but there was more to it than that. It was something about this woman. She was ballsy, sexy as fuck, and had an edge to her he found immensely appealing. The fact that she was so clearly turned on by him . . . damn, that felt good.

She undid the button of his jeans, lowered his zipper and pushed his pants down. Before he could regain control of the situation, she lowered herself to her hands and knees, freed his cock from his boxer briefs and licked up the length of his shaft.

"Holy shit," he ground out, tangling his hands in her hair. She closed her lips over his head and took him deep into her mouth, one long, teasing pull. Fuck, this was hot. Thirty minutes ago, they'd been complete strangers. And now here she was, still fully dressed with his cock in her pretty mouth. After several sweeps of her lips and tongue, she pulled back, letting the head of his cock rest against her mouth. She looked up at him through her lashes, rubbing him against her lips. She quirked an eyebrow at him, and just that eyebrow was so fucking sexy that his balls tightened. "I thought you wanted rough," she said, licking her lips and the head of his cock all at once.

Jesus Christ. Who *was* this woman?

He knew what she was asking, what she was inviting him to do, and he tightened his fists in her hair. He thrust his hips forward as he urged her toward him, fucking his cock into her mouth. She moaned enthusiastically and swallowed, her throat working around him. Wet heat engulfed him, sending searing pleasure licking up his spine. Goddamn, she felt good. Not just her mouth. Her fucking throat. With his hands still fisted tightly in her hair, he dragged her head back, watching as his cock slid free. Mascara was smudged below her eyes, giving her a debauched look that only turned him on more. Unable to help himself, he thrust back into her mouth, and she swallowed him again with a moan that vibrated through him. Christ, he could come like this, but that wasn't what he wanted.

Brooke was a gift, one he intended to unwrap and enjoy fully. Coming in her mouth—her sweet, gorgeous mouth—ten minutes in wasn't the plan. He pulled her hair, easing her away from his cock, and brought her up onto her knees. Tilting her head to the side, he nipped at her neck, biting softly at the curve of her shoulder, trailing hot, openmouthed kisses and bites up and down her neck. She moaned and writhed against his grip, a flush spreading across her skin.

"You have something else to wear home tomorrow?" he asked against her skin.

"Y-yeah. Oh, *God*," she moaned loudly when he sucked the skin just below her ear. He let out a gruff moan of his own, because fuck, her responsiveness was hot.

"Good." He released her hair, tangled waves falling around her shoulders, and gripped the front of her dress, ripping it open. She let out a gasp that grew into another moan when he tugged down her strapless bra, freeing her breasts. Circling an arm around her waist, he roughly palmed one breast, her nipple a hard peak against his hand. He dipped his head and scraped his teeth over the nipple of her other breast. Her head fell back and she made a series of incoherent sounds as he sucked her nipple into his mouth, not being gentle about it. Whimpers and moans and grunts, feeding both his ego and his erection. He managed to kick free of his boots, pants and boxer briefs, and then joined her on the bed, still tormenting first one breast and then the other. She reached behind her and undid the zipper of her dress. It fell off her, the torn fabric pooling around her knees, leaving her in only a red lace thong.

He eased her down onto the bed, shoving her torn dress to the floor. She wrapped her fingers around his cock, stroking him while he devoured her with his eyes. Blond hair fanning out around her, makeup smudged around her eyes, red patches on her neck and throat from his stubble. Lips swollen from kissing, from sucking his cock. Gorgeous little breasts, barely a handful, topped with small, light pink nipples. Her body was long and lithe, all soft skin and toned muscles.

So fucking sexy that he couldn't have conjured anything more perfect had his life depended on it.

He hooked his fingers into her thong and slid it down her legs, then tossed it over his shoulder. With his hands on her hips, he tugged her toward him and pushed her legs apart. He grunted appreciatively. Her pussy was bare minus a sweet little triangle of blond hair in the center of her mound. He settled himself between her legs, nipping and kissing at the insides of her thighs. She propped herself up onto her elbows, watching him with an adorably naughty smile on her face. He kissed her swollen clit and then inhaled deeply, wanting to memorize her scent. His mouth watered and his cock throbbed at how good she smelled. Like woman and sex and heaven. He closed his mouth over her and swirled his tongue over her folds in one long, slow lick.

"*Fuck*, Sawyer," she moaned, falling back onto the bed. The sound of his name on her lips in that strangled voice sent a bolt of heat streaking through him, like lightning, and the need to make her come seared through him. With long, slow, teasing kisses, he explored her, tasting her, drinking in the sounds of her sighs, her moans. Her hips shifted under his grip, and she writhed against him, wanting more. He nipped at her, licking and sucking and teasing. She tensed, her moans getting louder, and he sucked her clit into his mouth, swirling his tongue over and around it, but only for a second. Bringing her to the brink, but not letting her come. Letting it build.

Wanting it to be something she'd remember, and he knew he shouldn't be thinking that way. It didn't matter if she remembered him. Tonight was all that mattered. It hit him that it was for the best that he had her only for tonight, because fuck, he could get lost in her. Lost in a way he couldn't afford. Lost in a way that would end in heartbreak.

He backed off, going back to teasing kisses and licks, moving his lips and tongue over her wet, swollen flesh. Her hands slid into his hair, her nails raking across his scalp.

"More," she panted out, and he smiled against her as her hips shifted restlessly. He deepened his kiss, tasting and exploring again, sliding his tongue over her clit in slow, swirling strokes. Her hands tightened in his hair. "Oh, fuck, don't stop. You are *so good* at this. Oh, shit. Shit!" She tensed and then bucked against him, coming hard with long, loud moan.

But he wasn't done. He'd just made her come, but somehow it wasn't enough. He felt greedy for her—for her taste and smell, for the sounds she made for him, for how fucking good she made him feel. He slid his hands up her thighs and pushed her legs back until her knees were practically at her shoulders. Working his mouth over her clit, he slipped a finger inside her, slowly stretching her as she contracted around him. He added a second finger, curling them up as he ate her.

She clamped down around his fingers and screamed, her clit pulsing as she came against his mouth for a second time. He kissed the backs of her thighs as she came down, riding out the waves of pleasure, but he left his fingers inside her, still fucking her, stretching her out.

"I need more," she said, her voice husky. "I need you inside me. Fuck me, Sawyer." She looked up and met his eyes. "Hard and rough like we both want."

He slipped his fingers free of her body and sucked them into his mouth, savoring her taste. He quickly retrieved his jeans and pulled a condom from his wallet, tearing it open and rolling it on as he climbed back onto the bed. He kneeled in front of Brooke, guiding her trembling legs so that her ankles rested on his shoulders. He notched the head of his cock at her soaking wet entrance.

"Tell me again," he said, his voice hoarse.

"Fuck me, Sawyer. I need your cock inside me."

He groaned and pushed into her, swearing as he went. She was so wet, so hot and tight around him. So perfect. He swiveled his hips, working himself in deeper, and her back arched up off the bed. Their eyes met, and he stilled, buried deep inside her. Something unspoken passed between them. A connection tinged with sadness, because they both knew this was only for tonight. But he pushed it away, just wanting to feel good.

He pulled his hips back and thrust his cock into her at full force this time, and she cried out, her hands fisted in the duvet. With his hands tight on her hips, he started to fuck her in earnest, hard and deep, Brooke's throaty moans urging him on. His balls slapped against her as he buried himself over and over again, giving in to what he needed and losing himself in her body. In how good she felt.

How good it felt not to hurt, even for just a little while.

Brooke cried out, and liquid warmth flooded his cock. She was so gorgeous, so responsive and uninhibited that as his balls tightened and heat pooled low in his gut, his chest cracked open, and something that felt a hell of a lot like regret wormed its way in. Brooke pulsed around him, coming hard, her limbs shaking, his name falling from her lips, and he followed her over the edge, his cock throbbing as he came buried deep inside her.

Chapter Two

"WHAT THE HELL happened to you?" Dani Harris pulled off her sunglasses and shoved them up onto her head, pulling her black curls away from her face as she scrutinized Brooke. Feeling as though she were floating, Brooke dropped into a chair across from her friend on the terrace of Dixie Kitchen, an upscale breakfast joint on Peachtree that was a must for Brooke anytime she was in Buckhead.

"What do you mean?" asked Brooke, shrugging innocently and pulling the coffee Dani had already ordered for her toward herself. She took a sip and set down her cup, breathing in the fresh, warm air. A few clouds dotted the clear, blue sky, the Atlanta skyline rising up and gleaming in the sun. Old-school soul music played through the restaurant's speakers, mingling with the sounds of traffic and conversation.

Dani arched an eyebrow and pointed at her with a spoon. "You look tired, but glowy. Beard burn on your neck." Her eyes skimmed over Brooke, and it was as though she could still feel Sawyer's hands and mouth on her. She ached between her legs, but she clenched her thighs together against the throb thinking of Sawyer elicited. "You *almost* covered up that hickey with makeup. Another layer would've done it. Bet you've got fingertip bruises on your hips and thighs. And I know none of that is courtesy of Peter, whose wife practically dragged him out of that reception last night." Dani snorted. "Fucking pathetic. Him. Not you." She dropped her spoon onto her saucer with a clatter, and the breeze stirred the air around them, the elegant tan-colored umbrella over their table flapping softly. "So. You got fucked, and well, from the Cheshire cat grin you're sporting. Spill."

The waitress came by just then, sauntering away after they'd ordered their fried green tomatoes, pimento cheese, fried chicken and buttermilk waffles.

"I went to the hotel bar to cool off last night after shit went down. And I ended up bringing this guy—this *stranger*—back up to my room. You should've seen him, Dani. Gorgeous. Body of a god. Like Thor."

"Where did he rate on the Dickter scale?"

Brooke laughed. "Let's just say he'd give Thor's hammer a run for its money." She shivered despite the warm air around her.

"Did Thor have a name?"

"Sawyer." Brooke chuckled. "I don't even know his last name. Shit, I don't even know where he's from." A wave of . . . not sadness, that wasn't the right word, but *something* tugged at her, vaguely and delicately melancholy.

"So what happened?"

She settled back in her chair and told Dani the entire story of how Sawyer had picked her up in the bar. How in control and *masculine* he'd been. How they'd had freaking fantastic sex—twice—and then he'd kissed her, said thank you, and left. She'd fallen into such a deep, relaxed sleep that when she'd woken up, for a second, she thought she'd dreamed it. But she was deliciously sore, her muscles tired, and her body completely satisfied.

By the time she was finished with her story, not sparing any of the dirty details, their food had arrived. Dani shoveled some chicken into her mouth and then sawed off a bite of waffle. "So you didn't get any of Thunder Dick's details? I mean, I can't really put out a BOLO with just a first name and a description of his equipment."

Brooke laughed, and there was that tug in her chest again. "No. And you know I hate this expression, but it was what it was. We both got it." And they had. The rules, the expectations had been implicit. She couldn't change them after the fact, no matter how much she might want to. She couldn't remember the last time she'd been so instantly drawn to someone. The chemistry between them had been immediate and intense. She'd never experienced anything quite like it.

Dani snickered. "Yeah, you both got it."

"You know what I mean. We understood that it was just for last night. We both needed that, I think." Her mind flashed back to the sadness she'd seen in Sawyer's eyes, and she wished she'd talked to him more. Hoped he was okay. That whatever had put the pain there would get better. Hoped that spending the night with her had helped him, really had been what he'd needed.

Dani nodded, not judging. They'd met on the job a few years ago, and while they didn't work together anymore—Dani had been promoted to Homicide about a year ago—they were still close. "Speaking of last night, you wanna press charges against what's-her-face? Peter's wife? Ugh." Dani stuck out her tongue, making a disgusted face that basically summed up Brooke's feelings.

Brooke shook her head. "Nah. Not worth the mess. I'm still waiting to hear about that detective opening in HEAT. Last thing I need right now is drama. I've already been turned down once before. It would be satisfying as hell to slap cuffs on her, but I don't want to do anything to hurt my chances."

Dani nodded, chewing thoughtfully. "I hear you. Man, I can't believe you're up for HEAT. So badass."

"Hey, Homicide's pretty badass." But Brooke smiled because Dani was right. It was no secret that Atlanta had one of the highest crime rates in the country. A few years ago, HEAT—the High-Risk Evaluation and Action Team—had been created to address some of the most dangerous crimes plaguing the city: drugs, weapons, human trafficking, and gang activity. It was an elite unit of detectives, without a doubt. Brooke had already passed the physical test, the written test and the first interview. She had a second interview tomorrow, along with a glowing recommendation from her current captain. She'd applied for Homicide a year ago, but the rejection hadn't deterred her. No, it had only motivated her to work harder and do what she needed to do to earn that detective shield.

"It is, but it's not the same as HEAT. The undercover shit is so cool. I'm gonna be jealous if you get in."

Brooke laughed. "Let's wait and see what happens. But I have a good feeling about this."

"You're in a disgustingly good mood this morning."

Brooke laughed again and popped a piece of tomato in her mouth. Damn. Even her jaw was sore. "Let me tell you something, my friend. Spending the night getting your brains fucked out and coming over and over does wonders for a woman's outlook on the world."

"Mmm. I'll bet it does."

And it was true. She'd woken up feeling happier, more optimistic, more satisfied and alive than she had in a long time.

It really was a shame she'd never see him again.

SAWYER YANKED OPEN the door to The Speakeasy, cool air washing over him and raising goose bumps on his skin as he stepped inside and out of the muggy evening air. A storm had blown in and out over the afternoon, leaving behind a gray sky and a fuzzy rainbow. He'd never been one to look for signs and symbols, and he wasn't a religious guy, but from his desk in the HEAT bullpen, he'd stared at that rainbow until it had faded. Wondering. Hurting. He'd spent hours sifting through the case files on his desk, feeling both restless and unfocused, trying to keep his gaze away from Ryan's empty desk, which sat directly facing his own.

He sighed as he moved further into the bar, wrapping his grief and his guilt tighter around himself like a blanket, until it was part of him. Maybe, with time, it wouldn't feel so heavy. Maybe.

DeMarcus waved him over, the others already seated at their regular table. As he approached, Sawyer tried not to stare at the empty chair where Ryan had always sat. He fought the urge to rub a hand over his chest, where a dull ache was throbbing. Ryan was supposed to be here. But in the span of a few minutes, everything had gone sideways.

Everything. And now everything felt like nothing. Empty and cold and unreal.

He dropped into his usual seat, between Jack and Ryan's empty chair. Without a word, he reached for a glass and the pitcher of beer on the table. Once he'd poured himself a pint, he sat back and sipped, surveying his colleagues. There was no bragging about recent arrests, no ball busting, no raunchy jokes, no shop talk.

A silence hung over the table like a rain cloud, gray and heavy.

"How you doing?" he asked Amelia, who was staring into the bottom of her half-empty pint glass as though it held the answers to all of life's burning questions.

She hitched one shoulder, not looking up, and Sawyer's heart hurt for her. She'd joined their team two years ago, and she and Ryan had been dating for nearly a year. Had dated. Past tense, now.

She reached into her purse and chucked a small box onto the table. Sawyer's stomach lurched, because he knew exactly what was in that box.

"His parents found this. In his sock drawer, when they were . . ." She cleared her throat. "You know."

Jack reached for the box and popped it open. The small diamond ring caught the light, sparkling softly. His light blue eyes narrowed and he shoved a hand through his dark blond hair. "*Shit.*" He glanced up, the lines around his eyes softening. "I'm sorry, Ames."

Sawyer rubbed a hand over the back of his prickling neck and then took a healthy swallow of beer. It hadn't occurred to him to warn Amelia or Ryan's parents about the ring. In the midst of his own pain, he'd forgotten about it. Now he felt like an asshole.

Nothing new there.

"I tried to give it to his parents, but they told me to keep it." She spoke the words in a flat, monotone voice, sounding unlike herself.

Sawyer frowned. "Did you drive here?" he asked, his

eyes darting to the window as he scanned the parking lot for her Harley.

"Nope. Took a fucking Valium and called an Uber. I can't feel any more today."

A silence settled over the table, and Sawyer drifted back into his thoughts, both welcoming and pushing away the onslaught of memories that pelted him like hail each time he let his mind go idle.

"You gonna keep it?" asked Jack, raising an eyebrow.

Amelia snatched the ring box back and snapped it shut. "Why? You want it, Posh Spice?" Jack came from money and good-naturedly took a lot of shit for it. He and Amelia were partners, and this kind of sparring was completely normal for them.

Never had normal felt so weird.

Jack sipped his scotch and smiled, a teasing glint shining in his eyes. "Bit smaller than I'm used to."

"I'll take Things Your Date Said Last Weekend for $500, Alex." Sawyer made the joke Ryan would've if he wasn't dead. As soon as the words were out of his mouth, he felt bad, knowing that he probably shouldn't be cracking jokes. But after a heartbeat of silence, they all laughed, Jack shaking his head, Amelia smiling ruefully down into her beer. The knot in his chest loosened slightly. He topped up his beer, feeling both guilty and relieved that they were laughing.

"Yeah, I'm gonna keep it," said Amelia, slipping the velvet box back into her purse, an unreadable expression on her face. He watched her take a couple of deep breaths before she propped her elbows on the table, leaning forward. "Ryan would've wanted me to."

They all nodded, and Sawyer couldn't stop himself from thinking about all the things Ryan would've wanted had his life not been cut short.

Amelia sat up and squared her shoulders, blinking away the hurt that had clouded her eyes just a second ago. "Let's talk strategy. What's our game plan for bringing down this *hijo de puta*?"

Sawyer's mind lurched back to that night, somehow only two weeks ago. He and Ryan had been parked in an unmarked police vehicle, staking out one of drug lord Ernesto Hernandez's known associates, following up on a tip from one of Ryan's CIs about the Baracoa cartel. They'd been doing surveillance for hours without any sign of Hernandez or his associate, and Sawyer had ducked out to make a coffee run.

Not sixty seconds later, someone had slipped into the vehicle and shot Ryan in the head at point blank range. They had no physical proof it was Hernandez, but Sawyer had recognized his voice over Ryan's radio when he'd tried to signal for help. The dash cam had caught a shadowy figure matching Hernandez's build running away from the scene. But a snippet of voice on the radio and a man's silhouette on the dash cam weren't even close to enough to move on Hernandez, even if Sawyer knew down to his bones that he was the one who'd killed Ryan.

When Sawyer had returned to the car less than five minutes later, Ryan was already gone. Sawyer's stomach heaved as he remembered the lifeless sheen of Ryan's eyes, bits of blood and bone and brain spattered over the car's interior. Someone had tipped off Hernandez that he was being investigated, and the murder was clearly a message to the APD to back off.

Fat fucking chance of that.

Guilt gnawed at him as the scene played back again, searing itself into his brain.

If he hadn't left to get the coffees . . .

If he'd checked out Ryan's CI—who'd clearly set them up—more thoroughly . . .

If Ryan had gone to get the coffees instead . . .

If. If. If. The word beat against his skull, vibrating through him and chasing away the tiny bit of comfort from joking around.

DeMarcus sat up straight, mirroring Amelia's posture, the dim light from above gleaming against his bald head. "None of you should even be working right now," he said, his deep voice carrying a gravelly undertone. A beat of silence passed as he let his words sink in. "Raise your hand if you've seen the department's therapist." All hands stayed firmly down. No fucking way did Sawyer want to go talk to some stranger about what had gone down. Talking wouldn't bring Ryan back, and it sure as hell wouldn't make him feel better.

DeMarcus sighed, a rumble of resignation. "I would

strongly encourage all of you to take some time. Make sure your heads are on straight. But I can't force you to take leave." He paused, waiting for all of them to meet his gaze as he swept his dark brown eyes over the table. "But don't think for a second that I won't mandate your asses to therapy, or send you to the records department if I feel you're not fit for active duty. I want Hernandez as badly as all of you. But I will *not* allow you to put yourselves or your colleagues in danger because you've got a vendetta against him. Anything not completely by the books, and I'll bench your ass faster than you can say Tim Tebow. Understood?"

They all nodded, the mood at the table shifting back to somber.

"With all due respect, Cap, time is the last thing I want right now," said Sawyer. "I want to do my job and put this motherfucker in prison." Anger won out over sadness, and he curled his fingers around his glass. He wanted justice, for Ryan, and for himself and Amelia and what they'd lost.

"I can't deal with being alone right now," she said, tracing her finger around the rim of her glass. "I can't stand silence, or sleeping. I need this. You don't want me working the Hernandez case, I get it. But let me work. It's all I have." Her voice wavered on the last syllable.

DeMarcus nodded. "I know. I'm sorry, Amelia. It's my job to look out for all of you. It was my job to look after Ryan, and I . . ." He shook his head, and Sawyer's chest tightened, his guilty heart beating sympathetically for the captain. "If you guys say you're good, I trust you."

"Any word on when someone new might be coming in?" asked Jack, toying with his glass as he voiced the question they'd all pretended wasn't weighing on their minds.

DeMarcus nodded slowly. "New hire's been chosen. She'll be in next week."

"Internal?" Amelia asked, finishing her beer and pouring herself another glass, killing off the pitcher.

"Yeah, internal. I can't really tell you much yet, since it's not white shirt official, but we're just waiting for some *t*'s to be crossed. She's impressive, though. Ran track in college, black belt in kickboxing. Degree in criminal justice from the University of Georgia. She was given the Meritorious Service Award last year for her role in the crackdown on the illegal bars in Adair Park. I think she'll be a good fit." He glanced at Sawyer, who knew they were all waiting for him to respond.

"Doubt she'll be half as good as Ryan." He shrugged, noticing how tight his shoulders were. "Maybe I should just be on my own for a bit."

DeMarcus shook his head. "Listen, I get it. But that's not how this unit works, and you know that. If you're not ready for a new partner, I respect that, but it means you're desk surfing until you are. So it's your call."

Raindrops spattered against the window looking out over the parking lot, the sky opening up in a sudden downpour that matched Sawyer's mood. He didn't want to be stuck behind a desk—he needed to be out there, tracking that fucker Hernandez down and making him pay for what he'd done. And he couldn't do that if he didn't suck it up and accept the fact that next week, he'd be working with a new partner.

Somehow, the idea of someone else sitting at Ryan's desk, working with him on cases, felt more final than watching Ryan's casket disappear into the ground. As though a part of him had been hoping it was all a giant, tangled nightmare that wasn't really true. That life wasn't really marching on without Ryan. Not to mention that figuring out how to work with someone new right now was pretty much the last thing he wanted to do. He just wanted to focus on crushing the Baracoa cartel like the cockroaches they were. No distractions.

He glanced up and realized the entire team was staring at him, waiting for him to say something. "Fine. Last thing I want is to be stuck behind a desk."

That seemed to satisfy the captain, so Sawyer returned his attention to his beer, hating every single second of this. Being here without Ryan. Having to suck it up and accept a new partner. All of it.

A waitress came by and set down a bottle of Patron, four shot glasses, a salt shaker, and a bowl of limes. Jack slipped her his black AmEx and winked at her, watching her ass appreciatively as she sauntered away. He pulled the cork on the bottle and poured four shots, sliding the glasses toward each of them and then raising his own. "To Ryan."

"To Ryan," they all echoed before shooting the tequila back and shoving limes into their mouths. Sawyer savored the burn the liquor cut down the center of his chest, welcoming the feel of something other than the hollow pain he'd been living with for the past two weeks.

He wasn't sure he'd ever be quite whole again.

Chapter Three

THE ELEVATOR DOORS opened and Brooke stepped out into a swirling cacophony of voices and activity. The third floor of the APD's Criminal Investigations building—a nondescript red brick building on Peachtree that looked more like a boring government building than anything else—was devoted to HEAT, the High-Risk Evaluation and Action Team. The bullpen lay before her, with its rows of desks laden with computers, phones and files. Bulletin boards on the wall were covered in neatly arranged pieces of intel, parts of ongoing investigations. A hallway to her right led toward the holding cells, while the hallway to her left led to the interrogation rooms. The captain's office sat at the far end of the bullpen, and just adjacent to it was what looked like the briefing room.

Large windows lit the space with bright morning

sunshine, and the scents of coffee and industrial cleaner hit her nose as the elevator doors snapped shut behind her. Voices melded together, phones rang, printers whirred, fingers clacked against keyboards. Laughter erupted from somewhere near the coffee machine. The energy was almost palpable. These detectives were the best of the best—the smartest, the strongest, the bravest, the most determined.

And now she was one of them.

Excitement shot through Brooke as she raised her hand and fingered the shiny new detective shield hanging around her neck. She took a few steps into the bullpen, conscious of the fact that several heads had swiveled in her direction. Smoothing a hand over her ponytail, she stood up straight. Given the situation she was coming into—replacing a fallen officer—she knew she'd have some ground to make up. Impossibly enormous shoes to fill. But she had to try, both for her own career and for her new teammates. The only way through was forward, and maybe she could play a role in that.

Her stomach fluttered with nerves as she moved toward the captain's office, and she noticed that everyone was wearing jeans and T-shirts. She suddenly felt like an overdressed rookie in her navy-blue pantsuit. She wondered if she should ditch the jacket, roll up the sleeves of her blouse, try to look a little less keen. She needed to make a good first impression on her team, and she knew that she had about seven seconds in which to make one. If they immediately judged her as uptight, or as some brownnosing rookie, she'd have an even harder time building a rapport.

Before she could make up her mind, the captain spotted her and rose from his desk, waving her into his office. Captain DeMarcus Hill was an attractive African American man with a shaved head, brown eyes and a big smile. Something about his friendly face made him look younger than he likely was, but she knew that he was a force to be reckoned with it. One of APD's youngest recipients of the Medal of Honor, he was known to be tough but fair, with an analytical mind and the ability to remain calm when shit was hitting the fan.

"Detective Simmons, welcome," he said, shaking her hand and then gesturing for her to have a seat. God, *Detective* Simmons. That would take some getting used to. Right now, it still sent a nervous thrill charging through her. She'd worked so damn hard to get here that it didn't feel quite real. As though a part of her was waiting for someone to jump out with a camera and say, *"Just kidding!"*

"Thank you," she said, crossing her legs and sitting back in her chair, hopefully projecting an outward calm she didn't quite feel.

Captain Hill folded his hands on his desk. "It's not typical that someone gets their first crack at detective work in HEAT, but I have to say, you impressed us, and I think you'll be a good fit."

She nodded, flushing with pleasure at the captain's compliment. "Thank you, sir. I'm grateful for the opportunity."

He smiled and then tipped his chin toward the bullpen behind her. "There are forty HEAT detectives in total, all organized into subteams of four detectives each. One of the members of your subteam will be your assigned partner. You'll work your assigned cases together. The work we do can be incredibly dangerous, which is why investigations are never conducted solo. There's also inherent value in working as a team—puzzle pieces of investigations come together quicker with two—or even four—minds. Because of that, I try to connect partners who I believe will play to each other's strengths. Who will complement each other with skills in areas where the other is perhaps weaker."

She nodded, wondering what he thought her weaknesses were. "Understood."

His smile faltered and he sighed, leaning back in his chair. "As you know, you're coming on during difficult circumstances."

"I never knew Detective Walker, but I'm sorry for his loss."

The captain blew out a long breath. "The APD has lost eighty-seven officers in the line of duty, and sadly, Walker won't be the last." He leveled his gaze at her, as though trying to impress on her what she was getting herself into.

She didn't flinch. She was nervous about making a good impression on her team, but when it came to actual police work, she was fearless. "But if we can bring down Ernesto Hernandez, that'll at least be something. Justice for Detective Walker." She'd read the briefing about Walker's death, even though, given the undercover nature of the investigation, many of the details had been redacted.

The corner of Hill's mouth tipped up in a smile. "I think you'll get along just fine with your new teammates. Walker wasn't just their colleague, but their friend. They're hungry to see Hernandez rotting in a cell."

"Believe me, even though I didn't personally know Walker, I get it. My parents were killed in a hit-and-run when I was nine. Although it didn't bring them back, watching the man who'd taken them from me have to pay for what he'd done did bring me some peace. Some healing, I guess." She shrugged, wondering if she was oversharing. "It's partly why I became a cop—if I can prevent those tragedies from happening, or bring people to justice after the fact . . . well, that's worth something. It was worth something to me."

For a moment, she held his gaze, and something passed between them. An understanding, not man to woman, or superior to subordinate, but cop to cop.

His voice was quiet when he spoke. "I'm sorry about your parents."

"Thank you."

"You know what makes a good cop, Brooke?" He leaned forward, his eyes suddenly bright and intense.

"I have my own theories, but I'd like to hear what you think, Captain."

"It's the ones who don't forget what it's like to be civilian. It's the ones who have a deep-seated understanding of what it is they're protecting. What they're fighting for. And because we understand the value of that, we do whatever it takes, day in and day out, without hesitation. And sometimes we pay for that dedication with our lives." His gaze drifted to the far wall, where a picture of Ryan Walker hung. "You get that. It's what drives you, and it's why you'll be an asset to HEAT." He cleared his throat roughly, blinking away the sudden brightness in his eyes. "Come on, I'll give you a tour and introduce you to your new partner."

He stood from his desk, indicating that Brooke should follow him. Smoothing her hands down the poly-cotton-blend pants she was really starting to regret, she followed him out of his office, taking mental notes as he showed her around, pointing out the briefing room, giving her a tour of the cells and interrogation rooms, and making sure she knew where the essentials were—coffee machine, bathroom and vending machine. And while she maintained an even pace with him, she kept having to snap her attention back to what he was saying because her focus was pulled into the energy of the room, again and again. *This* was where she belonged.

As the captain finished up his tour, a feeling even more intense than the nerves, than the excitement, than the need to work hard and impress, settled over her: a sense of coming home. As though everything in her career had been leading up to today. A culmination and a beginning, all in one.

"Any questions?" he asked as they made their way back toward the bullpen.

She shook her head, her eyes dancing around the room. All she wanted was to meet her partner and dive in. To start doing the work she was so hungry for. To prove to everyone that she was worthy of the detective shield hanging around her neck.

"Great. You need anything, you can come to me. Now let's go find your team." He started walking toward the far back corner of the room, to a set of desks near one of the windows. A man and a woman stood with their backs to the room, talking to a partially visible man. All she could see of him was a pair of scuffed brown boots and worn jeans, his feet propped up on his desk and crossed at the ankles. The desk directly facing his was empty. Did her new partner—her first—always put his feet up like that? Because she didn't want to write her reports while staring at the dirty treads of his lug soles. She hadn't even seen him yet, and she could distantly hear the strains of *The Odd Couple* theme running through her mind.

"Everyone, this is your new team member, Detective Brooke Simmons." The man and woman turned around, their eyes cool and appraising, their expressions neutral and unreadable. "This is Detective Jack Ward, and Detective Amelia Perez." Brooke extended her hand and shook with Ward and Perez, exchanging polite greetings. Jack looked as though he'd stepped from the pages of *GQ*, with his perfectly styled blond hair, piercing blue eyes and strong jaw covered in an artfully manicured layer of stubble. He wore a black T-shirt stretched tight across his muscular chest and a pair of dark jeans. Amelia was pretty in a stern, don't-make-me-kick-your-ass kind of way. Her shiny dark brown hair framed her face, and her black tank top and tight jeans showed off a sleek, muscular frame. She was beautiful and strong, but what Brooke found most intriguing was the haunted look around her eyes, emphasized by the dark circles.

"Nice pantsuit, Hillary," she said, smirking at Brooke. For a split second, Brooke froze, turning the words over in her mind and holding Amelia's gaze, looking for an edge. She relaxed slightly when she didn't find one, happy to take the good-natured hazing.

Brooke smiled, tilting her head. "I've got a few spares; wanna borrow one?"

Amelia smiled, but the pain in her eyes stayed exactly where it was, untouched. "Nah, not really my style. We're a bit more casual here. As you may have noticed. With your detective skills." She tapped her temple in a smart-ass gesture.

Brooke bit her lip, hiding her smile. It was a shame

Perez wasn't her new partner—she liked her. "Right. A little more Gap, a little less sale rack at JCPenney."

Amelia winked at her. "Something like that."

The captain gestured at the man who was still sitting and only partially visible. "And this is your partner, Detective Matthews." The captain shot Matthews, who still had his feet up on the desk, a dirty look. There was a heavy sigh, the clap of a file folder hitting the desk, and then the boots disappeared. Jack and Amelia parted and everything inside Brooke went very, very still.

Because standing less than three feet away from her was Thunderdick Thor himself. Wearing a gray Henley, low-slung jeans, a badge around his neck and a scowl cold enough to freeze hell. One after the other, reactions fired through her body.

A warm tingling in her chest and between her thighs at seeing him again.

A nervous wriggle in her belly.

A happy little kick in her heart.

And a confused scramble in her brain, because he did *not* look as though his chest was tingling or his heart was beating a bit faster. Not even a little.

"Shit," he said, the word barely a whisper. His eyes held hers and a wave of heat passed through her, settling low in her core. The memory of feeling pinned by that gaze came back to her, and she licked her lips and then swallowed.

God, had she fucked this up before it even started?

Had her now-infamous bad judgment when it came to men struck again?

Her heart raced in time with her mind as her thoughts whirled around her brain. Her Sawyer was Detective Sawyer Matthews. Sawyer was her new partner. Sawyer, with whom she'd had the hottest sex of her life a little less than two weeks ago. Everything about their night together came rushing back to her—the intensity of their connection, the numerous orgasms he'd given her, the haunted sadness that had hung around him like a shadow. Had that been about Detective Walker? He'd clearly been just as hungry for a distraction as she'd been, and now, knowing who he really was, that part of the night suddenly made a lot more sense.

He cleared his throat and swallowed, staring at her as though she'd suddenly grown a second head. He looked so fucking sexy standing there, all brooding intensity and tightly coiled muscle, that she wanted to lick him, even though he didn't look happy to see her. In fact, he looked . . . pissed. Was that about her, or about him not wanting a new partner? She was inclined to go with the latter. Either way, she couldn't deny that a part of her was happy—very happy—to see him again, even if it did muddy the waters on the first day of her promotion.

At least she knew she didn't hate him. That had to count for something, right?

"Hey," she said, realizing that the silence was starting to stretch between them.

The captain arched an eyebrow, his gaze flicking between them. "Do you two know each other?"

"No," barked Sawyer before snatching up his discarded folder and marching toward the photocopier on the other side of the bullpen.

The captain closed his eyes and sighed. "I apologize for Detective Matthews. He can be . . . a bit rough around the edges. It's been a difficult time. He and Walker were close."

Brooke nodded, absorbing that small piece of information. Sawyer's name had been redacted from all the reports she'd read about Ryan Walker's death. Knowing that they'd been close made her hopeful that his reaction to her was about losing his former partner, and didn't really have anything to do with her. She was a big girl. She could let bad manners roll off her shoulders. She knew how not to take things personally.

Amelia let out a low chuckle. "Rough around the edges?" She peered at Brooke, her gaze sharp and assessing. "He's a grumpy motherfucker. Get used to it."

Brooke glanced over at where Sawyer was jabbing at the photocopier harder than was necessary, his shoulders tight. "I think I can handle him." Heat flushed over her skin as she remembered all the ways she'd handled him only a couple of weeks ago.

Grumpy motherfucker or not, they had some air to clear. They'd had sex—so what? They were both adults. Just because they'd bumped fun bits didn't mean they couldn't work together, couldn't be friendly. The only certainty was that now that they were partners, anything more happening between them was 100 percent off the table. It was completely against regulations to be romantically involved with an assigned partner—everyone knew that.

Brooke cleared her throat. "Besides, he's been through a lot. I can sympathize."

Now it was Amelia's turn to stare at Brooke as though she'd sprouted a second head.

Jack said nothing, leaning a hip on the empty desk—Brooke's new desk—and watching everything with casual interest. The captain looked as though he wanted to say more, but then shook his head. "Briefing in ten. Welcome to HEAT, Simmons."

SAWYER STARED UNFOCUSED at the sheets of paper as they collected in the photocopier's tray, the machine still humming away in front of him, the scent of toner wafting up into the air. He didn't need fifty copies of next month's schedule, but wasting paper was better than standing there in front of Brooke, dumbstruck and gaping like an idiot.

Once, during his first year as a rookie patrol officer, he'd pulled someone over for running a stop sign. When he'd gotten out of the cruiser to ask for their license and registration, he'd been so nervous and amped up that he'd accidentally shifted the cruiser into neutral instead of park. He'd barely made it to the pulled-over car's window before his cruiser had started rolling backward into the intersection. He'd had to chase it nearly thirty feet, dive inside and slam on the brakes. The entire thing had been captured on the dash cam and it had taken him months to live it down.

And yet somehow this, seeing Brooke again, knowing she was going to be his new partner . . . it felt like an even bigger moment in his career. Just as bad, and just as embarrassing with the way he'd stood there staring at her as though his brain had suddenly checked out for annual leave.

"Fuck," he said, rubbing a hand over the back of his neck as he tried to sort his shit out. He took a breath and closed his eyes, but when he did, all he saw was Brooke spread beneath him, her eyes glazed with pleasure and her legs wrapped around his waist as he buried himself deep inside her. God, she'd been perfect that night. Exactly what he'd needed, and although he'd known it was only for that night, he'd had a hard time making himself get dressed and leave the hotel room. The entire drive home he'd been half-tempted to do a U-turn and go back for round three. He couldn't remember the last time a woman had pulled him under the way she had, surprising him in a dangerous way, like a small wave with a shockingly big undertow.

And that was why this wasn't going to work. They couldn't be partners. He couldn't deal with this right now. Didn't need the distraction, the reminder of what he couldn't have, while trying to figure out an in to the

Baracoa cartel. He owed Ryan justice. And to get it, he'd
need to be focused and dedicated. Not twisted in knots
over Brooke. Who he barely knew, and yet who he knew
felt like heaven and tasted like sunshine. Who eased
that chasm inside him, not healing it up, but making
it a little less dark. Who made it the tiniest bit easier to
breathe. Or, at least, she *had*, just for a few hours.

He hated to split up Jack and Amelia's partnership—
they were good together, in sync and with skills and
personalities that complemented each other—but it
was the only option. He'd ask one of them to partner
with her instead. Or even better, ask the captain to
shuffle someone else onto the team and move Brooke
elsewhere. Maybe even off HEAT, since the thought of
seeing her every day in the bullpen caused a weird tug
in his chest.

A completely irrational surge of anger flared up his
spine. He knew this situation wasn't in any way Brooke's
fault, and yet he felt so tangled up and confused that he
couldn't help but blame her a little bit. Which was selfish and unfair, but there it was. He had a job to do, and
doing that job with her . . . fuck, it wasn't going to work.
He didn't see how it could.

Ryan's death had broken him, and he'd depleted
all of his strength, all of his emotional reserves, just
putting himself back together. Brooke was a layer—a
tempting, gorgeous, off-limits layer—he just couldn't
handle right now. He'd been carrying around so much
pain and guilt and other fucked-up shit that he didn't

have room to shoulder anything else. He knew all of that probably made him an asshole, or at least, reaffirmed his asshole-ness, but he couldn't really bring himself to care. He was used to feeling like an asshole. It was just part of who he was now. Like his eye color, or his height. Intrinsic and unchangeable. Maybe even in his DNA.

He heard the sound of footsteps behind him, heels clicking on the tile, and he knew it was her before he'd even turned around.

"So, let's just acknowledge that this is kinda weird, okay?" Her voice hit him somewhere low in his gut, and he braced his hands on the photocopier, as though it could somehow steady him. But nothing in his world was steady anymore. Schooling his face into a neutral expression, he turned around.

Her blond hair was pulled up into a ponytail, showing off her long, elegant neck, while her pantsuit hid her slender, athletic frame. Her arms were crossed over her chest, but there was nothing challenging in her expression.

"'Weird' is one word for it," he said, leaning back against the photocopier and mirroring her crossed arms.

She nodded slowly, studying him. "Let's just agree to—to leave it in the past. Pretend it never happened." Her eyes caught his, and the fire in her gaze was so scorching it was as though flames were licking at his skin. He shifted his weight, his jeans getting just a little bit tighter. This was bad. So, so bad.

"Sounds good to me."

She bit her lip, hesitating slightly before she continued. "I'm sorry about Detective Walker. I understand you were close."

"Mmm." He nodded, not saying anything more. Not trusting himself to say anything more.

"How long have you been part of HEAT?"

"Few years."

Her lips pressed into a thin line and he could tell she wanted to roll her eyes. She squinted at him and moved her hands to her hips. "So . . . are you pissed that *I'm* your new partner, or that you *have* a new partner, period?"

"Does it matter?"

Her eyebrows drew together. "Yeah. It does." She cleared her throat. "It matters to me. I've busted my ass to get here, and if this isn't going to work because of whatever shit you've got going on, let me know now." She took a small step closer. "Do *we* have a problem, or do *you*?"

He snorted, trying to ignore the flicker of heat teasing up his spine at the intensity flashing in her eyes. "Easy there, Robocop. Relax." Even though he did have a problem—God, he'd known she was smart from the moment he met her—he found himself getting his back up and not wanting to admit that she was right. Maybe he even wanted to prove her wrong.

"This is me relaxed."

He let out a low chuckle. "No, it's not. I've seen you *relaxed*." He regretted the words instantly, and the way they made something in her eyes darken. So much for putting distance between them. No, he had to go and fucking flirt with her. Like a moron.

A few heavy seconds passed before she spoke. "Can I ask you something?"

He grunted, the word *distance* running through his brain, searing itself onto his synapses.

She took a step closer, glancing around the bullpen before speaking. "If you're local, why were you in a hotel bar?"

He shrugged despite his surprise at her question. "Because I was looking for something very, very temporary." It was probably the most honest thing he'd said to her so far.

She flinched and then nodded. "Right. Yeah. Makes sense."

From behind him, the photocopier made a grinding noise, followed by a loud series of beeps. With a sigh, he turned back to face it and opened it up to unsnarl the paper jam. Everyone in the bullpen called the photocopier Bob Marley, since it "always be jammin'."

"I've got smaller hands, let me," she said, stepping around him. He watched helplessly as she slipped her hand in the machine and tugged the crumpled copy free. She frowned slightly as she glanced down at it, and then at the completed copies in the tray. A smile tugged at the corners of her lips. "Planning to give the whole department your schedule?" She reached forward and zipped her thumb along the corner of the stack of pages. "Lotta copies here."

He said nothing, just retrieved his stack of useless copies and slammed the machine back together a little too hard.

She held out the half-mangled page to him, her lips scrunched to the side in a way that made him want to kiss the shit out of her. "You want this one too?"

He ground his teeth together and pulled it from her hand, unable to stop himself from remembering how those fingers had felt curled around his dick. How she'd tasted, smelled. How just for the few hours he'd spent with her, he hadn't hurt.

"I don't have time to look out for a baby detective right now," he said, his voice coming out even gruffer than he'd intended.

Her eyes snapped to his, the teasing heat in her gaze cooling to something even more intriguing. "Let's get a couple things straight. We're partners. Partner means equal. We're a team, and I don't need you to babysit me. I wouldn't be here if I wasn't qualified and able to do this job. Yeah, I'm new and have some shit to learn, but that doesn't make you better than me."

Well, damn. There was that spark that had drawn him to her right from the start. "Didn't say I was better than you. But you can't deny that you're green. And I don't have time for green." It was as good an excuse as any.

Her lips pressed into a firm line, and he could tell that she wanted to say more, but was carefully weighing her options. She shook her head and then turned, joining the stream of people heading into the briefing room. After giving her a several-second head start, he dumped his stack of papers into the recycling bin and then followed her in.

It wasn't right how fantastic her ass looked in that pantsuit.

Slowly the neatly arranged black plastic chairs in the briefing room filled with detectives. At the front of the room, there were a few pictures of biker gang members taped to the whiteboard, along with a known cartel member, a man known only as the Sheriff because of how many times he'd been shot. In the far-right corner, the captain stood behind the podium emblazoned with the APD shield, shuffling a few pages. Brooke had taken a seat next to Amelia. Avoiding her gaze, he dropped into the empty seat beside Jack.

"Everything cool?" asked Jack, leaning toward Sawyer and keeping his voice down, letting it blend with the hum of other voices in the room.

Sawyer crossed his arms over his chest, studying the pictures tacked up to the board. Fucking Desperados. Atlanta's biggest biker gang, they were almost as bad as the Baracoa cartel in some respects. "Yeah, fine."

"You hate her." It wasn't a question. As much as Jack pissed him off sometimes, he had to admit that the man was one of the best when it came to reading people.

But he was off base here. Sawyer didn't hate Brooke; he hated the situation.

He shook his head. "Don't hate her. Just resent having a new partner." A half truth.

Jack raised his eyebrows. "Sure. Right."

"What? You can't deny that this sucks." God, he sounded like such a whiny little shit. Maybe because he was being one. Fuck.

"Doesn't mean *she* sucks. Give her a chance before you write her off."

Instantly he remembered the feel of Brooke's lips around his cock, cradling her face as he took and she gave. He propped one ankle up on his knee, fighting a losing battle against the blood flowing south.

"I'm not writing her off. But I don't have time to hold some new detective's hand. I don't deal with rookies. Not in the past, and especially not now."

Jack frowned at him and sighed. "Just . . . try to be like, ten percent less of a dick to her, okay? For the team?"

"I wasn't a dick to her."

Jack let out a low chuckle. "Right."

Before he could say anything else, the captain had cleared his throat, causing the room to quiet down.

"I know everyone's got full schedules today, so I'll make this quick. First, please welcome Detective Brooke Simmons, the newest member of HEAT. She'll be working with Matthews, along with Ward and Perez." Brooke turned and waved at the room, her posture relaxed and confident. A round of nods and murmurs went around the room, and Sawyer could feel several sets of eyes on him, probably wondering how he was taking having a new partner.

"Second, some good news. Search warrant for the storage facility came through." The captain stepped out from behind his podium and handed Jack a single sheet of white paper, folded in thirds. "Ward, Perez, Matthews, and Simmons will execute."

Adrenaline surged through Sawyer as he stared at the piece of paper in Jack's hand. In the weeks since Ryan's funeral, this search warrant was the first break in their case. And while this wasn't directly tied to the Baracoa cartel, Sawyer and his team had a hunch that it could be, and any lead was worth investigating.

The captain continued, moving to the whiteboard. "Allow me a few moments to bring Detective Simmons up to speed." Brooke leaned forward in her seat, her expression intense and focused as her eyes darted back and forth between the captain and the whiteboard. "For months now," the captain continued, "we've suspected that the Desperados are involved with the Baracoa cartel, storing and moving weapons and drugs for them. Since Walker's death, Desperado activity has ramped up, leading us to believe that the Baracoa cartel knew they were being watched even more closely. For the past two weeks, Ward and Perez have been conducting close surveillance on known Desperado members—" at this, he pointed at the pictures up on the board—"and have traced a significant amount of activity back to a storage facility in the Bluff. Ward was able to subpoena the facility's records, cross-referencing names assigned to the storage lockers with known Desperado members." He tapped the picture of a man named David Bowman, who looked to be in his early forties, with short black hair and a handlebar mustache. "We found a hit, which was enough to secure the search warrant." He nodded at Jack. "Excellent work, Detective. I want you to take the lead on this. Go in, investigate the unit, and bring any Desperado members you find in for questioning. Keep an eye out for Bowman, as well as these two known associates." He pointed at the other two pictures, and then moved on to the grainy image of the man known as the Sheriff. He was white, in his mid-to-late thirties, with closely cropped brown hair and a layer of scruff covering his jaw. His arms were covered in tattoos, but the picture on the board wasn't clear enough to make out what they were. "If you see him, do not engage." He glanced at Brooke. "He's a lieutenant with the cartel, and is extremely dangerous. He seems to run most of the cartel's day-to-day operations." Brooke nodded, taking in the information. "We'll send a couple of cars of patrol officers over with you. Hopefully we strike gold here and can start knocking over some dominoes when it comes to the Baracoa cartel. Questions?"

Sawyer shook his head, his foot bouncing on his ankle with the need for action.

After the captain had updated them on several

other ongoing cases, he dismissed everyone, and with fresh adrenaline pumping through his veins, Sawyer headed straight for his locker, not waiting for Jack. Or Brooke.

Once at his locker, he yanked his Henley off over his head and replaced it with a plain black T-shirt. Then he slipped his Kevlar vest on and adjusted the straps. After he'd checked the clip on his Glock 22, he slid an extra magazine into the front pocket of his vest. Hopefully this was just a routine search that would turn up some good evidence against the cartel, or the biker gang, or both. But it was always best to be prepared.

A few lockers down, Jack tugged on his own vest. "This is probably her first raid, you know," he said, and Sawyer didn't have to ask who he was talking about. "Good opportunity for you to show her the ropes."

"She doesn't want my help. Made that much clear earlier."

Jack's movements stilled and he arched an eyebrow. "Right, but she's your new partner."

Sawyer shrugged, doing his best not to let any of his emotions show. "I called her a baby detective, and she said she didn't need babysitting, so we're square."

"I'm not saying babysit her. I'm saying show her what we do. I'm running point on this. I can't coordinate everyone and show her what's what." Jack finished adjusting his vest and sighed as he approached Sawyer. "I know you miss him. We all do. But that's not Brooke's fault. Don't take your grief out on her."

"I'm not," said Sawyer, but the words sounded hollow even to his own ears.

Jack studied him for a second, rubbing a hand over his mouth. "All right." He didn't seem convinced, but he didn't press any further. He clapped Sawyer on the shoulder and headed out of the locker room.

Brooke and Amelia met them by the elevator, both geared up and ready to go. Brooke had ditched her suit jacket and blouse, leaving her in a sleeveless top that showcased her toned arms, her vest snug around her torso. If this was her first raid, she didn't look nervous or unsure of herself. No, she looked calm and determined, her eyes bright with the kind of excitement he knew well. As they waited for the elevator, she glanced over at Sawyer as though she wanted to say something, but then changed her mind when the doors slid open.

Once down in the parking garage, the team followed Jack out to his department-issued navy-blue Nissan Altima. The majority of unmarked police vehicles in Atlanta were either Chevy Malibus or Ford Tauruses, and the public knew it, which was why special investigative units such as HEAT avoided using those vehicles like the plague. Instead, they had their own garage that housed a variety of vehicles, ranging from typical four-door sedans to minivans and sports cars. The key was to use whatever would blend in and draw the least amount of attention. From the outside, the cars all looked just like any other car on the road, but had radios, dash-mounted computers, and light bars hidden in the grills.

Sawyer reached for the front passenger-side door handle, but Amelia hip-checked his hand out of the way. "Don't think so. My partner's car, I get shotgun." She wrenched the door open and dropped into the passenger seat. With a shrug, he maneuvered his long legs into the back seat of the Altima. Lucky for him, unlike regular cruisers with their hard benches and Plexiglas partitions, these vehicles still had standard back seats, with actual upholstery and seat belts. Brooke slid in beside him, not saying anything.

"I'm not sure what we're going to find," said Jack, as he headed south from the station. "I'm thinking drugs and possibly weapons. But we've seen enough Desperado activity to get the warrant, and we've picked up intel and chatter indicating communication between the Desperados and Baracoa. No sign or mention of Hernandez, though." His last sentence hung in the quiet air of the car, heavy and unsatisfying. "But if we find what we're looking for today, we'll have grounds to move on both the Desperados and Baracoa. And hopefully whatever they're hiding in that storage locker points us in the right direction." Drugs and weapons were traceable, and if they followed the breadcrumbs, and if Baracoa was in fact involved here, those breadcrumbs might just lead to Hernandez.

Sawyer nodded, eyes scanning the cars as they wound their way into the Bluff, one of Atlanta's most dangerous areas. Brooke shifted in her seat beside him. The sun streaming in through the windows caught the golden strands of her hair. He shifted too as he remembered how good that hair had felt wrapped around his fist. He tore his gaze away from her, looking out the window. Dilapidated houses with overgrown lawns, some with boarded-up windows, lined the street, the sidewalks cracked and dirty. A pile of garbage sat beside an abandoned warehouse—a likely hub for gang activity. Unable to help himself, he glanced back at Brooke again and a completely unexpected surge of protectiveness tightened his chest. Suppressing a growl, he shoved it away.

Follow the evidence. Build the case. Bring that motherfucker Hernandez down. That's what he needed to focus on. Not on the overwhelming grief, or the gnawing guilt. Not on the gorgeous woman sitting next to him, with whom he knew he could forget the grief and guilt fueling him. He needed that fuel. It was all he had right now.

They pulled up to Big Al's Storage just off of the 20. A large red-and-white sign advertised "Indoor, Climate-Controlled Storage—First Month Free!" Two police cruisers and four uniformed officers waited for them, along with an APD forensics van. A late-September heat wave gripped the city; the sun beat down from overhead and the air was stifling, probably almost a hundred degrees. Within seconds of stepping out of Jack's car, Sawyer could feel his vest sticking to his T-shirt, a layer of sweat coating his skin.

The storage facility was a two-story beige stucco building with peeling paint and lime-green trim. A chain-link fence circled the parking lot, topped with barbed wire. If this was where the Desperados were stashing drugs for the cartel, it was a good choice. Easily accessible, nondescript, and air-conditioned. Humidity was hell on drugs, messing with the chemistry and potency. A handful of cars dotted the gravel parking lot, and as Jack spoke with the sweaty, overweight, middle-aged man in charge— Big Al himself, apparently—Sawyer took a stroll, checking out the cars, looking for anything suspicious, like expired license plate decals or visible weapons. Taking some space to get his head straight. Nothing jumped out at him, and he rejoined his team.

Jack waved Sawyer over. "He says the units we're looking for are on the upper floor. While we search, he's gonna get us a list of all his employees so we can check them out, look for connections."

Sawyer nodded, hyperaware of Brooke's presence beside him.

Jack motioned to the uniformed officers. "Canvass the lower floor. Look for anything suspicious, and keep an eye on the exits. Perez and I will check out unit 214. Matthews and Simmons will investigate unit 222." He passed Sawyer one of the sets of keys Big Al had handed over.

With the four other officers in tow, they headed into the building. Black corrugated metal doors lined the concrete hallways, and bright fluorescent lights shone down from above. The entire floor was silent, save for the hum of the air-conditioning and the echo of their footsteps.

Jack jerked his head to the left, and Sawyer nodded, watching as he and Amelia split off down the adjacent hallway to investigate their locker, leaving him alone with Brooke.

"For what it's worth," she said, her eyes trained directly in front of her, sweeping back and forth across the hall, her hand resting casually on her holster, "I'm here to do whatever it takes to bring this fucker down. He killed one of our own. I didn't know Walker, but this still feels personal to me."

He grunted and nodded, not sure what to say to that. Not sure what to say about anything that had happened so far this morning.

They approached their storage unit, their footsteps slowing in unison as they both saw it: the padlock was open, the shackle looped around the storage unit's latch. Silently he met Brooke's eyes and gestured for her to back up. She frowned briefly but then took a few soundless steps backward, drawing her gun in a smooth, fluid movement. With it trained at the door, she nodded.

Moving silently, he crept forward and leaned toward the door, listening intently for voices, movement, anything.

He bent and pulled the storage locker's door up, and immediately found himself staring down the barrel of a gun. A wave of nausea churned through his stomach as he straightened, leveling his Glock at the man in front of him. Sweat broke out on his palms.

David Bowman, one of the Desperados from the whiteboard at the briefing, moved toward him and out of the locker, shadows playing across his face. "I'm not going down for this. No fucking way."

"Hey!" Brooke said from behind Bowman, her voice sharp and challenging, and Sawyer's stomach clenched, icy terror flooding his veins. He froze, unable to move, unable to speak, unable to pull the trigger on his Glock as Bowman whirled, his gun swinging toward Brooke. A dizzying fear swept over him, making everything seem as though it was in slow motion. With perfect timing and lighting-fast precision, Brooke threw an impressive roundhouse kick, knocking Bowman's gun out of his hands.

The fog lifted and Sawyer saw his chance, barreling into the man from behind, taking him down to the floor, hard. The man hit the concrete with a grunt, struggling against Sawyer. Brooke hurried over, pressing a knee into Bowman's back, helping to subdue him.

"Here," she said, a pair of cuffs dangling from her fingers. He took them and slapped them on Bowman.

"Police, don't move!" Amelia's voice cut through the air, and she ran toward them, her gun trained on the biker. Jack was right behind her, his weapon also raised.

"Matthews, Simmons, you good?" he called out.

"Yeah, we're good. He was in the locker." He jerked his head toward the open locker behind them. "Better be some good shit in there." He stood and hauled the man to his feet, passing him off to two of the patrol officers who'd come running at the shouts. He closed his eyes and forced himself to take a couple of deep breaths, trying to dispel some of the adrenaline still pumping hot and fast through his system. He felt the urge to reach for Brooke, to check on her, but instead he turned away.

Amelia stepped into the locker and let out a low whistle. "I'd say we hit the mother lode. Damn."

Sawyer stepped into the drug-crammed locker. Clear plastic containers filled with crystal meth. Dozens of large plastic bags filled with marijuana. A towering pile of cocaine bricks, stacked neatly along one wall. Jack yanked on a pair of gloves and then opened a large suitcase. Wads of hundred dollar bills came spilling out. Another large suitcase yielded at least a dozen automatic weapons, some with the serial numbers scratched out. Several smaller cardboard boxes sat in the far corner, stamped with the letters *MBR*. Crouching down, Sawyer opened one of the boxes and found plastic bags filled with diamond-shaped pills in a rainbow of colors.

"You ever seen these before?" he asked, and Jack, Amelia and Brooke all came over. Everyone shook their heads.

"No. Any idea what MBR means?" asked Amelia.

Jack shrugged. "No, but I'm hoping our friend can tell us when we get him back to the station." Jack plucked his radio off his shoulder. "Can we get foren-sics up to start processing this stuff?"

"You sure you're good?" asked Amelia, laying a hand on Sawyer's shoulder as he moved past her on his way out of the locker. Brooke and Jack were still examining the pills.

God, he was pretty fucking far from good. "Yeah, I'm fine."

She must not have believed him, because she let him have the front seat on the way back to the station.

Chapter Four

"Hey," said Jack, dropping a couple of folders onto Brooke's desk—case files for her to get caught up on. She looked up from her phone, pressing Send on the text message to Dani: Thunderdick Thor is my new partner. FML.

"Hey," she said, sifting through the folders and rolling her neck against the weariness settling between her shoulders. Talk about a killer first day on the job. Sawyer, the raid, the mountain of paperwork—it was a lot to process. "How did the interrogation go?"

"I'll tell you at the bar. We're all going for a drink and you're buying." He tipped his chin toward the elevator where Amelia was already waiting, a motorcycle helmet under one arm. "Let's go."

It was after six, and while technically she could've clocked out an hour ago, no way was she going to be the first one to leave, especially on her first day. "Yeah, sure," she said, grabbing her purse from the bottom drawer of her desk and then glancing up at Sawyer. He was scrolling through something on his computer, squinting at the screen, deep in thought. "You coming?"

He looked up at her, something she couldn't quite name flickering across his face. He glanced in the direction of the captain's office. "Got something I need to run by Hill first. I'll catch up with you."

Hey, at least it wasn't a growly no. Hooray for small victories. Because she wanted to make this work. Not just because she liked him, or because this promotion was important to her, but because she wanted to do her part in bringing Walker's killer to justice.

Brooke nodded and followed Jack and Amelia out to the staff parking lot. Without a word, Amelia headed off to a Harley parked near the doors.

"Come on," said Jack, leading them toward a sleek red vintage car. "I'll give you a ride."

When they were a few steps away, she stopped dead in her tracks, her jaw nearly hitting the pavement. "Get the fuck out. This is *not* your car."

Jack laughed and stroked the hood lovingly, the classic red paint gleaming in the fading light. "Oh, but it is. A 1961 Ferrari 250 GT Berlinetta, and she's all mine."

He held the passenger side door open for her and

she slipped inside, wondering how the hell a cop could afford a car like this. She'd scrimped and saved for her newer model Toyota Corolla.

"Nothing says 'I'm undercover, please don't notice me' like a hunk of junk ride like this," she said, wondering if her fishing was obvious. He started the engine, a throaty rumble vibrating through the car. The interior was done in buttery-soft caramel leather, with red and chrome finishes on the dash. Everything about it screamed money and luxury.

"Hunk of junk? I should kick you out. Blasphemy!"

"But I don't know where the bar is, so who'll buy your drinks?"

He pulled out of the parking lot, his rich laugh filling the car. "I like you, Simmons. You did good out there today. Don't let Matthews scare you away."

"Don't worry," she said, letting Jack's compliment ease some of the tension that had been knotted between her shoulders since that morning, "I've wanted this for a long time. I'm not going anywhere." She leaned back against the headrest, watching the streetlights flicker to life as they headed north toward Midtown.

"Glad to hear it."

At least she knew Jack wanted her around. She'd have to work on Sawyer. Maybe with a beer or two in him, he'd open up a little. Maybe.

A few minutes later, they pulled up to a gray-and-white brick building with a black awning over the large front window. "The Speakeasy" scrolled across the awning in flowing white script. The inside of the bar was classy and understated—not what she'd been expecting, but then again, she usually hung out with beat cops, not detectives who (somehow) drove Ferraris.

Golden lighting illuminated the wooden planks on the ceiling and shone down onto the white brick bar. Bottles lined the backlit shelves, glowing with an inviting warmth. The low murmur of voices and laughter mingled with the Stevie Wonder song playing through the bar's sound system. Jack waved at one of the waitresses, who gave him a heated once-over.

Brooke nudged him as they wove their way toward the table at the back, where Amelia was already waiting for them. "Waitress was checking you out."

"That's Celia. We're, uh, acquainted."

"Meaning she's seen more than just the inside of your Ferrari."

Jack winked at her, and she had to admit that after navigating around Sawyer's surliness all day, Jack's easygoing charm was a welcome change. "You catch on quick."

She tapped her temple. "All part of the job."

As they neared their table, she couldn't help but notice that the sadness she'd seen on Amelia's face earlier was back. She sat staring out the window, toying with her necklace, her eyes soft and melancholy. It was yet another observation about her new team that Brooke tucked away as she tried to get to know them and figure out her place.

"Sawyer say what he needed to talk to Cap about?" Amelia asked by way of greeting as Jack and Brooke sat down on either side of her. They both shook their heads.

They'd just ordered a pitcher of beer and a plate of nachos when Brooke spotted Sawyer's broad shoulders in the doorway. It was amazing the way he made the bar suddenly feel a little bit smaller. As though he somehow shifted the gravity in the room and became the center around which Brooke's attention revolved. He was wearing the same gray Henley and beat-up jeans that he'd had on earlier, and as he approached the table, she noticed that his hair stuck up at a funny angle on one side of his head, as though he'd been running a hand through it. He nodded at everyone, taking the empty seat next to her.

She had the urge to scoot her chair closer, but fought against it. She could feel the warmth of his body next to her, only a few inches away. But those inches might as well have been miles, because he wasn't into her, resented her presence, and even if those first two items weren't true, the fact that he was her assigned partner made him completely off-limits anyway.

God. She *really* needed to figure out a way to recalibrate her dude radar, because hers was forever pointing her in the wrong direction. Not only that, but she was wasting brain cells on her attraction to him when she needed to be focused on figuring out a way to make this partnership work.

"What were you talking to the captain about?" asked Amelia.

Sawyer poured himself a pint from the pitcher the waitress had just set down. "Nothing important. You order food?"

"Yeah, fish tacos," she said, still toying with her necklace.

Sawyer made a face like he'd just smelled something rotten. "Fuck you guys." He turned in his seat, ready to call Celia over.

"They ordered nachos," said Brooke, not quite following whatever the joke was.

Sawyer pointed at Jack. "I hope they're covered in black olives."

Amelia threw her head back and laughed and Brooke took a sip of her beer, feeling completely lost. This was one of the biggest challenges that came with joining a new team. She didn't speak their language yet. Didn't know any of their inside jokes, or hot spots, or little codes. And based on the way her three colleagues were laughing about fish tacos and black olives, she had a feeling that her learning curve was pretty freaking steep.

The waitress brought their nachos, setting the platter down on the table. Sawyer reached for his glass, and she couldn't help but watch, almost transfixed, as his muscles moved beneath his skin. The way his big hand wrapped round his glass and raised it to his mouth, his throat working as he swallowed. Heat churned in her stomach as she remembered the feeling of that mouth on her, those fingers inside her.

"Right, Brooke?" Jack's voice cut through her lust-induced haze, and she forced her attention back to the conversation happening around her.

"Sorry, I zoned out there. Long day. 'Right Brooke' what?"

"Feels good to get an arrest on your first day."

She nodded, picking up her beer and relaxing back into her chair, trying to ignore the mental tug of Sawyer sitting right beside her. "Yeah, although you guys did all the work to make it happen. That was your warrant, based on your surveillance." She nudged Sawyer, smiling at him. "Wasn't just my arrest."

He didn't react.

Jack shook his head. "And that's why I don't miss patrol at all. Patrol's reactive. But a lot of what we do is proactive. Preventing crimes instead of dealing with the fallout."

"How long have you been on?" she asked. Sawyer shifted in his seat beside her, reaching for a nacho. His arm grazed hers, and a warm tingle worked its way across her skin. She focused on Jack, keeping her expression casually neutral.

"Got hired as a beat cop over ten years ago. I did a stint in major crimes when I first made detective, then joined HEAT three years ago."

"And what about you?" she asked, nodding at Amelia.

"Started on patrol when I was twenty, spent a few years in Vice. Came to HEAT two years ago." She nodded at Brooke. "How long you been on?"

"Seven, almost eight years."

"You think you're gonna miss patrol?" asked Jack, picking the black olives off his nacho.

Brooke shook her head, glancing over at Sawyer, who didn't seem interested in participating in the conversation. "I like what you said about patrol being reactive. It's treating the symptoms instead of the cause, you know? Plus the whole dynamic of patrol gets old. The hours of boredom followed by several seconds of terror."

Sawyer leaned forward, resting his elbows on the table. She traced the rippling lines in his forearms with her gaze. "Several seconds of terror, like when your partner goes all Karate Kid on a fucking biker with a gun?"

Her head whipped around so fast that her ponytail slapped against her cheek. His blue eyes bored into hers, his face a stony mask of hidden emotion. Holy shit, was he pissed at her? She'd thought everything was fine— not that he'd said anything to her either way. Talking and Sawyer didn't really mix, apparently. That, and she'd spent her afternoon buried in paperwork while Sawyer and Jack had questioned Bowman.

A silence had fallen over the table, so she forced herself to laugh. "Aw, were you worried about me?"

An intensity flashed in his eyes. His jaw clenched,

and he looked so raw, so masculine, so grumpy, that she wanted to climb into his lap and do fun, dirty, forbidden things with him. "Things could've gone sideways real fast."

Jack sighed, pushing a hand through his thick blond hair. "Jesus Christ, lighten the fuck up. Brooke knows what she's doing."

Sawyer squinted at Jack, not looking convinced.

"Listen," she said, touching Sawyer's arm. His head swiveled in her direction. "This was day one. I'm sorry if . . . I didn't mean to scare you or make you think that I didn't have things under control. We'll figure out a way to work together. We'll find our rhythm." His eyes met hers, a dark heat flashing in his gaze, and she knew he was remembering just how well they'd found a rhythm together. Then he glanced down, and she realized her hand was still on his arm. He pulled his arm back, shifting away from her touch.

It stung, but she couldn't stop replaying their night together. Couldn't stop her stomach from dipping and swirling when she looked at him. Couldn't stop the buzzy rush of attraction that flooded her system like adrenaline when she was around him. But they couldn't be anything other than colleagues, and she had a new job to focus on.

"Hey." Amelia's voice was sharp as she kicked Sawyer under the table. "I hate that Ryan's not here even more than you do. But what happened with Ryan isn't Brooke's fault. You're being an asshole, even for you."

Another silence fell over the table, the tension palpable. Sawyer shrugged and took a sip of his beer, seemingly unconcerned with being an asshole. Fine. She couldn't control how Sawyer reacted to her presence on the team, and she had the feeling that trying to control anything Sawyer did was probably a losing battle. But she wasn't going to let that stop her from doing her job, or hoping that maybe things could shift between them—even if they couldn't shift in the direction her body kept remembering.

"You get anything good out of Bowman?" asked Amelia, steering them back on track.

Some of the rigidness went out of Sawyer's shoulders and he leaned back in his chair. "Not a lot, but it's more to go on than what we had before." He crossed his arms over his chest, which made him look even bigger. God, she wanted to sink her teeth into those biceps. Dammit. "Bowman runs security for the cartel, but said he had nothing to do with the drugs or the weapons we found. He was guarding the storage locker, probably against getting hit by another gang."

"So he's basically a security guard," said Brooke.

Sawyer nodded. "So he says. He gave us a few other names, bikers doing shit for the cartel. We'll follow up with those and see if anything shakes out."

"What about the pills? He say what they were?" Amelia's eyebrows rose as she lifted her beer to her lips.

Sawyer shook his head. "Said he didn't know what they were, or what *MBR* means."

"We should get Vice in on this," said Jack, adding to his growing pile of discarded black olives. "See if they've seen the pills before, or know what *MBR* is."

"Yeah, I agree." Sawyer nodded. "Bowman didn't have much to say, but if we can trace those pills, we might actually have a solid lead on the cartel. Especially if they're exclusive to Baracoa."

Jack popped a nacho into his mouth. "Here's hoping." Then he turned his attention to Brooke. "Okay, Simmons, let's have it. Craziest on-the-job story. Everyone's got one. I'll show you mine if you show me yours." He wiggled his eyebrows, and she laughed.

She tapped her fingers against her lips, keenly aware of Sawyer's eyes on her. "Craziest? I think that'd have to be Leotard Chester."

Amelia leaned forward, a rare smile on her face. "Oh, I'm liking this already. Leotard Chester? Here for it."

Brooke leaned forward too, her arms braced on the table, the feel of Sawyer's gaze on her warming her skin. "This happened last year. I'm on night shift, it's maybe one in the morning. Radio's pretty quiet, and I'm driving down Decatur. All of a sudden, I see this guy walking down the street in a supertight leopard-print leotard and ripped fishnet stockings, carrying a pillowcase stuffed with clothes. So I roll up on him to see if he's okay. As soon as I get out of my cruiser, I see him toss a baggie of drugs into the bushes and then he takes off. So I chase him, catch him, bring him down, and his leotard, I guess it, uh, shifted while he was running, so now his balls are, like, hanging out."

The table let out a collective groan.

"Right? I cuff him, and I'm trying to get him to relax, to tell me why he ran. He doesn't have ID on him, and he'll only tell me that his name is Chester. And then things got real weird. I go and pick up his pillowcase, and it's filled with women's underwear, all of it different sizes, and . . . none of it clean."

Another groan from the table.

"So I'm trying to talk to him, but I can't because he's now singing at the top of his lungs about how much he loves panties. He even had, like, a little jingle."

Jack waved his hand in front of him. "And how did it go?"

"I'm not gonna sing it, but the words were something like,

> 'They call me Leotard Chester
> I walk around in scanties
> Not because I'm a jester
> But because I love panties!'"

The table burst out laughing—even Sawyer. She gave them a second to get it together before continuing her story. "I'm trying so hard not to laugh, and also trying to figure out what the hell to do with this guy. Turned out he'd stolen the items from a nearby laundromat."

"Speaking of balls," Jack said, but Sawyer cut him off before he could continue.

"I'll take Things You Wish You Had for $500, Alex."

Jack flipped him off and continued talking. "When I was still in patrol, I arrested the same guy over twenty times for riding his bike naked in public. I always knew it was him thanks to the helpful sign mounted on the back of his bike."

"What'd it say?" asked Brooke.

"'Stay back, oversize equipment.'"

They all laughed even harder. "If I had a dime for every naked dude I've had to deal with, I'd be living on a tropical island by now," said Amelia, shaking her head and then taking a sip of her beer.

"Why are the naked people never the ones you'd want to see?" asked Sawyer, and they all laughed in agreement. For a brief second, their eyes met, and she knew he was thinking about her naked. Or maybe lust swirled through her was because she was remembering the muscled perfection hiding under his clothes.

"What's your crazy cop story?" Brooke asked Amelia. The table went quiet, and she shook her head, once again fingering the necklace around her throat, which Brooke could now see had a simple diamond ring threaded onto it. Sensing that she'd inadvertently stepped into murky waters, Brooke redirected her question, smiling at Sawyer. "What's yours?" she asked, wondering if he'd get all grumpy and quiet again.

He smiled at her and something inside her lit up.

"Oh, man, it's gotta be the snake. My first year on, we get this call—the Atlanta Zoo can't seem to find their python. It's missing. I tuck that away, go about my day, and I'm searching this house—we'd arrested the guy for assault and violating his probation, and then I hear it. This soft, low hissing noise. I turn, and the biggest fucking snake I've ever seen in my life is coiled in the corner, its head moving back and forth. Staring at me. Like I'm lunch." He shuddered. "I hate snakes. I fucking hate them. And this thing is huge."

"So what did you do?" she asked.

"Radioed for help, grabbed a broom that was in the corner and when it darted at me, I used the broom to pin it against the wall. Someone else came in and between the two of us, we managed to get it outside. The zoo people had shown up with a snake bag by then, so we dumped it in there." He shuddered again. "Snakes."

"So if I'm the Karate Kid, I guess that makes you Indiana Jones, huh?" she said, sending him a teasing smile.

He chuckled down into his beer. "Guess so."

It was such a small thing, but it still felt like a win.

Jack's phone rang and he excused himself to take the call. Amelia rose and headed for the bathroom, leaving Sawyer and Brooke alone at the table. A slightly awkward silence hung in the air, and Brooke traced her finger through the condensation from her beer glass on the table.

"So, uh . . ." started Brooke, trying to figure out

what to say to him. It felt strange that even though they'd had crazy, out-of-this-world sex, she didn't really know anything about him. "Too bad about the Braves, huh?" They'd failed to make the playoffs—again—disappointing everyone but surprising no one.

He took a sip of his beer and nodded. "Yeah."

She chewed her lip and decided to go for straight-up honesty instead of fishing for topics he might be interested in. "I don't know what to say to you."

He shrugged. "You don't need to say anything."

"Listen, we're working together and what happened is in the past. I want to make this work. This job's really important to me."

An expression she couldn't quite name flickered across his face just before he popped another nacho in his mouth.

"It's important to me too. I mean, every job's impor-tant, but this one . . ." He let out a long sigh.

"I get it. This one's everything."

He looked over at her, his head tilted. "You do get it, don't you?"

"Why wouldn't I?"

Amelia returned to the table and he shook his head. Okay, so it hadn't been the world's most scintillating conversation, but it was something.

SAWYER LEANED FORWARD, pretending he cared about scooping up the last nacho. But he didn't. Sure, nachos were great, but really he just wanted an excuse to lean in close to Brooke and take a deep breath. Like a diver pulling as much air into his lungs as he could before submerging himself in the cold, dark waters, he wanted to pull a small piece of her deep inside himself. To let that be enough to sustain him because he couldn't have more.

Amelia stretched and then retrieved her helmet from under the table. "All right kids, I'm off. See you in the morning, bitchachos." As she left, Sawyer wondered how she was sleeping these days. Nightmares? Tossing and turning restlessly, unable to shut off the images flashing through her mind? Or in a deep, prescription-drug-induced sleep? Because on any given night, he could check one or all three of those boxes.

Brooke nodded goodbye and then reached for her purse, the tip of her tongue playing against the corner of her mouth in an unconscious gesture as she counted out enough cash to cover their tab. Why did every tiny thing she did make him feel like he was about to jump out of his skin? It was unsettling. Unnerving. There was no fucking way he could work like this.

And that was exactly why he'd gone to the captain and respectfully asked that Brooke be transferred off the team, which probably made him an asshole. Maybe he'd even hinted that Brooke wasn't ready for HEAT, that she was too green to be an asset right now.

That last bit most definitely made him an asshole; no "probably" about it.

Brooke glanced over her shoulder to where Jack stood, leaning against the bar and flirting with the waitress. She laughed and ran a hand up Jack's arm, who then settled himself on one of the barstools, his attention fixed on her.

Brooke sighed. "Looks like I've lost my ride." Shaking her head, she pulled her phone out of her purse. "Guess I'll call an Uber."

Maybe it was because he felt guilty for what he'd done in the captain's office, but he couldn't stop himself from opening his mouth. "Don't. I'll give you a ride back to the station."

She turned to look at him, blinking slowly. Then she nodded, her ponytail grazing her cheek. "If you're sure."

"Not gonna leave you stranded here while Casanova does his thing," he said, standing and jerking his thumb toward the bar.

She stood too, her chair scraping against the floor. With her boots, she was only a couple of inches shorter than him, and he was surprised how much he liked that. How much he liked her lithe, athletic frame. His ex-wife, Krista, had been petite and curvy. Exactly the type he'd always gone for.

Then again, she'd also broken his heart. At first, she'd been into his badge and uniform—but it turned out that interest had only ever been on a surface level, because she hadn't understood what she'd signed up for when she'd married a cop. She'd resented the long hours, the secretive nature of the work, the stress Sawyer had sometimes brought home with him. She'd fallen in love with an idea, not reality, and the fighting had started about a year into their marriage. Ultimately, she'd asked him to choose—the job, or her. He'd chosen the job.

He didn't regret his choice now; the job was part of who he was. It was as though she'd asked him to cut off his arm to prove his love for her. He'd loved her, but the fact that she hadn't understood him, hadn't gotten who he was at his core . . . it had really fucking hurt. For months after they'd split, he'd wondered if he'd made a mistake and chosen wrong, but in the end, he knew it hadn't really been much of a choice. Policing was in his blood, and he couldn't change his identity, even if it meant losing a woman's love. He'd accepted that this was his path, and if he was destined to walk it alone, so be it. He'd always be a cop, and he'd long since given up on finding a woman who understood that he and the job were one and the same. Quite simply, going through the divorce had changed him and how he now saw dating and relationships. He'd made a heartrending choice in the past, and the last thing he wanted to do was get himself into a situation where he'd be forced to make another.

"Hey," Sawyer called as they headed toward the door, Brooke in tow. "I'm gonna drive Simmons back to her car."

Jack tossed a half-hearted wave over his shoulder, completely preoccupied. Sawyer rolled his eyes and held the door for Brooke, her scent making his gut tighten as she passed by him. He ground his teeth together, fighting back the lust heating his blood and making him want to reach for her.

"So be honest," she said, falling into step beside him as he walked toward his gray Ford F-150. "How'd today go?"

He shrugged. Tomorrow it wouldn't matter how today had gone. The captain had seemed receptive to his request, and he'd never turned down a favor for Sawyer before. It wasn't necessarily standard to request a partner change, but given everything that had happened over the past three weeks, Sawyer figured he was due a little leeway. "Fine."

She blew out an impatient breath. "Fine? Great. Thanks for the feedback." She bit her lip and shook her head, as though deciding if she wanted to say more. "No, you know what? It's not fine." They reached his truck and she leaned a hip against the passenger side door. "I'm trying to do my job. That means working with you. That means we have to talk. So if you've got something to say to me, let's hear it."

Her eyes were bright, flashing defiantly. Heat licked up his spine and he stepped into her space and pressed his palms against the truck on either side of her, caging her in. She took a deep breath, her nostrils flaring. His gaze dropped to her mouth, but he forced it back up to meet her eyes. His face was inches from hers when he spoke. "*Hey*?" he said, his voice low and gravelly as he echoed back what she'd said in the storage facility earlier that day. "Fucking *hey*? I had him. You shouldn't have . . . You scared the shit out of me, you know that?"

Her eyes held his in the semidark parking lot, her chest rising and falling, not quite touching his. She swallowed and then she relaxed back against the door, some of the stiffness going out of her shoulders. "I'm sorry. I didn't . . . I'm sorry I scared you." She pressed a finger into his chest, and he glanced down, steeling himself against her touch. "But you didn't have him, Sawyer, and you wouldn't have had him without me. I'm sorry about Walker. I'm sorry for what you've been through. But that's not on me. And everyone—Jack, Amelia, the captain—seems to know that except you. You can't push me away because of Walker."

"This doesn't have anything to do with Ryan."

She pursed her lips together and nodded slowly, dropping her finger from his chest. "Yeah. Sure."

The air seemed to thicken and pulse around them. Her lips parted as she stared at him, something that almost looked like a challenge shining in her eyes. It would take less than a second to slip his arms around her, pull her against him and reclaim that gorgeous mouth.

But getting involved with an assigned partner wasn't just frowned upon—it was a fireable offense.

Didn't matter if he couldn't stop thinking about how she'd felt, how she'd sounded, how she'd tasted— she was off-limits, fully and completely. He reached behind her and pulled the truck's door open. "Get in the truck, Simmons."

She smiled at him and turned, hauling her sexy ass up into the cab of his truck. Once she'd tucked her long legs inside, he closed the door and took his time crossing around to the driver's side, getting his shit together. Something he seemed to be doing a lot around her.

Something he'd hopefully not have to deal with anymore in the very near future.

He slid behind the steering wheel and started the engine. Luke Bryan came blaring out of the speakers, and he hastily reached for the knob on the dash and turned the volume down.

Brooke tipped her head toward the radio. "Love him. I saw him at the Lakewood Amphitheater last summer."

"Me too." His brothers, Hunter and Logan, had come to the city for the weekend. Ryan had come to the concert too. It had been a nice distraction from Sawyer's divorce. The loss of his marriage had left him reeling in a way he hadn't known how to handle.

"Small world."

He grunted in agreement. Truthfully, the world was a little too small for his comfort right now. He tightened his grip on the steering wheel as he maneuvered his truck out of the parking lot. He just needed to get

Brooke back to her car at the station before he did something he'd regret. Then she'd be out of his hair, even if she wasn't out of his brain.

"Can I ask you something?" she asked, swiveling her head to look at him. He kept his eyes on the road and grunted again.

"What the hell's the deal with the Ferrari?"

Sawyer chuckled, the question easing some of his tension as he rolled to a stop at a red light. "You ever heard of the Ward Group?"

"The huge real estate company?" Her eyes widened as she made the connection. "That's his family?"

Sawyer nodded. "Yeah. They don't get along, but he's a trust fund kid. His big fuck-you to them was refusing to have anything to do with the family business and becoming a cop."

"Hard to imagine Jack not getting along with anyone. You, on the other hand . . ."

"Hey, I get along fine with my family," he said, hating how much he liked this. Just driving in the dark, shooting the shit.

"Brothers and sisters?"

"Two brothers. I'm the middle. Hunter's the oldest, and he's in the air force, stationed up in Charleston. Logan's the baby. He's a firefighter in Savannah."

Brooke sucked in a breath and grimaced. "Ouch. I'm sorry."

He laughed as he turned onto Juniper Street. The rivalry between cops and firefighters was notorious and longstanding. "What about you? Brothers and sisters?"

The smile faded from her face and she shook her head. "No. Just me."

He wanted to know more, but he kept his mouth shut and his eyes on the road. There would be no getting to know her better. They sat in silence for a few minutes, nearing the station.

"My turn," he said. "The blood on your dress the other night. Were you being straight with me?"

She groaned. "Yeah, Sawyer. I was."

"Please tell me you're not still dating that guy."

She blew out a breath but didn't answer for several seconds, probably debating whether or not to challenge him about why he even cared. "No. I'm not still dating that guy." She shook her head, turning her attention out the window.

He stopped at another red light and glanced at her, feeling both angry and indignant on her behalf. What kind of asshat would fuck her over, not realizing what he had?

"One more question," she said as they pulled into the station's parking lot. "Amelia's necklace. There's a diamond ring on it and every time someone mentions Walker, she touches it. Were they . . . ?"

He put the truck in Park, the familiar ache radiating through his chest. "Yeah. They were together. His parents found the ring after . . . after." He swallowed thickly, emotion clogging his throat.

Brooke's face tightened, a shadow of pain flickering across her features. "I'm so sorry. I can't even imagine . . ." She took a deep breath. "I lost my parents when I was a kid, so I know what it's like to lose someone close to you. To feel like your world's been turned upside down."

He switched off the ignition. "You lost your parents?"

She nodded rapidly, her ponytail bouncing behind her. "When I was nine. Hit-and-run accident."

The ache in his chest bloomed into something tender and raw. Parents gone. No siblings. Alone. "Foster care?"

She shook her head. "No, my grandparents, my mom's parents, took me in and raised me, made sure I had a good, happy childhood. My grandfather died a few years ago, so it's just me and Nan now." Pain shone in her eyes, and he found himself shifting closer.

"I'm sorry, Brooke. I'm sorry." And he was. Sorry for her loss. Sorry for being an asshole. Sorry she'd probably hate him tomorrow.

She undid her seat belt and moved a bit closer. "Thanks." They were completely alone, shrouded in darkness in the silent cab of his truck. The traffic on Peachtree was minimal, the lot filled with empty cars. Cocooned away with her like this, his instinct was to give some of the comfort she'd given him the other night back to her. For the sake of . . . fuck, of everything, he needed to figure out a way to squash it down and ignore it.

He reached for her, his hand grazing against her

waist, but he grabbed her door handle instead, pushing open the passenger side door. "Goodnight, Simmons."

Brooke stared at him for a second, confusion and something he couldn't name flickering across her face. But after a moment, she grabbed her purse and slipped out of the truck.

"Night, Sawyer. Thanks for the ride."

She slammed the door behind her without a backward glance.

Chapter Five

IT WAS NEVER a good thing to get called into the captain's office first thing in the morning. Brooke may have been a baby detective, as Sawyer—frustratingly sexy, maddeningly tempting Sawyer—had called her yesterday, but even she knew that. Second day on the job, and she was already getting hauled into the principal's office.

The captain had called her over before she'd even had a chance to sit down at her desk or grab a cup of coffee, and the stern look on his face had her wiping her damp palms on her jeans as she made her way toward his office. Her spine tingled, as though she could feel the eyes of her colleagues on her. Had she done something wrong? Had she managed to fuck everything up after just one shift?

Her pulse hammered in her temples as she stepped

into his office, forcing a professional smile onto her face. Back at her old precinct, she'd been able to read her commanding officer, but Hill was new to her, and she had no idea if this was typical, or if she was about to get her ass handed to her.

The captain gestured at one of the empty chairs facing his desk, and before her butt hit the upholstery, Sawyer stepped into the room and received an equally stern glare from the captain. It was unsettling the way her entire body lit up like Christmas at just the sight of him.

"Detective Matthews, have a seat." The captain gestured to the empty chair beside Brooke. She glanced over at Sawyer as he sat down, wondering if she could pick up a clue as to what this was about from him. But he didn't meet her eyes, instead keeping his gaze forward, focused on the captain's desk. His body language was tense and closed off, and something about the way he wasn't even looking at her set off an alarm bell deep in her brain.

Oh, God. Had someone told the captain about her history with Sawyer? Getting romantically and/or sexually involved with an assigned partner was a fireable offense. Had someone overheard something and reported them? A wave of nausea rolled through her stomach, and she swallowed, forcing herself to sit back in her seat.

The captain closed the door to his office and then took a seat behind his desk, folding his hands in front of him, looking unhappy as his eyes darted back and forth between them. Several seconds of silence filled the room before he finally spoke. When he did, his words did nothing to ease the churning in Brooke's stomach.

"Does someone want to tell me what the hell's going on here?"

"Sir?" Brooke asked, frowning while hoping she wasn't about to get fired. Until she knew what this was about, she wasn't saying anything more.

Sawyer said nothing—no surprise there—and sat stone still in his seat. A thick, almost suffocating tension seemed to fill the room. Unable to help herself, she touched her detective shield, wondering if she'd have to give it back a mere twenty-four hours after first putting it around her neck.

The captain sighed, his gaze narrowing as it continued to swing back and forth between them. Finally it settled on her. "Yesterday after you'd clocked out, Detective Matthews came and spoke to me. Specifically, he came and spoke to me about you. He requested that you be immediately transferred off his team, and implied that you weren't ready for HEAT. Can you think of any reason as to why he'd do that?"

Sawyer had gone behind her back and tried to get her booted from the team? The captain's words were like a knife to her chest. For a second she couldn't breathe. Couldn't think. Couldn't seem to focus on anything besides the panic and shock and anger rioting through her body. She felt as though Sawyer had pulled the rug out from under her, and that rug had been covering up a gaping black hole. Her mouth went dry, and she licked her lips, knowing she needed to say something.

She cleared her throat softly, glancing over at Sawyer and trying to keep her shock and anger out of her tone. "No sir, I can't think of a reason, and respectfully, I disagree. I believe I'm an asset to both this team and this unit. I don't know why Detective Matthews would've told you that." She hoped he couldn't pick up on the slight tremble in her voice. Blood rushed to her cheeks, a mixture of anger and humiliation heating her skin.

God, she was so stupid. She'd known that she had some work to do where Sawyer was concerned, but she'd never in a million years thought he'd go behind her back to the captain and try to get her removed from the team by making it seem as though she couldn't do her job. After last night—the beer and nachos, exchanging cop stories, the ride back to the station—she'd foolishly thought that everything would be fine. That they'd figure out a way to navigate around their physical attraction and maybe even become friends.

But she didn't make friends with assholes, so that ship had sailed. Assuming she still had a job here.

The captain nodded slowly. "You wouldn't be here if I didn't believe that." A small bit of relief trickled through her.

Sawyer still said nothing, staring ahead, not looking at her.

The captain sighed and leaned back in his chair. "Listen, I don't know what's going on between you two, if you have some kind of personal history, or if this is about you—" he jabbed a finger in Sawyer's direction— "needing to get your head straight about Walker being gone." He rubbed a hand over his smooth head. "Frankly, I don't care. We have over sixty open cases right now, including the Baracoa investigation. I don't have time for this shit." His words took on a tinge of anger, and Brooke sat up a bit straighter, hoping that this was a reprimand and nothing more.

"I'm sorry, sir." She didn't know what else to say.

He shook his head. "No need for you to apologize, Simmons." He leveled his gaze at Sawyer. "Contrary to what Detective Matthews seems to think, *I* run this unit, not him." He stood from behind his desk. "Whatever shit is between you, work it out. You're both adults, both detectives, and I expect you to behave professionally. I don't want to hear about this again. I won't have squabbles—personal or professional— derailing my unit. Am I clear?" With hardened eyes, he stared down at Sawyer.

He nodded. "Yes, sir. Understood." His deep voice came out rough around the edges.

"Briefing in ten." He shot each of them an intimidating glare. "Until then, I'll give you the room. Sort your shit out. That's an order."

"Yes, sir," they said in unison, standing as he left the room. The door latched behind him and Brooke's anger exploded, bubbling up out of her like boiling water.

"You fucking asshole!" She slammed her hands onto

her hips. "What the fuck, Matthews? What the *actual fuck*?"

He crossed his arms over his chest, staring at the floor, shaking his head. "I didn't have a choice, Brooke."

Anger crackled over her skin like electricity, and she forced herself to suck in a deep breath. "You didn't have a choice? Bullshit. I didn't do anything yesterday to give you the right to go to the captain and tell him I can't do my job. If you have some kind of problem with me, you should've come to talk to me. But oh wait, you don't do that. I'm so done with this *me caveman me no use words* shit."

He didn't flinch. "There was nothing to talk about. This isn't going to work."

"Why? Because of Walker? Because you don't like having a woman save your ass? Is this some kind of macho garbage?"

He shook his head. "No. You know we can't work together."

She took a step closer to him, narrowing her eyes as he met her gaze. "So this is because we had sex?"

When Sawyer spoke, his voice was low and fierce. "You're a distraction, Brooke."

She ground her teeth together. "I'm a distraction? The fuck does that mean?"

He took a step closer, erasing the distance between them. Despite her anger, her nipples hardened at having him so close. It was no wonder she responded the way she did to him, given her fucked-up radar for eligible men. "It means that I need to focus on bringing down the cartel and getting justice for Ryan, and I . . . fuck, I can't think straight around you."

"You can't think straight around me? That's the stupidest excuse I've ever heard."

"We've got a problem here, and I know I'm not the only one who sees it. You can't think straight around me either."

Another hot flare of anger erupted through her and she let out a frustrated grunt. She actually thought she might throttle him because he wasn't 100 percent wrong. She spun and marched a few steps away before turning back to face him. "So your solution's to make me look incompetent? You're a real piece of work, you know that?" He stared at her, a flicker of guilt flashing across his otherwise stony features. "You went behind my back to my commanding officer and made it sound like I can't do my job. What gives you the fucking right, Matthews? How *dare* you. How fucking dare you!" He opened his mouth, but she held up a hand. "No, for once I don't want you to talk because I need you to hear this. I worked damn hard to get where I am and I'm not going to let anyone take it away from me. Especially a macho caveman asshole like you." She looked away and shook her head, letting out a frustrated laugh. "I was willing to give you the benefit of the doubt because I know you're hurting, but you don't get to take your shit out on me, and on my career. This is over the line. Fuck, over the line doesn't even touch it. This is like setting the line on fire." She scoffed and shook her head. "I'm a distraction. God."

"With the shit we deal with, neither of us can afford a distraction. You can't deny that. This is complicated, maybe even dangerous. For both of us."

"Because we had sex." She blew out a breath and lowered her voice. "Even though nothing can happen between us now." She swallowed as she replayed their night together, arousal spiking through her, tangling with her anger. How was it possible to want to slap someone and get them naked at the same time?

He nodded slowly. "Because I can't stop thinking about it, and I need my head in the game." She wanted to throw a chair through the window. What kind of asshole had no qualms about throwing her career under the bus because he couldn't handle how he felt about her? And what did it say about her judgment that as pissed as she was, she still wanted him?

"Then let me uncomplicate it for you real quick. There will *never* be anything between us, Matthews. I think you're a selfish, self-centered asshole, and I don't want anything to do with you." She stepped forward and jabbed a finger into his chest, his muscles rock-hard against her fingertip. Heat flared in his eyes, and she couldn't tell if it was anger, lust or some messed up combination of both. "I'm here to do my job, and I'm not going anywhere. If you ever try to sabotage my career again, you'll have a hell of a lot more than distraction to worry about."

She didn't wait for him to answer before she turned and marched out of the captain's office, fighting the urge to slam the door behind her.

A SILENCE SETTLED over the captain's office as the door snapped shut behind Brooke, leaving Sawyer alone with his throbbing heart and raging erection. Maybe it was fucked up, but the fiery way she'd laid into him had turned him on. Then again, pretty much everything she did turned him on. Like she was his sexual kryptonite— she made him weak in ways he was powerless to resist. It had taken everything he had not to press her up against the wall and kiss her, which just proved his point that they couldn't work together.

He'd hoped that Hill would see his side of things, but apparently going to him had been a mistake. He hadn't expected him to haul both of them into his office. At worst, he'd thought the captain would simply ignore his request. He hadn't anticipated this, and he couldn't help but feel angry with himself, because he should've. He'd been so focused on getting some distance from Brooke that he hadn't thought it through.

More proof that he couldn't think straight around her. Normally everything he did was careful, measured and planned, with all outcomes accounted for. But he'd been sloppy in a desperate attempt to find a way to handle his attraction to her, and it had blown up in his face. Because although he hadn't thought it possible, he now somehow wanted her more. The way she'd stood up for herself and torn into him—which he'd deserved. The way his body responded to hers and caught him off guard.

It hit him with the weight of a ton of bricks that he could fall for her if he let himself. She was everything he hadn't known he'd wanted. Gorgeously sexy, smart, tough. She understood the job and everything it entailed—he'd never connected with someone over work before. The thought was sobering enough to make him realize it was for the best that she hated his guts now. Since she wasn't going anywhere, nothing could happen between them.

He pulled open the door to the captain's office and headed toward the briefing room, trying to convince himself it was a good thing that Brooke thought he was king of the assholes. At least maybe that would help them stay on track professionally.

It felt like cold comfort.

The briefing room was almost full, and he took a seat next to Jack—who, he noticed, hadn't shaved this morning and was wearing the same clothes as yesterday, his attention glued to his phone. It was always the way with him—he'd burn hot and fast with someone until it inevitably fizzled out after a week or two. As far as Jack Ward was concerned, the scariest word in the English language was *commitment*, and Sawyer had to admit he could understand.

He nodded at Jack as voices swirled around them, the usual focused energy filling the room. He took a deep breath, trying to settle himself after what had just gone down in the captain's office. The smell of coffee and Pine-Sol filled the air, and he scuffed his boot over an old stain on the carpet tile in front of him. Just as he looked up, a man he didn't recognize sat down in the empty chair next to Brooke. They shook hands, and he offered her a wide, friendly smile as they chatted.

Something cold started to burn deep in his gut, but with a shake of his head, he pushed it away.

Whatever. It was a free country. She could talk to whoever the hell she wanted.

His eyes bounced back to her, and something hot and possessive crashed through him at the way the man was looking at her with pure masculine appreciation. His gut churned uncomfortably. Fuck, he'd thought he could shove everything down into neat little compartments, keeping one emotion, one goal, one need separate from the others. Like lures in a tackle box. But nothing wanted to stay in its place, creating a chaotic snare he didn't know how to process.

The man held a manila folder in one hand, and he tapped it against Brooke's knee as he leaned in a bit closer, as though telling her a secret. The sound of her laugh was like a punch to the solar plexus.

Fun times.

Thankfully, the briefing started and the captain brought them up to speed on several ongoing investigations, assigning the day's various tasks—follow-up calls, interviews, recon. The unit-wide briefing was useful because it allowed for what the captain referred to as "cross-pollination." The criminal world—especially the world they dealt with—was small, and often one case was connected to another. Being aware of what the others were working on, of what leads they had, sometimes led to a break in something else.

So Sawyer was surprised when the captain dismissed everyone except him, Jack, Amelia, Brooke, and Prince Charming. Who, Sawyer noticed, also had a detective shield around his neck and couldn't seem to take his eyes off of Brooke.

The captain nodded at the newcomer. "Everyone, this is Detective Adam Jensen from Vice. The information he has is sensitive and confidential, and at this point, need-to-know." Sawyer nodded, suddenly understanding the cleared-out room.

The detective stood, and Sawyer found himself sizing Jensen up. A little over six feet, fit. Short, dark brown hair. Clean-shaven. The kind of nose that looked like it had been broken a couple of times, but the bastard was good-looking enough that it didn't seem to matter. Early thirties—probably around the same age as Brooke. No wedding ring. Sawyer immediately disliked him. Jensen glanced around at the team. "Ward reached out to me asking if I know anything about those funky pills y'all found in the storage unit."

"Do you?" asked Sawyer, the two syllables coming out gruff and low.

Jensen seemed unfazed. In fact, a cocky smile spread

across his face and he tapped the folder against his palm. "It's your lucky day, because hell yeah I know what they are." He pulled a picture of the rainbow-colored pills from his folder and tacked it to the board. "This, my friends, is called Tantrik."

"What can you tell us about it?" asked Amelia, leaning forward with her forearms braced on her thighs.

Jensen smiled, clearly not minding being the center of attention. Sawyer squinted at him. "Ready to love me? Because you're gonna love me." He winked at Brooke, who smiled back at him. He tapped the photo. "Tantrik is a combination of the street drug ecstasy and a controlled pharmaceutical—nonnarcotic—called sildenafil. It's used commercially as an erectile dysfunction drug."

"So it's like ecstasy for your dick?" Brooke asked.

Sawyer ground his teeth together. Why did Brooke have to say "dick" in that sultry voice of hers? Why?

Jensen pointed at her. "Bingo. The idea's that you take it, trip balls, have sex for hours and stay hard. I mean, if you need a drug for that sort of thing." He bounced his eyebrows in a way that implied he didn't. Brooke laughed, pink spots appearing her cheeks.

Sawyer couldn't remember the last time he'd wanted to punch someone so badly.

"So you obviously got your hands on some," said Amelia, gesturing at the board. "If you know what it's called and the breakdown."

Jensen nodded. "Yeah. Which brings us to—" he

reopened his folder and pulled out another picture "—Exhibit B. Also known as Exhibit Be Glad This Isn't You."

Sawyer sat forward in his chair, studying the picture, unsure what, exactly, he was looking at.

"Wait," said Jack, somehow managing to arch an eyebrow and squint at the same time. "Is that a . . ." He swallowed thickly. "Is that a dick?"

Jensen tapped the picture. "And circle gets the square."

They all let out a collective disgusted groan. The equipment in the picture was lumpy and engorged, with the skin shiny and tight. The skin had broken in a few places, leaving traces of pus and blood behind. The head was an angry-looking purple. Sawyer frowned, shifting uncomfortably in his seat.

Jensen continued. "This is what happens when you overdose on Tantrik. This sad-looking joystick belongs to a college kid named Chase Anderson. When he showed up in the ER, he told the doctor what had happened. The doc filed a vice report, which is how we got our hands on the rest of Anderson's supply and saw firsthand the damage it can do."

"Is the kid okay?" asked Brooke.

"Physically, yeah. The doctors were able to drain the excess blood and then treated him with medication. He'll heal. But I think the poor dude was pretty scared."

Jack and Sawyer both nodded sympathetically. "So, where'd he get it?" asked Jack.

"His girlfriend bought it for him, thought it'd spice things up. There's a club in Midtown called the Manhattan Ballroom."

"MBR," said Sawyer. "Is this at all connected to the Baracoa cartel? We caught someone from the Desperados guarding a storage locker where we found bags full of Tantrik. He copped to running security for the cartel."

Jensen shrugged. "That's as good a lead as any. We haven't been able to get hard evidence—sorry, no pun intended—that it's coming from them, but given that they pretty much run the drug scene in this town, and you found a bunch in a storage locker connected to them, there's an extremely good chance this drug is theirs."

"Did this Anderson kid say who sold his girl the pills?" asked Brooke.

"We pressed him for dealer specifics, but he didn't know anything. When we talked to the girlfriend, she admitted she'd bought it from a dancer there, but wouldn't give up more than that."

The captain nodded. "Thank you, Detective Jensen." He turned his attention to the four of them. "This could be our in to the cartel. Ward and Perez, stay on the Desperados—you're making good headway there. Matthews and Simmons, this is yours. This is an undercover, need-to-know op, and the objective is simple: infiltrate the dealers to find the suppliers. If the suppliers are the cartel like we suspect, we'll have a shot at taking them down."

"One other thing," said Jensen, his mouth twitching with a suppressed smile. "The Manhattan Ballroom is a strip club."

Sawyer and Brooke's eyes met, and he thought he saw the tiniest flicker of panic in hers. He'd been about to say something comforting and reassuring—hopefully—but then Jensen continued speaking. "A *male* strip club."

Brooke threw her head back and laughed. Sawyer felt frozen to the spot, unable to fully process what he'd just heard. Aside from Brooke, who was laughing so hard she had tears in her eyes, everyone stared at him.

He shrugged. He'd do whatever it took to bring down the bastards who'd killed Ryan. "Fine. I'll get myself hired at the club."

The captain nodded. "That's the plan. If you can't get hired, we'll reevaluate, try to find another way in."

"I'll get in," he said, feeling a clawing pressure inside his chest. He didn't want to do it, but it was the only way to try to make things right. "I'll make it work."

"And what about Brooke?" asked Jack. "I'm just trying to figure out how she can still work with Sawyer and back him up if he gets in."

"Easy," said Jensen, once again winking at Brooke. "Stripper groupie. You go every night, watch, hang out in the audience, pretend you're his biggest fan. Stay close and see what other connections you can make."

The smile slid off her face. Sawyer felt smugly satisfied that she wasn't laughing anymore. But then something else chased away the smugness, something he couldn't quite name. His stomach churned at the thought of having to strip and dance in front of Brooke, night after night. Brooke, who he couldn't have. Brooke, who hated him.

As much as he hated the acronym *FML*, he had to admit that this really felt like an *FML* moment.

The captain nodded. "Any questions?" Everyone shook their heads. "Let's bring these bastards down. Dismissed."

Everyone murmured in agreement, filtering out of the room and leaving Sawyer and Brooke alone.

Before he could say anything, she'd already pushed up out of her chair. "Maybe your stripper name can be Karma."

She turned and left the room, leaving Sawyer wondering how his entire world could've gone to such shit in the span of only a few weeks.

Chapter Six

BROOKE HAD HOPED that as the day progressed, she'd start to feel a little more . . . certain of the task ahead of her. But with each passing hour, all she felt was foggier and foggier. She was supposed to be Sawyer's backup under the guise of a stripper groupie? How was she going to watch that every night, knowing he was (a) completely off-limits and (b) an asshole?

And that was assuming that he'd (a) go through with it instead of coming up with an alternate plan, and (b) even knew how to dance in the first place.

As she followed him down to the parking garage, she couldn't help but think that this entire mission had *unmitigated disaster* written all over it.

Sawyer stepped into the small office and peered at the board where the keys to the various vehicles they had access to were kept. Even through the smudged windows, she couldn't help but stare at him. He rubbed a hand over the stubble on his jaw, and her eyes went to his arms. He reached up to take a set of keys and she felt an appreciative curl of heat low in her belly. It was like his muscles had muscles, popping and flexing fluidly as he moved. A set of keys disappeared into his massive hand and he emerged from the office, heading toward a vehicle without waiting to see if she was with him.

Right. The whole asshole thing. She stared at his toned butt as they walked, and so to compensate, she replayed their earlier conversation—the one where he'd tried to throw her under the bus and get her booted from his team because she was a distraction. As though he was so attracted to her that being around her was a challenge.

Yeah, well. Maybe she could relate to that. A little. Maybe.

But it didn't matter, because he was both her partner and a jerk, and if he thought he could just walk all over her and run things his way, he was sorely mistaken. New to the team or not, she wasn't his lackey.

"Keys," she said as she came up beside him, matching her stride with his. She held her hand out, palm up.

He kept moving, glancing over at her as though she'd just asked him if he believed in aliens. He slowed as they approached a newer model Mustang, shiny black. "I'm driving."

She scooted around in front of him and planted her butt against the driver's side door handle. "Keys."

He crossed his arms over his chest, making her mouth water, as always, and stared at her. "And you think you get to drive because?"

She shrugged and then jerked her thumb at the vehicle behind her. "Because this one's a bit more sophisticated than the Flintstones car. You know how to start it without scrambling your feet on the ground?"

He grunted and the tiniest smirk pulled at his lips. "Cute. Fine, you want to drive? What's the address of the club?"

Well, shit. She had it in her phone, but hadn't memorized it. When she didn't say anything, his smirk grew. He reached for the door handle, his hand grazing her hip. "Get in the car, Wilma."

She rolled her eyes, but moved away from the door. "Fine, but I get to drive next time."

"If you know where we're actually going, you can drive whenever you want."

As she crossed around to the passenger's side, she couldn't help but wonder if he was actually trying to teach her something here. About not overlooking details, about preparedness, about not relying on anything or anyone but herself for crucial pieces of information.

Huh. Maybe the jerk had a point about her being a baby detective. That set the acid in her stomach churning, and she cleared her throat as she dropped into the passenger's side seat.

They pulled out of the parking garage and headed north from the station toward Midtown, merging onto the highway. It wasn't quite three in the afternoon, so the usual traffic hadn't hit yet. Silence filled the car, and after several seconds of staring at the concrete barricades along the side of the highway, Brooke reached forward and pushed the knob on the console, turning the radio on. Beyoncé's "Drunk in Love" came through the speakers, and Brooke sat back in her seat. She'd barely returned her gaze to the window when the music changed, switching from Beyoncé to Sam Hunt. She glanced over at Sawyer, whose attention was on the road as he navigated the Mustang through the building traffic.

She reached forward and changed the station back to Beyoncé. Maybe it was bratty, but she didn't care. She hated the way he got under her skin, the way he took over seemingly every single situation, the way he'd made her think that everything would be fine and then humiliated her. The way he'd made her realize that she had more to learn than she'd thought.

The radio changed back to Sam Hunt. "Shotgun doesn't get to pick the music."

On their left, the Midtown skyline rose up, clear and sharp against the blue sky, which was dotted with a few fluffy clouds. Sawyer's gaze flicked to her, and she stared at him as she turned the station back to Beyoncé. "No? Then what's shotgun's job?"

"Shotgun buys the coffees," he said, using the controls on the steering wheel to change the station back. His jaw flexed and he rubbed a hand over his mouth.

"No deal," she said, once again turning the station back to Beyoncé. "I only buy coffee for people who don't try to humiliate me in front of my captain."

He let out a heavy sigh. "Fine," he bit out. "Pick a different preset and we'll both agree not to change it. Split the difference," he muttered, his grip tightening on the steering wheel.

"Fine." She hit one of the other presets and suddenly the synthesized chords of "Karma Chameleon" filled the car.

Sawyer made a disapproving noise and went to reach for one of the other preset buttons, but Brooke swatted his hand away. Electricity danced up her arm at the feel of his skin beneath her fingertips. "You promised."

He yanked his hand back, and a tension filled the car. After a second, he rolled his eyes and huffed out a growling sigh. Why was everything he did so impossibly sexy? She'd wanted to piss him off, annoy him, but this . . . this was kinda fun.

Near Tech Square, Sawyer pulled off the highway, weaving his way north until they turned onto a quiet side street.

"That's it right there," he said, pointing at a completely nondescript low-lying gray stucco building with white awnings. No signage. Tinted windows. The building looked clean and well-kept, with a gated area around the back. A few pieces of broken furniture lay beside the garbage bins. An Irish pub sat on one side, a juice bar on the other. A high-rise apartment building rose up directly across the street, with a dry cleaner, pharmacy and dog groomer taking up the business space on the main floor.

"I didn't realize there were strip clubs in Midtown," said Brooke, taking in the manicured boulevards and tidy sidewalks.

Sawyer shrugged. "If they're targeting college girls and young professional women with Tantrik, it makes sense. Yuppies and Millennials, especially female ones, aren't going to roll into the Bluff looking for drugs." He pulled around the block and then slid into a parking spot in an alley across the street. They weren't going in the club today—just scoping it out and doing some basic recon. The club was quiet and dark, obviously not open yet.

"Pretty small place," he said, and she studied him, trying to figure out what he was feeling.

She nodded. "If you're able to get in, it should be easy to figure out who the dealers are."

"I'll get in."

She arched an eyebrow. "Can you even dance?"

"Just because I'm a country boy doesn't mean I can't dance."

"That's not an answer." She curled her fingers into her palms, digging her nails into her skin to steel herself against asking him where he was from. There would be no more personal conversations.

"I'll figure it out." He swung his head to look at her. "I have to. For Ryan. This is our chance."

"I get that. But if you can't dance, they're not going to hire you."

He smirked and leaned a bit closer. "You and I both know I don't have any issues in either the hip movement or rhythm department."

Blood rushed to her cheeks, and she bit her lip, fighting back the butterflies flapping in her stomach at the memories he'd just conjured up.

"Oh, yeah? Maybe I faked all that. To spare your ego."

He leaned even closer, his eyes glinting. "Sweetheart, we both know you didn't fake a damn thing. Trust me. I can dance." He reached forward, slipping his arm behind her seat. Her nipples beaded and she held her breath as she tried to come up with a snappy comeback.

He pulled a digital camera from the back seat. Not reaching for her at all, but the camera. "Well, well, well," he said, his focus trained directly ahead.

"What?"

He raised the camera and started snapping pictures, adjusting the lens between clicks. "Look who it is. Headed toward the gate there."

Brooke followed Sawyer's gaze and smiled. "Holy shit. Is that the Sheriff?"

"Sure is. Going into the MBR with a backpack." He snapped a few more pictures as the Sheriff unlocked the gate and then disappeared inside the club.

When Sawyer lowered the camera, a grim smile

stretched across his face. "Fucking Baracoa. I *knew* they were involved."

Brooke nodded in agreement, her cheeks still a bit hot. "The fact that he's here is a slam dunk, for sure." She reached for the camera. "Let me see what you got."

He handed her the camera, their fingers brushing. The cheesy radio station they'd landed on started playing "I Wanna Sex You Up." Because of course it had. God, even the radio station was conspiring against her. How was she supposed to keep him at arm's length and remember that he was an off-limits first-class asshole if she kept being reminded of how freaking fantastic he'd been in bed? As she took the camera, Sawyer turned the volume down. Ah, so he'd noticed the song too. She couldn't help the tiny satisfied smile that pulled at her lips.

Forcing herself to focus, she flipped through the pictures he'd snapped, zooming in on the Sheriff's face, committing it to memory.

"Wow. You know, for a career criminal involved with a drug cartel, he's actually pretty good-looking." He was tall and fit, with short brown hair, and rugged features. He walked with a swaggering confidence that made it clear he wasn't someone who took shit from anyone.

"Jesus, you really do have terrible taste in men," Sawyer said, pulling the camera out of her hands.

She shot him a glare and then slowly arched an eyebrow. "Tell me about it."

He opened and closed his mouth, as though searching for something to say, but then the Sheriff emerged—without the backpack—and Sawyer resumed taking pictures, documenting the delivery they'd just witnessed.

"You know, maybe I won't need your backup on this," he said quietly, setting the camera down as he stared ahead, his eyes still trained on the club. "It's a small place, we've already got solid evidence. It'll be in and out, piece of cake."

"Right. And when you're dancing around in a man-thong, you're going to put your gun where, exactly?"

Much to her satisfaction, he actually blushed and rubbed a hand over the back of his neck. "I'll figure something out."

"It's too dangerous for you to work a case alone, and you know the captain would never go for it. Especially after what went down in his office this morning." She studied the club, watching the completely oblivious pedestrians stroll by on the sidewalk. "So, what's your plan? How are you getting in? I mean, that might be a challenge, right?"

He frowned and shook his head. "That'll be the easy part."

"Oh, really?"

"Yes, really. I have years of undercover experience. I know what I'm doing."

She waved her hand. "All right then, Obi Wan. Teach me. Show me."

He sat quietly for a moment, and then nodded, picking up his phone from where he'd tossed it on the dash. Pulling up the club's information, he dialed the main number listed and then put the call on speakerphone.

"Manhattan Ballroom." A woman's voice answered on the third ring. Brooke pressed her fingers to her lips, still giggling over the club's name. Sawyer rolled his eyes at her.

"Yeah, hi," said Sawyer, and Brooke's eyebrows shot up at the way his voice had lost all its regular gruff grumpiness. "I was wondering if you're hiring dancers right now."

"We're always looking for new talent. We have open auditions every other Tuesday. There's one next week."

"Great. What time?"

"Noon. Prepare an audition routine and show us what you got. You have experience?"

"Some, not a lot. Mostly smaller places outside of Atlanta."

"Sounds good, sugar. We'll see you next week."

The call ended and Sawyer tossed his phone back into the cup holder. "See?" he asked, shrugging. "Piece of cake."

"Oh, totally," she said, biting her lip. "Now all you have to do is come up with a stripper routine good enough to get hired."

Sawyer mumbled something that sounded an awful

lot like "fuck me" as he pulled the car out of the alley and headed back toward the station.

LATER THAT DAY, Sawyer sat with his feet propped up on his desk, crossing his ankles as he leafed through a folder, flipping through the case files Jensen had made copies of for the team. He scowled at Jensen's messy, scrawling signature along the bottom of one of the reports and with a heavy sigh, closed the file and tossed it onto his desk. With or without Jensen's intel, Sawyer would make sure Baracoa paid for what they'd done. The fantasy of seeing Ernesto Hernandez locked away for life in prison fueled him. Once he was behind bars, then maybe Sawyer would actually be able to breathe. Maybe he wouldn't feel like his insides were puréed chaos all the time.

Right now, it felt as though his brain was a blender, whirring and mixing his thoughts until he couldn't separate them, couldn't stop them from spinning and melting together. Ryan's death. Brooke. The Manhattan Ballroom.

His gaze slid to Brooke's empty desk, directly across from his. Jack was interrogating another member of the Desperados they'd just brought in, and he'd taken Brooke with him to give her the chance to observe and learn. As he stared at her desk, he rubbed a hand over his chest, a dull ache radiating right up the center. It felt like heartburn, but he recognized it immediately as guilt. Going to the captain and making it sound as though Brooke couldn't do her job because he couldn't handle his own attraction to her was shitty, plain and simple. He knew he should've found another way to handle their situation. A less selfish way, even though given that they couldn't happen, it was probably a very good thing she thought he was an asshole now.

He needed to remember all of the reasons why they were a bad idea. He shouldn't have flirted with her in the car earlier, but he hadn't been able to help himself. The words had simply come out of his mouth, as easy and natural as breathing. She broke through his walls without even trying, which meant keeping her at arm's length was crucial. Now that they finally had a break in the Baracoa case, the last thing he needed was to go and get himself fired.

"Idiot," he muttered to himself, pulling his feet off of his desk and waking up his computer. He needed to do the research he'd been putting off.

Normally he lived for undercover work. In the past, he'd infiltrated a weapons trafficking operation, various small drug operations, a gang of violent bank robbers, and in his biggest case, a human trafficking ring that kidnapped immigrant women and sold them into sex slavery. He was damn good at his job, and normally thrived on figuring out his way in.

Thriving wasn't the word to describe how he was feeling right now. Impersonating a criminal scumbag was one thing—he'd dealt with enough of them during his police career that blending in with them wasn't a challenge. But this . . . shit, this was a whole other ball game. Dancing, entertaining women, fitting in with the type of dudes who did this for a living. He knew he was attractive and could dance reasonably well, but what if that wasn't enough?

He opened his web browser and pulled up the club's website. The image of a man's bare chest—waxed and coated in baby oil—greeted him, while bright blue-and-white letters across the top proclaimed the club the "ultimate ladies night out" with the "hottest male strippers in Georgia!" He clicked on the gallery tab, scrolling through the current dancers. He looked at the pictures a bit more slowly, wondering who'd sold Chase Anderson's girlfriend the Tantrik, and if there was more than one of them dealing. Sebastian Steele. Dominick Valentino. Damian St. Vincent. Jack Hammer. At that last one, Sawyer scrubbed a hand over his face. Right. He'd have to come up with a cheesy stage name. He kept scrolling. None of the guys looked like seasoned criminals or hardcore drug dealers. More likely than not, the ones who dealt probably sold Tantrik on the side as a way to make a little extra money.

Below the photos were links to several video clips. With a sigh, he clicked on one. Several men stood on the stage wearing nothing but American-flag-themed Speedos, their chests bare and shining in the flashing lights as they danced and thrust their hips to James Brown's "Living in America." The music was almost totally lost, unable to compete with the excited squeals and shrieks of the audience.

He clicked on another video, watching as a man pulled a woman up on stage, sat her down in a leopard-print chair, and guided her hands all over his abs. Something pulled low in his gut. What if he couldn't get hired? What if he couldn't do this? It would be such a piss-off to get within grabbing distance of something solid on the cartel only to have it slip through his fingers because he couldn't find a way in. If he couldn't get justice for Ryan because he couldn't do his fucking job.

He clicked on another video, watching the same group of men dance in unison as shirtless marines, and he took some comfort in the fact that none of them seemed to be outstanding professional-level dancers. They were decent dancers with rhythm whose appeal was in their fit bodies, and while he didn't like to brag, he knew his body was on par with what these guys had.

He could do this. For Ryan. To bring the cartel down. To make Atlanta a safer place. He had to.

He hadn't been bullshitting Brooke when he'd told her that he could dance, but he knew he had a lot of work ahead of him if he hoped to get hired by the club. Closing the website, he navigated to YouTube and typed "male stripper" into the search bar. Pulling up various videos, he started taking mental notes on how they moved, how they played the crowd, the pace at which the items of clothing disappeared. Lots of hip movement. Lots of body rolls. Lots of flirty looks and winks. Basically, it was simulated sex disguised as dancing, in time to music. The keys seemed to be a buff chest, confidence and making it look like you were having the time of your life.

"I really hope that's research." Amelia's voice came from behind him, and he turned in his chair to see her standing a few feet away.

He nodded as she plunked down on his desk, facing him. "Yeah. I've probably forever ruined my YouTube search history."

She smacked him playfully on the shoulder. "Dude. That's what incognito mode's for."

He shrugged. "Too late now."

"So . . . how's it going? You think this'll work?"

He minimized the browser window, having seen enough buff dudes in G-strings for now. "We scoped out the club earlier and saw the Sheriff making a delivery, so that, along with Jensen's files, is grounds to infiltrate. I called, and they have open auditions next week, so I'll show up for that, try to get hired. Figure out who's dealing, see if I can get in on it to trace it directly to the cartel. We have every reason to believe that Baracoa are the ones supplying the dealers at the club."

Amelia nodded. "Good. This is really solid. And we'll help you, man. Whatever you need. I know this isn't your typical undercover shit." Her eyes widened and she snapped her fingers. "Hey, maybe we should all go out to a club this weekend so you can practice dancing. Test out your moves on me and Brooke. Maybe Jack will have some pointers. And if not, at least he'll probably pay for our drinks." She wiggled her eyebrows.

He nodded. "Yeah. Good idea." He normally hated clubs, but he had to admit that the idea of having an excuse to put his hands on Brooke, to dance with her, slow and sexy, flirt with her and see if he could turn her on, was massively appealing.

It was also massively stupid, seeing as hooking up with his partner could get him fired.

"I'll set it up and text everyone the details."

"You sure you're up for something like that?" he asked gently, not wanting Amelia to put herself in a situation she wouldn't be comfortable with. She'd been lying low since Ryan's death, and they'd all tried to give her some space. Going out dancing wasn't a huge deal, but maybe it was for her.

She waved away his concern. "I'm staying busy. Maybe this'll be good for me." She sounded less than convinced, but he didn't push it. "I'll text you." She pushed off of his desk and headed for the coffee machine, walling her grief away in a way he recognized because he knew he did it too.

Brooke emerged from the interrogation room, talking to Jack. Her badge bounced between her breasts as she moved, her jeans hugging her slender hips. She laughed at something Jack said, and Sawyer felt that sound like a kick in the gut.

Brooke didn't even look at him as she stopped in front of her desk, pulling her purse out of the bottom drawer and grabbing the blazer she'd left over the back of her desk chair.

"Going somewhere?" he asked, although the clock on the wall told him it was almost six.

She pulled her blazer on and then took her badge off, slipping it into her purse. "Yeah." She met his eyes. "I'm meeting Detective Jensen for a drink."

Sawyer was unprepared for the wave of jealousy that washed over him. Heat prickled uncomfortably at his chest. "Mmm."

"Is that caveman for *see you later*?" she asked, pulling her hair out of her collar.

He slowly shrugged one shoulder. "Cop-on-cop relationships are a bad idea."

"Mmm," she said, echoing him. "Thanks for the unsolicited opinion."

He cleared his throat. "Fine. Don't say I didn't warn you. I mean, I guess he's your type," he said, keeping his voice casual and disinterested.

"You don't know anything about my type."

He arched an eyebrow. "Don't I?" Shit. That had come out flirtier than he'd intended.

A slow smile spread across Brooke's face, but it didn't quite reach her eyes. "Are you jealous?"

He scoffed. "No," he lied. He shrugged, pretending to be interested in organizing the files on his desk. "I just thought you were done wasting your time on clowns."

"Wasting my time on men who turn out to be assholes does seem to be my specialty." Her voice had taken on a frosty tone, and he knew it was because he'd hurt her. Little pink spots appeared on the apples of her cheeks, and she turned to go. The acid churned in his stomach and before he could talk himself out of it, he sprang out of his chair, stepping in front of her and blocking her path. He should've let her walk away. Should've let her hate him. But seeing that hurt shining in her eyes . . . he couldn't. And yet he couldn't seem to get his mouth to form words, either.

She stared up at him, her pupils dilating, and then licked her lips. He sucked down a deep breath, trying to figure out what he wanted to say to her. She patted him on the arm as she stepped around him. "You enjoy your night," she called over her shoulder as she made her way toward the elevators. For her *date* with Jensen.

With a grumbling growl, he grabbed his gym bag from under his desk, needing to go work off his frustration.

Chapter Seven

BROOKE STUDIED THE line of people—all young, mostly attractive and well-dressed—on the sidewalk from the back seat of her Uber. Streetlights illuminated the red brick facade of Opera, the club in Midtown Jack had suggested a few days ago for their little night out. She swallowed and rubbed her palms on the skirt of her dress, then tugged it down self-consciously as the Uber slowed.

"Here's fine," she said, wanting to step out into the fresh air. Pushing the door open, she stepped out onto the sidewalk. Muffled bass thumps echoed into the night air, mingling with the voices of the dozens of people standing in line waiting to get in. The men wore casual clothes, most of them in T-shirts, jeans and sneakers, but the women were a bit more dressed up. Some were in cocktail-style dresses, skintight with cutouts showing even more skin. A few were in corsets and tiny skirts. It had been a long time since Brooke had gone out clubbing, and she hoped her little black dress would cut it. It had a halter-style neckline with straps that crossed at her throat, leaving a keyhole cutout between her breasts. It was nearly backless and hugged her body, the skirt ending several inches above her knees and showing off her legs. She'd added a pair of strappy black heels, a little red wristlet clutch, and sparkly drop earrings.

When Amelia had suggested they all go out dancing to help Sawyer get ready for his audition, Brooke had been a bit hesitant at first, but the idea had grown on her. She knew how important this investigation was for Sawyer and the team, and even though he talked a big game, he probably needed all the help he could get in the dancing department. While clubs weren't really her thing anymore, she'd actually been looking forward to tonight. Her heart kicked in her chest and her stomach fluttered. She was into the idea of dancing with him, touching him, letting herself fantasize for just a couple of hours that he wasn't both an asshole and her partner. She shouldn't have been, but she was, and she didn't know how to switch it off, as much as she knew she needed to.

Honestly, the fact that she was still so attracted to him after the shit he'd pulled was undeniable proof that her radar was fucked up, maybe beyond hope. Her adrenaline merged with the tiny tingle of fear wending its way through her. If she couldn't figure herself out and get her head straight when it came to men, she'd end up alone, her heart mangled from having been broken so many times. And while singledom had its perks, she didn't want to spend the rest of her life without someone in it.

She shook her head, pushing it all away. No wallowing allowed. Maybe a night of dancing and drinking and letting off steam was exactly what she needed to work off some of her tension—even if she'd be dancing with the source of said tension. Squaring her shoulders, she started to head toward the VIP line, as per Jack's instructions, and just as she looked up, she saw him. Sawyer stood about ten feet away on the sidewalk, staring at her. When her eyes met his, he started moving, closing the distance between them with long, easy strides, his eyes traveling slowly down her body and then back up. Her skin warmed under his gaze, and she hated the way she loved having his eyes on her. Having a claim on his attention. The way his gaze was filled with hunger and appreciation made something twist and tighten deep inside her.

He'd looked at her like that the night they'd spent together, and God, it had felt good having that masculine intensity focused on her, as it did now. He took a step closer, his eyes practically devouring her, just like when he'd been inside her, making her come while screaming his name. An achy twinge pulsed to life between her legs and she shifted her weight from one foot to the other.

She wanted to look away, but it was as though her eyes were drawn to him like a magnet. It was bad enough that she was fighting with her brain over him; it was worse knowing her body had gone full-on traitor. He wore a black T-shirt, jeans and sneakers, and it was unfair how sexy he managed to make those simple items look. He'd put a bit of gel or something in his hair, and something else was different too, but she couldn't quite . . .

"You shaved," she said, reaching up to touch his smooth jaw before she could stop herself. His skin was warm and surprisingly soft, and the lack of perma-scruff made him look younger and showed off the chiseled planes of his face. His eyes locked on hers and she took her hand back, curling her fingers into her palm. She turned to head into the club, needing some space, but his strong fingers circled lightly around her wrist, pulling her back toward him. Taking control in a way she was surprised she liked.

He leaned down, his breath warm against her ear. "Did you dress like this on purpose?" His voice was low and gruff, rumbling over her skin.

For some reason, she bristled at the idea that he knew she'd made the effort to look sexy for him. "Did I wear clubwear to a club on purpose? What kind of question is that?"

"You're wearing the world's tiniest dress. I've seen dinner napkins with more fabric."

"I didn't realize troglodytes used napkins." She

smirked at him. "*Troglodyte* means caveman, by the way."

The corner of his mouth tipped up. "I know what it means." He stepped a bit closer. "And I was asking if you wore that dress on purpose. For me."

She glanced up at him through her lashes and smoothed her hands down her dress, standing up a bit straighter, arching her back. "What, this?" Before he could answer, she gently poked his chest. "Newsflash: I didn't wear it for *you*."

"Really? Because this feels like a payback dress."

She arched an eyebrow. "A payback dress?"

"Yeah." He talked in a high-pitched voice. "I'll show that caveman what he's missing." And then he mimed flipping long hair over his shoulder.

Unable to help herself, her mouth fell open and she started laughing. "Oh my God. Are you being funny? You . . . you have a sense of humor?"

His eyes gleamed in the dim light and he shrugged. "I have my moments."

Asshole partner. Asshole partner. Asshole partner, she chanted to herself, clinging to the two words that summed up why they couldn't happen. Because, shit, if he added funny to the mix of everything else he had going on, she might as well just take her panties off right now and save him the trouble.

"Well, it's not a payback dress, because that would mean I care what you think. Which I don't." Lies, lies, lies.

His eyes did another slow sweep down and then back up. "Mmm," he growled, and then laid his hand on her lower back, guiding her toward the entrance of the club. Before she could stop herself, she'd arched into his touch, her spine tingling at the solid warmth of his hand on her. "Jack and Amelia are already inside," he said from right behind her, and then gave their names to the bouncer standing guard at the red velvet rope. He checked his tablet, stamped their hands and let them in.

They stepped into the club, and Brooke blinked as her eyes adjusted to the swirling, pulsing lights bathing the interior of the club in purple and yellow. The dance floor was crowded, filled with writhing bodies, all moving in time to the deafening music. Bass throbbed through the floor and vibrated up her legs. She took the tiniest step backward, taking it all in, and she bumped into Sawyer, her back against his chest. His body was so big, so strong and warm right behind her, and it felt too good. She moved to put some space between them, but his hand came to rest on her hip, his fingers flexing gently to keep her in place.

"Ames just texted me," he shouted in her ear. Goose bumps erupted over her skin at the sensation of his voice. "She and Jack are at the VIP bar." His fingers flexed again and she pressed back against him, earning a low rumble from somewhere deep in his chest when her ass brushed his hips. "Stay close," he shouted. "It's crazy in here and I don't want to lose track of you."

For once, she didn't argue with him, because staying close sounded good. Really good. Which was bad. Very bad. More and more, she was understanding what he'd meant when he'd talked about how distracting the pull between them was. As they wove their way through the crowd toward the bar, his hand still on her lower back, she had to wonder how she was going to focus on the investigation when he was dancing mostly naked on stage.

There was no easy answer; she'd just have to find a way to make it work. Not only was this investigation massively important to the team, but would be crucial to her career, as well. Getting a big win right out of the gate would prove to everyone that she belonged on HEAT. And if she could help put a drug dealing cop killer in prison, even better.

Sawyer lifted his hand from her back to wave at Jack and Amelia, who stood at the bar, a line of shots in front of them. Her skin still tingled from where he'd touched her. As they approached, Jack's eyes widened.

"*Damn*, Simmons!" he shouted, shooting her a grin. "Don't you clean up nice."

She tipped her head and smiled. "Thanks! You guys look great too." Jack wore a light blue button-down tucked into a pair of gray pants, and Amelia looked gorgeous, with her hair pulled up in a messy twist, tendrils falling around her face, and wearing a red body-con dress that showed off her curves. She smiled, playing with the ring around her neck.

"Shall we?" asked Amelia, eyeing the line of shots. Brooke nodded, knowing she'd likely need a drink or four to get through the night. They'd only just arrived, Sawyer had barely touched her, and she was already tingly and warm. Already struggling to remember that this was all part of the assignment. That it didn't mean anything because it couldn't *be* anything.

"What is it?" asked Sawyer, pointing at the line of clear shot glasses.

"Some kind of fancy infused vodka," said Amelia. She jerked her thumb in Jack's direction. "That's what we get for letting this guy order."

"Infused with what?" asked Brooke, picking up one of the glasses and sniffing it. It smelled sweet with a hint of spice.

"Vanilla bean, fig and cardamom," said Jack.

Amelia rolled her eyes. "Posh Spice strikes again."

Jack made a face. "Feel free to buy your own drinks if you're going to be picky."

The others lifted their shots, unwilling to turn down free premium alcohol. "Cheers!" shouted Jack, and they all clinked glasses. Tipping her glass to her lips, Brooke downed the clear liquid in one go, letting it warm her from the inside out and take the edge off her tension, or whatever the hell was making her stomach act like a washing machine stuck on an out-of-control spin cycle.

Everyone set their now-empty glasses down on the bar and Jack caught the bartender's eye, twirling his finger in the air in the universal sign for another round. She quickly refilled their glasses, giving Jack a lingering once-over as she poured. Brooke's fingers tingled pleasantly as she picked her glass back up, the first shot starting to do its work.

Jack held his glass up in the air. "Here's to getting our hands on those Baracoa fuckers."

"Hell yes," said Sawyer, and as they tossed back their drinks, Brooke wondered how he was really feeling about this assignment. Not that he'd actually tell her if she asked because that would involve talking and emotions, two things Sawyer seemed allergic to, but still. Maybe it was the vodka making its way into her bloodstream, but she felt a sudden pang of sympathy for him, making her want to find a way to check in with him, find out if he was really okay. To be a supportive partner.

Ugh. Damn vodka.

"All right, Magic Mike," said Amelia, tapping Sawyer's chest. "You ready to show us what you got?"

Sawyer took a deep breath, his nostrils flaring. After a beat, he nodded.

"Then let's go," she said and led them onto the dance floor. She found an open space toward the back of the VIP area and started moving to the music. "Okay, let's see what we're working with," she said, motioning for Sawyer to start dancing.

For several seconds he just stood there, looking at all of them. He tilted his head back and stared at the ceiling.

And then he started moving his hips and shoulders in time to the music, his hands coming up in front of him, open and relaxed. Brooke stood completely still, staring at him as he moved in time to the music. Well, shit, he really hadn't been lying when he'd said he could dance. He moved his body with a fluid confidence that completely surprised her. He pointed at Brooke, winked, and did a body roll complete with a little hip thrust at the end.

Amelia shrieked. "Oh my God, look at you! Two shots of vodka and you turn into Channing Tatum!"

He kept dancing, all smooth, sexy confidence. Heat churned through her. She'd thought this was going to be awkward and dorky.

Nope. She'd been wrong. So very, very wrong.

"Practice on Brooke," Amelia said, giving Brooke a little shove in his direction. "You can dance, but you need to be seductive."

Sawyer met Brooke's eyes and then took her hand, pulling her closer. The song changed to a slightly slower Latin beat, and he turned her so that her ass was nestled against his hips. With his hand on her stomach, he rolled his body, guiding her through the movement. Her muscles went limp as she gave herself over to his touch, her heart beating a furious tempo in her chest.

"That's good, but you need more hip movement," Amelia said, apparently Sawyer's self-appointed stripper coach. "As slow as possible."

Jack gave her a look, and she shrugged. "What? I've been researching. Can't ever tell me I'm not a team player."

Under Amelia's direction, he rolled his hips, grinding against Brooke, incorporating more moves as the song went on. Body rolls to the left and right. Hip thrusts that had her pressing her thighs together. He turned her so she was facing him, maintaining smoldering eye contact as he moved his gorgeous body to the music.

He took her hand and spun her away from him with ease, dancing a few steps around her so he had his back to her. Still moving in time to the music, he grabbed her hands and slid them over his abs so that she was practically hugging him from behind. As he moved, she could feel the muscles rippling beneath his shirt and she closed her eyes, remembering the sight of Sawyer in her hotel room, pulling his shirt off over his head.

"That's good!" said Amelia. "Move her hands more, like you're teasing her. Sell it!"

He guided her hands up his chest to his pecs, then back down over his hard stomach, and traced her fingertips along the edge of his jeans before sliding them back up. Brooke moaned, and she was immensely grateful for the loud music and the fact that her voice was muffled by Sawyer's broad back. Slick heat gathered between her legs as they danced. It felt as though everything in her body was throbbing along with the beat of the music.

One song blended into another and Sawyer moved Brooke in front of him again. Her skin felt like it was on fire from his touch, from being so close to him, from the desire pumping through her veins. His hand slid down her back and he pulled her closer, his scent invading her nostrils. He was wearing the same cologne he'd worn the night they'd slept together.

Still moving to the music, she arched up onto her toes as much as her heels would allow. "Did you wear that cologne on purpose?" she shouted into his ear, echoing his earlier question about her dress. He pulled back slightly, one eyebrow inching up as a smile spread across his face, seductive and slow.

She'd been keeping her arms by her sides, not touching more than she had to, but at that smile, she reached up and wound her arms around his neck. Wanting him closer. Wanting more. He dropped his hands to her hips, pulling her to him. She let out a tiny gasp when she felt him pressed against her, hard and thick beneath his jeans. She ground against him, earning a low, gruff sound from him, and felt her panties slide against her, soaked. Her clit throbbed for attention, for friction, and she rolled her hips against him again, whimpering. His hands tightened on her hips, his features tight with hunger.

"The way you're looking at her is really good!" Suddenly Amelia was right there, almost in between them, nodding her approval.

Brooke dropped her hands back down to her sides. Shit. For a moment, she'd completely forgotten about Amelia and Jack.

Sawyer glanced around. "Where's Jack?" He took his hands off her, and despite the heat of the bodies around her, she felt suddenly cold.

Amelia jerked her thumb over her shoulder. Brooke looked past her to see Jack dancing with two gorgeous women several feet away.

"What happened to the waitress, Celia?" asked Brooke.

Amelia shrugged. "Same thing that happens to all of Jack's women."

"I didn't realize he was such a *wham bam thank you ma'am* kind of guy."

Amelia shrugged again, frowning slightly. "I have a feeling he's not the one saying thank you." She turned her attention to Sawyer, poking him in the arm. "You're a way better dancer than I gave you credit for. Look at poor Brooke! She's all flushed and flustered."

Feeling suddenly self-conscious, Brooke took a step back and tugged her skirt down. Amelia wasn't wrong; she *was* all flushed and flustered, and even though dancing with him and getting turned on felt good—so damn good—it wasn't a good thing.

"I . . . I need some water," she stammered out, turning toward the bar and pushing her way through the crowd. "God, so stupid. Stupid, stupid, stupid," she chastised herself as she looked for an open space at the packed bar. She'd let herself get caught up in the moment, caught up in the act Sawyer was putting on. Let the feel of his body against hers obliterate everything else, including all the reasons they couldn't happen.

She ordered her water, and standing over here, a safe distance away from Thunderdick Thor, all of her reasons for keeping her distance felt so much more logical. So much more concrete. He was off-limits. He was a jerk. He was a distraction. She huffed out a breath, biting her lip. She really hated that he'd been right about that last part.

"Stupid, stupid, stupid," she muttered again, taking a sip of her water.

"Hey baby," came a slimy male voice to her right. She felt fingers on her arm and instinctively jerked it away, sloshing a bit of water over the rim of her plastic cup. An overly tanned man in his late twenties stood there staring at her with a creepy grin on his face. He wore a white button down and black pants, both garments a little too big for him. He moved closer to her, his eyes hovering on her breasts. "Wanna sit on my face?"

Brooke rolled her eyes. "Fuck off," she said casually, as though he'd asked her what time it was.

The man grabbed her arm. "That's not very ladylike. Maybe someone needs to teach you some manners."

She'd been about to break his hold on her arm—between her black belt in kickboxing and her police training, she was more than capable of handling herself—but she didn't get the chance. Sawyer appeared and shoved the man in the chest, sending him stumbling back a few feet.

"You heard the lady," he said, putting himself between Brooke and the scumbag. "Fuck off." Sawyer crossed his impressive arms over his chest and stared down at the man, not saying another word. The man stared at him for a second, but then shook his head, scurrying away and taking his probably teeny tiny dick with him.

"I had that under control. I was handling it," she said when he turned to face her.

"You're here with me. You shouldn't have to handle anything."

Their eyes met and something in her softened at the possessive, protective heat in his gaze. She swallowed thickly and took another sip of her water, needing to cool off. Because she was suddenly thinking how good it would feel to actually be with someone like Sawyer. Someone confident and protective and amazing in bed. Someone with a surprising sense of humor. A man's man who could take care of her, in every sense of the word.

So stupid.

The corner of his mouth kicked up and he reached for her clutch.

"What are you doing?" she asked, frowning up at him.

"Looking for the douchebag magnet you must have hidden in there."

She bit back her smile and held her clutch out, suddenly slapping it against his arm and pretending it was stuck to him. "Hey, whaddya know? It works."

He laughed, his eyes twinkling, and her insides softened, all warm and sweet like melted butter. "Nice try, but

I'm not a douchebag. I'll own up to asshole, maybe even caveman. But not douchebag." He pointed at a greasy-looking guy in a mesh tank top who was trying to grind with various women, none of whom wanted anything to do with him. "Now that's a douchebag."

She cocked her head. "Agreed. Fine. You're not a douchebag. Just an asshole caveman."

His lips twitched. "Don't get all sweet on me, Simmons."

She bit her lip and smiled up at him, and then pressed her fingers to her mouth, her jumbled emotions making every word, every action feel fraught with meaning.

He opened his mouth to say something, but then Amelia was there, tugging at his arm. She had a weird look on her face and her eyes were red, as though she'd been crying. "I'm gonna head home. You're good with the dancing, but if you need help coming up with a routine just let me know, okay? Jack's over there some-where, I think," she said, waving her hand toward the far corner of the VIP area, where a grouping of couches sat. She cleared her throat and toyed with her ring. "I've had enough fun for tonight."

Sawyer nodded. "We can walk you out."

She shook her head. "No, it's fine. I already ordered an Uber. Should be here any minute. You guys . . ." A sadness shone in her eyes and she cleared her throat again. "Have fun. I'll see you." Without waiting for a response, she turned and wove her way through the crowd.

"Should we go with her?" Brooke asked, frowning as she stared at Amelia's quickly retreating back.

Sawyer shook his head. "No, let her go. I had a feeling the party atmosphere might be too much for her."

An ache took root in Brooke's chest as she thought of what Amelia had lost. Not only the man who'd loved her, but the entire future she'd had laid out before her. Ripped away by Ernesto Hernandez. Bringing down Baracoa wouldn't just get justice for Ryan; it'd be for Amelia too.

"I think I need more practice," said Sawyer, bringing her back to the present. Oh, God. More dancing was probably a really bad idea, and yet it didn't feel like a bad idea. Nothing felt bad with him standing so close, looking at her like she was the only woman in the club. As though he could sense her hesitation—hell, he knew all the reasons it was a bad idea too—he took her hand and led her back out onto the dance floor.

He pulled her close immediately, his arms going around her waist, and it was as if they'd picked up exactly where they'd left off. Her skin warmed and tingled and an achy throb started up between her legs.

She slid her hands up his chest, then wound her arms around his neck. He was so big, so strong and solid. Even though she didn't need him to protect her, there was something immensely appealing in the thought that he could. It made her feel . . . safe. And feminine. As they moved to the music, she traced her fingers over his smooth jaw and he smiled at her. God, he was so devastatingly gorgeous when he smiled. He turned his head and brushed his lips against her palm, sending tingling sparks up her arm.

"We shouldn't be doing this," she whisper-shouted into his ear.

His hands dipped lower, his fingers brushing the top of her ass. "I know."

It was risky—what if Jack saw them?—but she couldn't seem to tear herself away from him, justifying somewhere in the recesses of her lust-addled mind that they were just dancing.

Right. And Mount Everest was just a hill.

Her eyes fluttered closed and she rocked against him, her clit throbbing almost angrily. Needy for him. As though he could read her mind, he slipped his muscled thigh between hers, and with his hands on her ass, ground it against her.

"Yes," she moaned out, hoping that the music had snatched the needy sound away. The throbbing intensified, and she tipped her head back, letting him guide her movements as he worked his thigh between her legs. He gave her ass a squeeze, his palms hot against her, and she swiveled her hips, deepening the grind.

"How was your date with Jensen?" Sawyer's voice rumbled in her ear.

She opened her mouth to tell him that it hadn't really been a date, not in any official sense, but he chose that minute to work her up and down his thigh, intensifying the throb between her legs. Making her feel empty and achy for him.

"Fine," she managed. She traced her hands up and down his chest, rediscovering its muscled contours with the tips of her fingers.

He gave her ass another squeeze. "Just fine? That doesn't sound very promising."

She shook her head. "I can't think right now."

"Fuck, me neither," he growled before burying his face in her neck. He kissed the skin just below her ear and then worked his way lower, his mouth hot and urgent against her. Everything inside her tightened at the feel of his lips on her skin, and she let her head fall to the side, giving him better access. If they were caught like this, it could ruin their careers, and yet in that moment, with Sawyer's mouth and hands on her, she couldn't bring herself to worry. His grip on her tightened and his movements started to lose their finesse as he kissed her neck, his teeth scraping against her. He nipped at her earlobe, giving it a gentle tug with his teeth that sent sparks of need shooting straight down to her core.

"I think about you constantly, Brooke. About us," he said, his lips brushing against the shell of her ear, causing her to shiver despite the heat swirling through her. Her legs shook a little with how much she wanted him. He was the only man she'd ever met who had the ability to turn her on like this. He sucked on the spot just below her ear, and she arched into him. "You see what you do to me?" His voice was low and rough as he took one of her hands and guided it back down his chest, not stopping at the waistband of his jeans this time but letting it rest on the impressive bulge straining against his zipper. "I'm hard as fucking concrete because of you."

He pulled his head from her neck and she met his eyes, wondering if hers were as glazed with desire as his. "Shit," she said, rubbing her palm over the ridge in his jeans. "If someone found out about this, we could be fired, and yet I can't stop wanting you, and I hate it, and—"

His mouth closed over hers, stealing the rest of her words with his kiss. With a moan, she opened for him instantly, slipping her arms around his waist. His tongue slid against hers, liquefying every bone in her body. He left one hand on her ass, bringing the other up to her face, cupping her cheek. She rocked her body against him, deepening the kiss, and he slid his hand into her hair and tugged gently, sending tiny zings of pleasure dancing across her scalp.

God, it was so wrong, but she would never get enough of the way he kissed. Rough and demanding in a way that she'd never have guessed she'd like. As though he was trying to claim her with just his mouth. She nipped at his lower lip, giving some of that roughness back to him, and he groaned, a deep, gruff sound that made her want to find out what else she could to do him to make him groan like that.

He broke the kiss, his hand still tangled in her hair. "I can feel how wet you are," he said, working his thigh against her. He dipped his head, kissing her neck as she practically writhed against him. "You're soaked for me, aren't you, Brooke?"

She whimpered and pulled his mouth back to hers, needing more. Knowing it was a mistake, it was stupid, and risky, but unable to stop herself. The kiss was slower and deeper this time, as though they were settling into each other after the frenzy of the first kiss. Her senses were alive with him, flooded with Sawyer. His scent, his taste. The sound of those low, gruff moans as his mouth worked against hers. The feel of his solid, muscled body.

He broke the kiss again. "I'm sorry I tried to get you kicked off the team."

His words were like ice water, instantly cooling her overheated system. What was she doing? Not only had this man tried to sabotage her career, but now she herself was risking everything she'd worked for by crossing a line with her partner.

Panic clawed at her chest, and she stepped back from Sawyer, needing some space away from him and the way he somehow managed to consume her.

"This was a mistake," she said, not knowing what else to do but run. She turned and Sawyer's fingers closed around her wrist, pulling her gently back toward him. He didn't say anything, his eyes holding hers. "I have to go." She hoped he understood that she meant *please let me go*. Because if he didn't, she didn't trust herself not to get swept up in him and do something colossally stupid. After a moment he did let her go, confusion, and concern, and lust all shining out at her from his gorgeous blue eyes.

She pushed her way through the crowd and into the cool night air, leaving the club and Sawyer behind.

Where they belonged.

Chapter Eight

———————————————————

THAT WEEKEND, GRAVEL crunched beneath the tires of Sawyer's truck as he wound his way up the unpaved road, Eric Church playing quietly from the stereo as he put more distance between himself and the city and all the shit he'd decided to leave behind for a couple of days. Pine trees stretched toward the blue sky on either side of him, beams of sunlight slanting through the needled branches. He slowed as he followed the road, and the trees started to thin, the gravel giving way to dirt. A clearing rose up before him and his family's log cabin came into view. A lacquered wood sign with the name *Matthews* stood at the edge of the clearing, and he smiled to himself as he drove slowly past. He remembered making that sign with his dad and his brothers over two decades ago, fighting with Hunter over getting to use the electric sander.

The log cabin, built by his father and grandfather about thirty years ago, wasn't big or fancy. It was less than a thousand square feet in total, but it had electricity and indoor plumbing, and stood on a quiet piece of land on the southern shore of Carters Lake. For Sawyer, it had always been a peaceful, happy place, and given everything that had happened over the past month, he'd found himself wanting to come up. He needed a couple of days away from the city to get his head straight, and given that the cabin was less than two hours north of Atlanta, spending his weekend off at the lake was a no-brainer. He and his brothers all used the cabin regularly, but given his proximity, Sawyer probably used it the most. His parents still used it, but not nearly as much as they once did.

The cabin was a place that felt like home. A place where the weight of the world felt a little less heavy. Where life felt a little less complicated. And right now, that was exactly what he needed. A couple of days here would give him the space to detangle everything—the undercover op and the potential link to Baracoa, Brooke, still missing the shit out of Ryan.

He parked his truck beside the cabin and hopped out, pulling in a deep breath of fresh air. The sun was warm, but the breeze was crisp, and while the leaves hadn't started to change yet, now that it was early October, Sawyer knew it'd only be a matter of weeks before they all exploded in color. Hopefully he'd be able to come back up for that. Keys in hand, he grabbed his duffel and the cooler full of groceries from the bed of his truck. He'd come back for the fishing gear later, after he'd settled in. He felt a welcome calm wash over him at just the thought of getting out on the lake. October wasn't great for fishing—bass season was pretty much over, and it was still too warm for rainbow trout—but he didn't care. This weekend wasn't about catching something—he'd brought burgers and steak and chicken, so he and Logan wouldn't starve if the fish weren't biting. It was about unplugging and getting away from it all. Letting the peace of being outdoors work out some of his tension, maybe help him find some clarity.

Considering he felt like he was carrying around a metric fuckton of tension these days, a little fishing was exactly what he needed. As he walked up to the porch, he glanced out at the lake, shimmering blue and rippling in the breeze. The cabin sat on the top of a gently sloping hill, and a set of wooden stairs led down to the dock, where Hunter's black aluminum fishing boat sat.

The breeze picked up, rustling through the black oak trees. A bluebird chirped from somewhere above and the lake lapped gently against the dock. The tightness in Sawyer's shoulders started to melt away. This was exactly what he needed. Just him and his brother, the lake, the fish, and fresh, clean air.

He unlocked the door and stepped inside, dropping his stuff in the entryway. It had been a few weeks since anyone had last been up here, so he moved from room to room, opening windows to freshen up the stale air.

The cabin was rustic, with wood plank floors, bead board walls and heavy beams crossing the ceiling. The main room at the front served as both living room and dining room, with a small L-shaped kitchen running along the back. A beat-up forest-green leather couch sat in the living room—the same couch that had been in his family's living room when he was a kid. A simple coffee table—one of Logan's high school shop projects—stood in front of it. A pair of worn armchairs flanked the wood-burning stove.

The two bedrooms now each held a double bed and simple furniture; the bunk beds he and his brothers had fought over were long gone. The tiny bathroom was barely big enough for a stall shower, toilet and sink. Sawyer frowned as he noticed the rust around the edges of the medicine cabinet, the worn patches on the linoleum. Maybe he'd have to get Logan and Hunter up here another weekend so they could fix it up.

With the windows opened, he retrieved his stuff from by the front door, dropped his duffel on one of the beds and then unpacked his simple groceries. Just as he was putting the last of the food into the fridge, he heard the rumble of an engine, Logan's blue Silverado pulling up beside Sawyer's truck.

"Hey man," Logan called as he lifted a cooler and a large backpack out of the back of his truck. Logan was the baby of the family, four years younger than Sawyer and seven years younger than Hunter. But even though he was the baby, he'd ended up the biggest of them all, towering over Hunter and even standing an inch taller than Sawyer. Sawyer was close with both of his brothers. As a kid, he'd tagged along admiringly with Hunter, and then done the protective big brother thing with Logan. As adults, they had each other's backs and stayed in touch despite the distance separating them.

Sawyer waved and met him halfway down the steps. Logan set the cooler down and pulled Sawyer in for a bone-crushing hug. When he was done cracking his ribs, Logan pulled back, his gaze going up to Sawyer's hair.

Logan frowned. "Um . . . did you dye your hair?"

"It's for work."

Logan pursed his lips, a *sure it is* smirk on his face. But as Logan studied him, the smirk faded. "Hey, are you . . ." He paused and shook his head. "Is everything okay?"

Sawyer let out a long breath. "Not really. Come on. Let's grab a beer." He wasn't much for sharing, but for once, he was glad he had Logan there to talk to.

He and Logan quickly unpacked the cooler and then grabbed two beers from the quietly humming fridge. They stepped out onto the covered wraparound porch, by far Sawyer's favorite spot at the cabin. Leaning his arms against the railing, he stared out at the lake, taking a sip of his beer and letting the peaceful scene before him wash over him. Settle him. He hoped it'd work its magic the way it always did.

Logan stood with his back to the lake, his assessing gaze on Sawyer. "So . . . what's eating at you?"

Sawyer shrugged, not even sure where to begin. Unsure how much to say.

So he said everything. He told Logan about the one-night stand, about Brooke being his new partner, about the investigation and upcoming undercover work. Naturally, it was the last bit that got the biggest reaction out of Logan.

"Whoa. Wait. Back it up a second," he said, his hands raised in front of him. "You have to go undercover as a male stripper?" He bit his lip, hard, clearly trying to keep it together.

"Yeah, yeah. Laugh it up."

Logan couldn't hold back his laughter any longer and let it fly, echoing out over the lake. Sawyer rolled his eyes and took a sip of his beer. Once Logan had collected himself, Sawyer continued. "Anyway, I have an audition on Tuesday. I've spent the past week coming up with a routine. Once I'm in, I'll figure out who the dealer is and work from there."

"But really what you're all in knots about is this new partner." It was a statement, not a question.

Sawyer nodded. For the past week, Brooke had kept her distance, vacillating between awkward and stiffly professional. Which, he reminded himself for what felt like the thousandth time, was a good thing. "She's . . . different. I don't know how to explain it, but she's under my skin, somehow."

"And that's bad?" Logan frowned at him.

"Hell yeah it's bad. We're partners. Getting involved would be a one-way ticket to unemployment."

Logan nodded slowly. As a fellow first responder, he knew what Sawyer's career meant to him.

"I just . . ." Sawyer shook his head and rubbed a hand over the back of his neck. "I was a dick and tried to get her kicked off the team."

Logan let out a low whistle. "And now she hates you. Which is good, but also maybe not good, because I haven't seen you all twisted up over a woman like this in . . . since, well. You know."

"I'm not all twisted up over her. I'm trying to figure out how to ignore the physical shit between us so I can do my damn job."

Logan shot him an amused smile and Sawyer glanced out over the lake, his words sounding hollow even to his own ears.

"Anyway, I apologized for trying to get her kicked off the team, but somehow that seemed to make things worse. And now, assuming I get hired, I'll have to strip in front of her on a nightly basis."

She'd run from the club, and now she was keeping him at arm's length. He'd given her exactly what she'd wanted and somehow that had pissed her off. She'd been ticked at him—and rightly so—for going to the captain behind her back, so he'd said he was sorry for what he'd done, and now she was . . . mad that he'd apologized?

Logan shrugged. "Women. I have zero advice for you there."

Even more confusing than her reaction to his apology was how he felt about her. He'd spent the past couple of years running from anything that felt like it could be . . . something, and now here he was, torn between pursuing and pushing away a woman who was completely off-limits. It was unlike him to break the rules, and yet something about Brooke made him want to toss the damn rule book out the window. He shouldn't pursue her, and he yet couldn't switch off the part of himself that wanted her. He felt it like an almost constant ache. He didn't understand it. Then again, he'd never been great at making friends with his emotions. All he knew was that it went deeper than physical attraction, and that maybe, after all this time, he was ready for something more than casual sex.

In fact, the only part of the situation that didn't confuse the shit out of him was his attraction to Brooke. She was gorgeous, and smart, and took her job seriously. He'd called her a baby detective, and maybe she was, but she was busting her ass and her policing instincts were sharp. She was funny, and didn't take shit from people. She had a spark that was immensely appealing, and their sexual chemistry was off the charts.

Logan drained the rest of his beer and clapped Sawyer on the shoulder. "It's a shitty situation, but I know you'll figure it out. Trust your gut. And it's not like she hasn't already seen the goods, so maybe it'll be fine."

It didn't feel fine. Not even a little bit. Everything was a jumbled mess—losing Ryan, the investigation and his nerves about it, the complicated situation with Brooke. Maybe there was a way through, but he couldn't see it right now.

Sawyer glanced at Logan and nodded, knowing his little brother couldn't solve his problems for him. "Yeah. Maybe."

"I'm gonna grab a quick shower and then I'll meet you down at the dock so we can take the boat out, okay?"

Sawyer nodded again and then finished his beer. The truth was, there were no easy answers. He felt as though whatever path he chose, there'd be consequences. To the investigation. To his career.

Sighing, he stared out at the lake. He rubbed a hand over his chest, the unfamiliar sensation of his T-shirt brushing against the smooth skin bringing him back to the present. Yesterday after work, he'd had his chest waxed in preparation for his audition. It had been the first time he'd ever done it, and he really hoped it was the last, because man, that shit had hurt. He'd come out of the salon with a new appreciation of what women went through. He'd also gotten a haircut, partly as a way to change up his look since he'd be undercover, and partly because he knew his regular eight-dollar Super-cuts special probably wouldn't hack it in the world of male stripping. So he'd shelled out at a fancy place, and he had to admit his new cut looked good. Shorter on the sides, longer on top, and they'd lightened it from a light brown to a dark blond to enhance the change and pretty him up even more. In the back of his mind, he wondered what Brooke would think of it, and then immediately decided that he shouldn't care, because he'd made the changes for the investigation.

The investigation in which she'd be watching him strip on a regular basis. A pressure he recognized as panic expanded in his chest.

He headed back into the cabin and grabbed another beer, then headed down to the dock. After taking off his shoes, he rolled up his jeans and hung his legs over the edge, letting the cool water slosh against his feet. He closed his eyes and focused on the feel of the sun on his skin, the sounds of the water lapping gently against the dock and the boat, the birds singing in the softly rustling trees above.

He pulled a deep breath into his lungs and cracked the beer open. Confusing mess with Brooke aside, the investigation was weighing on him as well.

He'd put together an audition routine by watching the *Magic Mike* movies and countless YouTube videos, but what if it wasn't good enough to get hired? What if their only solid lead on Baracoa vanished because he blew the audition? And if he did get hired . . . shit. It meant he'd actually be stripping in front of people. Putting on an act while dancing and taking his clothes off, all in the name of getting closer to the drug dealers.

He took a sip of his beer, the cool liquid sliding down his throat but doing nothing to calm him. He looked up at the sky, squinting at the clouds above, dragging his toes through the water. Wondering if Ryan could see him right now. Wondering what he'd say if he were here.

"I miss you, man," he said, his voice coming out rough around the edges. Setting his beer down, he reached into his pocket and pulled his phone out, opening up his saved videos and scrolling down to the one he'd watched probably a hundred times over the past few weeks. He hit Play, and the tinny sound of a group of people singing "Happy Birthday" echoed out over the lake. Ryan sat at the head of a crowded table at his favorite restaurant, a cake covered in flickering candles in front of him.

"Blow 'em out before I have to call the fire department," said the Sawyer who'd taken the video.

Ryan laughed and blew them out, everyone around the table clapping, Amelia smiling and laughing beside him.

"What'd you wish for?" she asked.

"Nothing," said Ryan. "I have everything I want right here."

"Do you need a knife to cut the cake?" a waitress asked Sawyer, and the video stopped abruptly.

That was the night Ryan had told Sawyer he was going to ask Amelia to marry him. His thirty-third birthday. His last birthday.

Sawyer tossed his phone down on the dock and wiped at his wet cheek with the back of his hand.

Nothing made sense anymore. Nothing. This wasn't how things were supposed to go.

He picked up his beer and stared out at the lake, thinking about Brooke and wondering if he'd gotten so caught up in missing Ryan that he'd started missing out on life.

Chapter Nine

THE WHIR OF the blender filled Brooke's grandmother's kitchen as late afternoon sunshine streamed in through the window. Nan's white-blond curls bounced as she shuffled across the floor to grab a pair of margarita glasses from a cabinet. At ninety, Nan was still quite spry, but Brooke could tell that her hips were bothering her more and more. She had a cane, but she hated to use it, worried that she'd become dependent on it. Stubborn and spirited, as always.

"Brooke, honey, grab the salt, would you?" she asked over her shoulder as she set the glasses down on the counter. Brooke nodded and started rummaging around in the pantry. She was less familiar with this kitchen than the one she'd grown up in. But selling the house and moving Nan into the retirement community after her grandfather died had been the right thing to do. Her grandmother was still independent, but help was just around the corner if she needed it, which made Brooke feel a bit better.

She found the salt and sprinkled a layer onto a plate, while her grandma dipped the rims of the glasses in lemon juice. Brooke watched her, taking in her little pearl earrings and red blouse, the same shade of pink lipstick on her lips that Nan had worn for as long as she could remember. The way she hummed softly to herself as she salted the rims and then poured the margaritas into each glass, her movements sure and steady. Brooke hoped she was still as healthy and with it at ninety, almost as much as she hoped her grandmother had a long time left.

Sometimes she daydreamed about throwing her a huge surprise party for her one-hundredth birthday. Nan reaching one hundred would give Brooke ten more years with her. And yet ten years didn't feel like nearly enough. So she tried to live in the moment when she was with her, to soak it all in while she had the chance. To memorize even the mundane moments like these ones, because she knew they were what she'd miss most when Nan was gone.

"Come on, let's go sit outside," she said, handing Brooke her glass. "My bones could use some sunshine."

She followed her grandma out to the little patio off the kitchen, and settled herself into one of the wicker chairs. Brooke had barely taken a sip of her drink before Nan was on her.

"So. You going to tell me what's wrong?" She arched an eyebrow, studying Brooke.

She shrugged, taking another sip of her drink, fighting back her wince. Nan always made her drinks strong. "Nothing. Just a lot going on with work and the new job and everything."

"Really? Because you've seemed as though you've got something on your mind. A few days ago on the phone, and again today. More than just the stress of a new job."

Brooke licked at the salt on the rim of her glass, avoiding the question. She refused to lie to Nan, and the truth was, there *was* something on her mind: a six-foot-four muscled jackass named Sawyer. God, making out with him in the club had been such a mistake. What if Jack had seen them? What if she'd done something stupid like go home with him?

"You haven't started seeing that weasel Peter again, have you?" asked Nan, eyeing her over the rim of her glass.

Brooke shook her head. "God, no. I haven't even talked to him since the night I found out he was married."

"Good." She pursed her lips, as though debating if she should say what she was thinking.

"Out with it. What?"

"I was talking to Doris, and she was telling me that her granddaughter just got engaged. A man she met on . . . I think it was Timber?"

Brooke bit her lip, hiding her smile. "Tinder. As in lighting a fire."

"Oh. I thought it was Timber since the point is to find some available wood."

Brooke snorted, almost choking on her drink. Nan looked at her, a naughty twinkle in her eye. If the woman hadn't raised her, she might have been scandalized by Nan's dirty sense of humor, but it was one of her favorite things about her.

"Available wood would be nice. Emphasis on the available," she said, toying with the stem of her glass. "And I appreciate the sentiment, but I have enough man problems right now without adding Tinder dudes into the mix."

Nan's eyes narrowed. "Ah. So there is someone."

Brooke shrugged. "Not . . . not exactly. It's complicated."

"Give me the abridged version." She settled back in her chair and took a long sip of her drink. "Maybe we can uncomplicate it."

No way was she telling Nan about the one-night stand she'd had with Sawyer the night she'd broken up with Peter. She tucked a strand of hair behind her ear and sighed, trying to figure out where to dive in. "I guess the simplest way to explain is that I . . . I have a thing for my new partner. His name's Sawyer, and since we're partners, nothing can happen between us, but . . ."

"There are sparks anyway," Nan finished for her. She waited for Brooke to continue, but when she didn't, she waved a wrinkled hand in the air. "Pfft. That's not so complicated."

"He's also a jackass who tried to get me kicked off of his team because of those sparks." Irritation, hot and prickly, flared in Brooke's chest as she remembered how humiliated and angry she'd felt.

At that, Nan threw her head back and laughed. "God, men are so stupid sometimes. I'd have hoped they'd have made some progress between my generation and yours, but apparently not." Nan took a sip of her drink and set it down on the little glass table, then reached over and patted Brooke's hand. "It sounds like he's as hung up on you as you are on him if you've driven him to that kind of idiocy. I assume you let him have it after that little stunt?"

Brooke nodded. "Damn right."

Nan's eyes twinkled again. "And let me guess: that only made the sparks brighter?"

Given the way Sawyer had kissed her the other night at the club, yeah. It was safe to say the sparks were only intensifying. "But we can't happen. Not only did he disrespect me and interfere in my job, we can't date because we work together. And that's assuming he even wants to date me."

"Oh, he does. He wouldn't have his knickers in such a twist if you hadn't gotten under his skin."

Brooke hated the way the butterflies in her stomach swarmed at the idea of actually being with Sawyer, a mixture of giddiness and fear swirling through her. "But it doesn't matter because being romantically involved with an assigned partner is a big fat no-no. I could lose my job."

Nan got quiet and stared up at the sky for a minute before reaching for her drink and taking a big sip. "I've never told you this, but when I first met your grandfather, he was engaged to someone else."

Brooke's mouth fell open. "What? Nan, you hussy."

Nan smiled ruefully. "It's true. We met at a USO dance in 1945, and the night we met, Brooke, honey, there were sparks. So many sparks I couldn't see straight. He told me he was engaged, but as the night went on, that seemed to matter less and less. I knew we were meant for each other. I'd never had an instant connection like that before."

Brooke's mind flew back to the night she'd met Sawyer, how she'd felt almost instantly drawn to him, how she'd never had chemistry like that with anyone. "So what happened?"

"We spent a wonderful night together and then he broke off his engagement. His family was so upset, as was hers. And boy, did his parents hate me at first. It wasn't an easy road, not by a long shot. But we found a way to make it work, because we knew what we'd found was worth fighting for. Sometimes the timing and the circumstances are absolute crap, but if what you have is special, you figure it out. You can't make an omelet without a few broken eggs along the way. That's what your grandfather always used to say." She sighed, her eyes faraway and misty. "My point is," she said, shaking her head and turning to look at Brooke, "don't close yourself off to something just because the path is hard. I know you've been dating and trying, but maybe you're taking the path of least resistance with these men. And my darling, you're not a least resistance kind of girl. You need someone to challenge you and push you and maybe even piss you off sometimes. That's who you are."

She took a sip of her drink, letting her grandmother's words sink in. She couldn't deny that there was some truth in them—okay, fine, maybe a lot of truth—but they also didn't make her situation any clearer. She was attracted to Sawyer and felt a connection to him, grumpiness and all. But he'd crossed a line, and they were about to start an undercover operation. "I can't risk my career for something that might not go anywhere," she said, nibbling at a chunk of salt. Maybe it was unfair of her to expect her ninety-year-old grandmother to understand. Times were different now, and Brooke wasn't going to give up her dream job for a man. Fuck. That.

Nan leaned forward and cupped Brooke's cheek. "Oh, my sweet, stubborn girl. You'll figure it out. I know you will. And if he really is the man for you—which it sounds like he may be—you may not have a choice."

Chapter Ten

BROOKE SHOVED THE last bite of her burger in her mouth and then wiped her hands on her napkin as she chewed. She'd missed out on her weekly Monday tradition of beer and burgers with Dani last week because they'd both been so busy with work, Dani with a bank robbery turned homicide, and Brooke getting settled in to her new position. She was glad they'd been able to pick it back up this week—as important as her job was to her, she didn't want to disappear into it and be one of those people who never had time for friends and family.

Over the course of their meal, she'd filled Dani in on as many details as she could, which, truth be told, wasn't many given the undercover, need-to-know parameters of the investigation. Instead, she'd focused on telling her what an ass Sawyer was, to which Dani had only smiled cockily and held her hand up to her ear, asking Brooke if she could hear wedding bells too.

Brooke's phone buzzed from where she'd laid it face-down on the table, and she picked it up in case the message was work-related. Gone were the days where once she'd clocked out, she was off duty, and no one would bother her with calls, texts or e-mails.

Sawyer: I need a favor.

Dani pointed at Brooke's phone with a ketchup-laden french fry. "Is that Thunderdick?"

Brooke sighed as she typed out her reply. "Yep. It's like the universe is punishing me for something."

Brooke: Can't right now. I'm busy. Ask Ward or Perez.

One of Dani's eyebrows arched and she leveled a Dwayne Johnson-worthy stare at Brooke. "Uh-huh. Or maybe it's pushing you together." Dani leaned forward, her elbows on the table. "The morning after you slept with him, you were happy. Glowing, even though a part of you was sad you'd never see him again."

Sawyer: Can't. You're the only one who can help me with this.

Brooke huffed out a breath and rolled her eyes as she typed out her response.

Brooke: What is it?
Sawyer: I need you to come over.
Brooke: To your house?
Sawyer: It's more of a cave, but yeah.

Despite herself, Brooke smiled. Why did he have to go and be funny? The sudden appearances of his sense of humor were immensely appealing and had the effect of a battering ram on the walls she was trying to keep in place.

Brooke: What's the favor?
Sawyer: I'll explain when you get here.

She should've typed out *no* and then stopped responding, but hesitated with her thumbs poised over the screen. She couldn't let whatever the hell was going on with her and Sawyer interfere with her ability to do her job. One, because her job was important to her, and two, if she let him become a distraction, she'd prove him *right*. She almost shuddered.

Brooke: Fine, but on one condition.
Sawyer: Name your terms, Simmons.
Brooke: I get to do all the driving for the next week.

Sawyer: Deal.

Brooke: Damn, that was fast. I should've asked for a month.

Sawyer: Too late now.

"Hello? Earth to Brooke?" Dani waved her hand in front of Brooke's face as her phone buzzed with another text from Sawyer with his address. "Let me guess: Thunderdick calls?"

Brooke reached into her purse and threw down enough cash to cover her beer and her burger. "I'm sorry. It's a work thing."

Dani smiled. "*Sure* it is." She leaned back, one arm bent over the back of her chair. "You're a detective, I'm a detective, so let's talk evidence. Exhibit A: the first night you spent together, which blew your mind and wrecked your lady parts for a week. Exhibit B: he's hot as shit."

"How do you know what he looks like?"

"Duh. I looked him up in the APD database as soon as you said he was your partner. He could be a long-lost Hemsworth brother."

"Exhibit A for the defense: he's my partner. Exhibit B: he's an asshole."

"Exhibit C: he apologized because he knows he fucked up. Exhibit D . . ." She snorted. "The nickname Thunderdick isn't arbitrary."

"You done?"

"One more. Exhibit E: he fires you up in a way I've never seen before."

Brooke slung her purse over her shoulder and threw her hands up. "Because he's infuriating!"

Dani just laughed, finishing her beer.

"Did Nan put you up to this?"

Dani shook her head. "Nope." She fished out her own wallet. "Didn't need to. You can pretend you're blind or illiterate all you want, but the writing's on the wall. You just don't want to see it because you're stubborn and scared to get hurt."

Brooke grunted and scuffed her foot on the floor. "Would everyone *please* just mind their own business and stop trying to convince me that Sawyer Matthews is the man for me? He's my partner. It's never going to happen in a million years."

Dani held up her hands in a placating gesture. "Fine, fine. Just answer this: where are you headed right now?"

Brooke toyed with the strap of her purse. "It's a work thing."

"So, the station?"

Brooke sent Dani a flat look. "His house."

Dani laughed, and Brooke turned to go.

"Enjoy your work thing," called Dani. "Bring condoms!"

Brooke flipped her off over her shoulder as she left the restaurant.

Less than twenty minutes later, she pulled into the parking lot of a well-kept condo complex on the outskirts of town, practically in Smyrna. The lawns separating

the three-story condo buildings were neatly manicured, dotted with mature trees. Low brick walls, covered in hanging moss, separated the condos from the parking lot. Three identical buildings faced each other, arranged in a triangle, all done in light brown siding, and trimmed with black shutters on the windows and white railings along the balconies. In the triangular courtyard, she caught a glimpse of a pool and a tennis court. She pulled into a spot designated for guest parking and, following the signs, made her way toward unit 2001 and knocked on the black metal door.

Sawyer opened it almost immediately, and her heart picked up its pace. He was wearing a simple white T-shirt and jeans, his feet bare. She'd seen his newly styled, lighter hair at work earlier that day, and she still wasn't quite used to it. Combined with his smooth jaw, it made him look younger. Less grizzled and more polished.

Somehow in the two weeks she'd been working with him, he'd managed to get even hotter.

"Hey," he said, holding the door open and inviting her in with a causal wave. "Thanks for coming over."

She slowly stepped inside, her arms crossed over her chest. "Uh-huh. So, what's up? You said you needed a favor."

"Yeah. Let me, uh . . ." He rubbed a hand over the back of his neck, his muscles flexing against the cotton of his T-shirt. "Let me show you." Sighing, Brooke toed her shoes off and followed him inside.

Sawyer's condo was surprisingly nice, and not even a little bit cave-like. Light wood floors and off-white walls made the space feel bright, and framed photos hung on nearly every wall. She wanted to stop and look at them, maybe even ask him about them, but he'd disappeared farther into the condo, so she followed him.

Immediately to her right was the kitchen, small but nicely finished with cherry wood cabinets, black granite countertops and stainless steel appliances. A table and four chairs sat in the breakfast nook that separated the kitchen from the living area, which held a couch, coffee table, and gigantic flat-screen TV mounted to the wall. A cabinet beside the couch was filled with books and DVDs. She could see what she was pretty sure was a balcony along the far wall of the living room, but she couldn't be sure since the white wooden slat blinds were closed.

Sawyer moved into the living room and picked up the coffee table from in front of the couch, carrying it into the hallway off the living room. Then he went and grabbed one of the dining chairs from around the table and brought it into the living room, setting it so its back was nearly touching the windows.

Brooke watched all of this with her arms crossed, her purse still slung over her shoulder, her curiosity growing by the second. Not only her curiosity, but an unsettling restlessness at being alone with him in his living room. As though just the change in location had some of her defenses crumbling, and she couldn't let that happen, causing an internal tug of war.

"So?" she asked, moving her hands to her hips.

He stopped fiddling with the chair and turned to face her. "I need to practice my routine. On a person. And I can't do it on Jack for obvious reasons, and Amelia . . . it would be way too weird."

Oh, God. Now she understood what the chair was for. She swallowed thickly and licked her lips. "I didn't bring any singles."

His lips twitched. "This one's on the house. My audition's tomorrow, and I need to practice."

"I . . . I'll laugh. I'll ruin it for you."

He took a step toward her, something in his eyes darkening. "I promise, you won't laugh."

"I've never been to a male strip club," she said, her voice sounding strained even to her own ears. "I don't know what kind of feedback to give you."

He reached out and took her hand, pulling her closer. "You're a woman." He shrugged. "Tell me if it's hot. If there's something I should do differently. And I know you'll be honest with me. Tell me if it sucks." His features tightened. "I can't fuck up the audition."

She closed her eyes and sighed, her stomach swirling with what felt a lot like nervous anticipation. "Fine." She pulled her hand from his and stalked over to the chair, dropping her purse on the floor and sitting down.

He moved back toward the kitchen and pulled his phone out of his pocket, placing it beside a small Bluetooth speaker on the kitchen counter and then hitting Play. The opening strains of a sultry R and B song filled the air and he took a couple of slow, sexy steps toward her, his eyes holding hers, the atmosphere in the room shifting. He ran his big hands up his body, making his T-shirt ride up and giving her a glimpse of his abs. Her throat went dry, her heart fluttering in her chest. He rolled his body, a slow, controlled movement that was surprisingly sexy. He took a few more steps toward her and then slowly pulled his shirt up off over his head, letting it drop to the floor.

Her eyes widened when she saw that he'd waxed his chest, the lack of hair making his muscles look even more defined. A dull throb started up between her legs and she fought the urge to shift in her chair. He did another body roll, showing off his gorgeous physique, and then swung one leg forward, jumping and dropping down into a fluid, graceful push-up. Her eyes widened and then she gasped as he spread his knees and moved his hips against the floor, his entire body undulating. He rose to his knees and slid closer to her, planting his hands on either side of her chair as he climbed gracefully to his feet, his body rocking directly in front of her. Close enough that she could smell him. Close enough that it'd be nothing to reach out and touch his smooth skin. Her lips tingled, the urge to test out that new smoothness with her mouth almost overwhelming.

Still moving to the music, he slowly pulled his belt from his jeans and let it fall to the floor beside his discarded shirt. He popped open the top button on his jeans, and she was suddenly having a hard time remembering to breathe. His movements were so confident, so relaxed and sexy. He did another body roll as he stepped closer and then dropped his hands to her knees, pushing her legs apart. He planted his foot between them, stepping up onto her chair and then dropping down so that he was straddling her without putting his weight on her in an effortlessly seductive move.

She sucked in a sharp breath, her nipples tight, her inner muscles clenching. With his arms over the back of her chair, he thrust his hips against her, a slow, rocking grind in time to the music. She heard a breathy, trembling moan and realized it had come from her mouth.

Eyes locked on hers, he took her hands and guided them to his abs. She traced the ridges of the rippling muscles, her hands sliding up his chest as he rose from the chair and then dropped to his knees in front of her. He paused, his face inches from where she ached for him, and he took a deep breath, his nostrils flaring before he rolled up over her body. Suddenly his hands were on her ass and he'd lifted her clean off the chair as though she weighed nothing, moving her up and down as he rocked his hips, his body still moving to the music as he simulated having sex with her. As the song started to fade out, he slowly dropped to his knees, laying her out on the floor, thrusting his hips over her.

The song ended and a silence fell over the living room, Sawyer still poised over her. Her body felt like a giant throb and she couldn't think. Could barely breathe. Her hands shook and her pulse hammered in her throat. Everything inside her felt tensely coiled, wound tight with arousal.

"So?" he asked, his voice rough around the edges as he looked down at her, seemingly in no hurry to get off her.

Words. She needed words. "I'd ride you. I—I mean hire you," she stammered out.

"Would you?" he asked, and let more of his weight rest against her. His massive erection pressed against her thigh. The feel of him against her, the evidence that he was just as aroused as she was, made her weak, and in that moment, she didn't care.

The air seemed to ignite around them and suddenly his mouth was on hers, his kiss hot and urgent. Desperate and hungry. She wound her arms around him, pulling him closer and letting out a shivery moan as his tongue slid against hers.

Oh God, this wasn't just a bad idea. It was the *worst* idea. And yet it felt too damn good to even think about stopping. Too damn right.

Sawyer broke the kiss, his breathing labored as he looked down at her. He pushed a lock of hair out of her eyes. "Brooke." There was something in his tone, something pleading and seeking, and she knew what he was looking for.

Permission.

She slid her hand between them and undid his zipper, reaching into his pants and stroking him, the weight of him hot and smooth in her palm. "Yes. Don't stop. I can't stop," she said, her thumb trailing over the bead of moisture on the head of his cock.

He groaned and pulled her hand out of his pants, guiding her arms above her head and pulling her shirt off. He yanked her bra down, freeing her breasts, and closed his mouth over one aching nipple, sucking it hard and deep into his mouth. He scraped his teeth over her sensitive flesh and then soothed the bite with his tongue before turning his attention to her other breast. She threaded her hands into his hair, moaning and arching into him, writhing against him as he tormented her with his mouth, teasing her nipples into sharp peaks. So good, but not nearly enough.

His mouth still on her, she flung one arm out to the side, reaching for her purse and knocking it over, sending its contents spilling across Sawyer's living room floor. A lip gloss tube rolled by as he ground his hips against her, and she rocked up into him, frustrated with the clothing separating them. Groping blindly as his teeth clamped down on her nipple, she found what she was looking for and thrust the condom at him.

He growled and took it, moving off her so he could shuck his pants and boxer briefs. With desperate, jerky movements, she tossed her bra aside and then managed to wriggle out of her jeans and panties. By the time she'd kicked free of them, he'd finished rolling on the condom, and with an arm around her waist, pulled her back underneath him and pushed into her in one fluid movement. They moaned in unison as he filled her, inch by delicious inch.

Oh God. She was fucking Sawyer again, when that was the last thing she should have been doing. He withdrew and then slid back in, deep—so damn deep—filling her with his gorgeously thick cock, and she wrapped her legs around his waist and let it all go. This, whatever this was between them, she was powerless to fight it right now.

He groaned and tangled a hand in her hair, slamming his hips against hers as he fucked her hard and deep, taking her without mercy, biting at her neck. She cried out his name and he rode her harder, giving them both what they'd been dying for for two weeks now. He swiveled his hips, dragging his cock out of her, a slow, unbearably sexy movement that reminded her of the way he'd danced for her.

She clenched around his retreating cock, and then let out a long, loud moan as he slid back in, filling her up. He felt incredible inside her, as though he was made for her. His hand tightened in her hair, winding her tighter, pushing her higher, until his body inside hers was all that existed for her. White-hot pleasure seared through her, and she scored her nails down his back as he somehow managed to get even deeper, hitting a spot inside her she'd never felt before. Sparks exploded over her skin and it felt as though her insides were melting, her entire body open and his for the taking.

Too much. It was all too much.

Gripping her legs around his waist, she rolled him under her and rocked her hips, slowing the frenzied, frantic tempo down as she rode him. He squeezed her hip with one hand, the other trailing up over her stomach and to her breast, her nipple hard against the roughness of his palm.

She'd wanted to take control back, fighting against getting so lost in him she'd never find her way out, but maybe this new position had been a mistake, because now he was looking up at her, lust and possession and adoration all shining out at her from his hooded blue eyes.

She could feel every throb of her heart against her ribs like a kick drum, and she knew the adrenaline and excitement pounding through her were partly caused by the way Sawyer was looking at her. Like she was beautiful and perfect and everything he'd ever wanted. Never had a man looked at her like that. Only Sawyer. Maddening, off-limits Sawyer.

He moved his hand from her hip and slipped it between her legs, working his fingers against her clit, and everything inside her tightened and then exploded in hot, heavy throbs as she came, sudden and sharp. She rode him harder as shockwaves of pleasure trembled through her, his name falling from her lips. An intense shiver coursed through her and her movements faltered.

Still buried deep inside her, he sat up, lifted her and

tossed her onto the couch as if she were a sack of feathers. From behind, he pulled her up onto all fours, his hands on her hips as he slid back inside, his hips rolling against her ass. She gripped the armrest for support and pushed back against him, taking him deeper.

He groaned, an immensely gratifying growl. "This. I've wanted this since you set foot in the bullpen."

She moaned, close to coming again. Already. As though he had some magic formula for taking her from zero to sixty with minimal effort.

Or maybe it wasn't magic. Maybe it was just him. Them, together.

"You make me nuts, Brooke. All I think about is being inside you. Fucking this insanely sweet little pussy and driving you as crazy as you drive me." She gasped and moaned, partly in surprise, but mostly at how hot it was to hear Mr. Strong-and-Silent talk dirty to her. Not just dirty. Filthy in a way she'd never fully admitted she loved. She shivered again despite the heat swirling through her.

"It's working." Her nails scraped against the fabric of the couch, that restless need coiling tight in her belly, her clit heavy and throbbing.

He smacked her ass, tingling heat dancing out across her skin and making her clench around him. "Good. Because you're going to come for me again." His hand slid up her spine and into her hair, and then he wrapped the strands around his fist and tugged. Her back arched as he slammed into her from behind, her body pulling at him, searing hot pleasure scorching through her. He dropped down over her, his chest pressed to her back, his hips rocking against her as he worked himself in and out of her in a frenzied rhythm. "It's so fucking good with you. So goddamn perfect."

"I know. Fuck, I know." Her words came out as a half sob, half moan.

"Rub your clit and come for me, sweetheart. I want to feel you soak my cock again."

With a trembling hand, she reached between her legs and touched herself, circling her swollen clit with her fingers. Exactly the way she'd touched herself, alone in her bed, after dancing with him at the club. He took her hard and deep, growling out her name, and she came again, contracting around him as pulsing waves of pleasure crested over her. Every stroke of his cock in and out sent her spiraling higher, prolonging her orgasm into something beautiful and intense.

"Fuck! God, Sawyer!" Unable to support herself any longer with her shaking, boneless arms, she fell forward, pressing her face into the couch cushion.

His movements became stiffer and jerkier, his grip on her hips bruising, and a few gorgeously deep thrusts later, he cried out, pulsing inside her as he came. A silence fell over the room, and she realized how loud they'd gotten.

His breathing heavy, he pulled out of her and collapsed on the couch, pulling her against him. She was too limp, wrung out from the two orgasms, to protest.

With his legs sprawled out in front of him, he settled her against his chest. She could feel his heart hammering against her cheek, and she knew hers was beating just as fiercely.

He pushed a hand through his hair. "Jesus," he said, his voice low. He ran a hand up and down her back, and it felt so good to sit there with him, naked and sated. Too good, especially given that what they'd just done could get them fired. Too good, and too . . . her mind flashed back to the way he'd looked at her.

That wasn't just sex. It had been more. And she couldn't do more—she couldn't risk her career, so anything she was feeling needed to stay firmly locked down where it couldn't do any damage.

She rose from the couch and started tugging on her clothes. Once she was dressed, she collected the spilled contents of her purse, shoving tampons and gum and pens back in. The entire time, she could feel Sawyer's eyes on her, like a heated weight. Watching her and not saying a damn word about what they'd just done.

It didn't matter how much she'd enjoyed it. It didn't matter that she wanted to do it again. None of that mattered, because sex with Sawyer shouldn't have happened. End of story.

She turned to face him, her heart catching in her throat at how gorgeous he looked, still naked, his incredible body on display. His hair disheveled, his chest slick with sweat. Looking more relaxed than she'd seen him all week. She cleared her throat. "That shouldn't have happened."

A small smile tugged at the corner of his mouth. "Probably not. But it did."

She cut him off before he could say anything more, forcing the lie to her lips. "You know this doesn't mean anything, right? Doesn't change anything?"

Hurt flashed in his eyes, gone almost as quick as it came. "Oh, yeah. No. We're cool. Totally cool. Thanks for your help with the audition."

She nodded, biting her lip as she took a few steps backward. "Good luck tomorrow." And then she turned and left, wondering how she was supposed to put this mistake behind her.

SAWYER DIDN'T COME in the next morning before his audition, and Brooke couldn't decide if she was relieved or disappointed, so she kept herself busy by getting caught up on other case files related to Baracoa and letting off steam in the gym. Trying to keep her mind and body occupied so she wouldn't think about Sawyer and the fact that they'd had mind-blowingly hot sex. Again.

And she'd almost managed it too, until her phone buzzed with a text message. She glanced up at the clock on the wall. Just after one PM. Audition complete.

Sawyer: I start tomorrow night.

Before she could figure out what to say to him, her phone buzzed again.

Sawyer: She said the scratches on my back were a nice touch.

"Shit," she whispered, tossing her phone onto her desk and dropping her head into her hands as she tried to figure out what the hell she was going to do.

Chapter Eleven

AT EIGHT THIRTY the following night, Sawyer walked in through the back door of the Manhattan Ballroom, feeling as though he'd eaten rocks for dinner. The back-pack slung over his shoulder contained things he'd have never in a million years guessed he'd need for an under-cover op. Shiny, glittery man-thongs, baby wipes to clean up sweat in undesirable places, a jar of hair pomade, an extra razor, lotion, cologne, deodorant. He'd ordered the thongs online and paid extra for overnight delivery so he could try them on at home first and not look like a complete rookie in front of his new crew. He'd barely slept last night, his mind too busy with everything. The first day of any new op was always nerve-racking, and this one especially because of what was riding on it.

The door shut behind him, and he found himself in a narrow, dimly lit hallway. It didn't matter how many times he'd done it, he always felt naked on the first day of an undercover op—no gun, no badge, no radio. Exposed and obvious, as though the group targeted for infiltration would see through him in a heartbeat. But he knew from experience that it was just a matter of settling into his new role and that he was damn good at what he did.

Following the sound of male voices at the end of the hallway, he turned a corner and pushed through a black velvet curtain.

"Hey! New guy!" called out a voice, and all five heads in the dressing room turned in his direction.

"Fuckin' time we got some new blood up in this joint."

"Jade never hires anyone who comes to those open auditions. We thought they were just a way for her to get a free show every other week."

They all laughed at that. Jade, the club's manager, had been one of the people at his audition yesterday, and had hired him on the spot.

Someone clapped him on the shoulder from behind. "You made it." Patrick—the other person present at his audition—stood beside him. "Everyone, this is Ryan," he said, using the alias Sawyer had given at his audition. He'd picked the name so he wouldn't forget the reason he was doing this. He noted the way Patrick seemed to be in charge. He was older than all the other dancers—probably close to forty—and clearly had a say in who got hired at the club. He was a few inches shorter than Sawyer, but fit and lean with short brown hair and a deep tan.

Patrick pointed at a college-aged kid who looked like your typical frat boy. Messy brown hair, cocky douche-smirk on his face. "This here's Danny, and then over there we got Jesse," he said, pointing at an extremely attractive guy in his early thirties. Dark brown hair, bright blue eyes, perfect smile. "That's Shawn," he continued, pointing at a ripped black guy with a goatee doing push-ups in nothing but his boxer briefs. "And Hurley," he said, waving his hand at a guy wearing a biker's bandana with several tattoos decorating his muscular arms. He sat on a leather sofa against the far wall, smoking a joint.

Patrick turned to face Sawyer, smiling and tapping his own chest. "And you know me already. Come on, I'll give you a quick tour before the show starts." Sawyer nodded, following Patrick. He crossed to the other side of the room, near the leather couch, and pulled back a beaded curtain. They emerged onto the small stage, raised maybe four feet off the ground.

The club itself was small. The stage with a runway sat at the back of the room, facing a sea of tables and chairs. Even at full capacity, it probably held only about a hundred people. Which, Sawyer had to admit, was a relief. Hopefully half of Atlanta wouldn't have seen him in nothing but a thong by the time this was done and Hernandez was rotting in jail. But even knowing that the club was small did nothing to alleviate the nerves running through him at the thought of taking his clothes off for strangers.

A bar ran along the front of the room, brightly lit with pink and purple neon lights. From his vantage point on stage, he could see the club's entrance was to the right of the bar.

"You get two hundred a night as your base, and you keep any tips you make," said Patrick, hands on his hips as he surveyed the empty club. "Show's two hours long, and we work Wednesday through Saturday. Open with a group number—which you'll have to learn— then we work the crowd, and then move on to solos. I introduce everyone, get the crowd nice and riled up for you in between. Little thunder helps to make it rain. You got your shit ready?"

Sawyer nodded. Jade had told him to have a new routine ready for tonight, one that didn't rely on a lap dance. Too bad he hadn't had the chance to practice this routine on Brooke. In fact, they'd barely spoken since she ran out of his condo so fast he was pretty sure she'd left a little cartoon puff of smoke behind her. He clenched his jaw and pushed the thoughts of Brooke away. He didn't need that kind of distraction right now, when his focus should've been entirely on the investigation—not on his hot-as-hell partner who could get him fired.

"Good man. What about a stage name?"

Sawyer rubbed a hand over the back of his neck. "Lance Silver."

Patrick smiled. "Lance Silver. I like it. You can start learning the group numbers tomorrow. We rehearse Tuesday through Friday at 2 p.m. Just show up here."

"No problem."

"You'll see how it all goes down tonight. After the solos, we do hot seats."

"Hot seats?"

"They didn't have those at the other clubs you worked at?" Patrick looked at him, a puzzled frown on his face. Shit.

"Nah. They were small. Amateur. Just group numbers, solos, working the crowd."

"Ladies pre-book the hot seats. They get a chair on stage and a dance from whoever they choose. One song is fifty, two songs seventy-five. They book you, that money's yours too."

Sawyer nodded. "How many of those you do a night?"

"Almost everyone goes for the two-song deal, so five or six. If we're short on hot seats, we'll throw in another group number."

Patrick gave him a quick overview of the stage, where the exits were, how to work the runway, good spots to hop down into the crowd, and then led him backstage again and back into the dressing room.

"You can grab one of the empty lockers over there," he said, and then waved his hand at the shelves standing in the middle of the room, interspersed with free-standing mirrors. "Props are there. There's something you need and can't find, just ask Allan." A skinny, nerdy-looking guy who was arranging a set of matching construction helmets waved without looking up from his work. "Costumes are there. You can bring your own, or you can use ours. White tanks, pre-cut so they rip better, are in the drawer over there. Questions?"

Sawyer shook his head, taking it all in, wondering which one of them had sold Chase Anderson's girlfriend the pills. If he could figure out who was selling, he could start dropping hints that he was short on cash, and then hopefully get in on the action.

But first, he had to make friends. Make the guys think he was one of them so they'd let him in. Patrick disappeared to go do a final sound check, leaving him with the main group.

"So, you a cop?" asked Shawn, and everyone went quiet.

But this wasn't Sawyer's first rodeo, and he knew a test when he saw one. He chuckled and picked up a fireman's helmet from the prop shelf. "Nah." He put the helmet on. "Not tonight, at least."

They all laughed, and the tension that had been hanging in the room dissolved.

"So, you danced much before?" Jesse asked, a friendly smile on his face.

Sawyer gave a half shrug. "A little. Just smaller places, in Savannah, and down in Florida."

"What brought you to Atlanta?"

"Club I was working at closed and I went through

a shit breakup, so it was time for a change," he said, blending true elements of his own life with his cover story. The most successful undercover identities stuck as close to the truth as possible without compromising the investigation's goals.

A sympathetic murmur ran through the group. "Well, you're in the right place if you're looking for re-bound pussy," said Danny as he rubbed moisturizer into his arms.

"Danny, easy with the lotion." Hurley stood from the couch and started taking his clothes off. "You'll have nothing to jack off with later when you go home alone."

They all laughed. It almost felt like any other locker room. Good-natured ribbing. Naked men.

Hurley stripped completely and then pulled on a glittering gold thong, arranging his junk.

Okay, so not really like any other locker room. They all started to get changed for the opening group number.

Time to blend in.

Sawyer claimed an empty locker and then pulled his T-shirt off over his head and stuffed it inside. His belt, jeans, and boxer briefs followed. He took his wallet— containing a Georgia driver's license and credit cards with the name Ryan Williams on them—out of his jeans and stuffed it in his backpack.

"Hey, new guy! Check you out. Not bad," said Danny, nodding his approval. "I can see why Jade hired you."

"Where you work out?" asked Shawn.

Sawyer started tugging on his white bedazzled man-thong. "Couple different places. I'm trying to get a personal training business started." He started doing up the snaps on his tear-away jeans.

Shawn nodded. "I hear that. Been saving up to open my own restaurant for a while now."

Sawyer tucked away the piece of information that Shawn needed extra cash to get his business off the ground. Pants in place, he crossed the room to grab a pre-cut tank top and pulled it on over his head. "What kind of restaurant?"

At that, Shawn's standoffish nature seemed to fade away and his face lit up. "Picture this: Burgatory. As close to heaven as a burger can get you."

Sawyer laughed. "I like it, man. Cool idea."

"Thanks. Menu would have deluxe, gourmet burgers, fries, shakes, cocktails. Just need to save up enough cash so I can qualify for a small business loan."

Sawyer nodded. "What about you, kid?" he asked as he checked himself out in the mirror, running his fingers through his hair and fiddling with it, mimicking what Jesse was doing beside him. He glanced over at Danny, who wasn't answering him. "What's your deal? You just here for the pussy?"

"Something like that," he answered, dousing himself in cologne.

"Danny had a scholarship to Emory, but lost it.

Doesn't want to tell his parents," said Jesse. "He's trying to stay afloat without them knowing."

"Sucks about your scholarship," Sawyer said to Danny. So. There were at least two guys who needed money badly.

"Whatever." Danny shrugged. Sawyer made a mental note to double-check what school Chase Anderson and his girlfriend went to. He was pretty sure the report had said GSU, but he'd ask Brooke to go back over it to see if maybe there could be a connection between Danny and Chase.

Sawyer took Hurley's abandoned spot on the couch. "So, you guys hook up a lot? What's the vibe like here?"

"The vibe here is fucking great," said Hurley, sorting through the rack of costumes. "You don't need to go home alone if you don't want to."

"Unless your name is Danny and you seem to have a knack for hitting on the bride-to-be in every bachelorette party that comes in here," Jesse teased.

"Fuck you, man," he shot back good-naturedly. "Only happened a couple times. And one of them said yes anyway."

Jesse sat down on the couch beside Sawyer. "Some of us hook up regularly with women. Like Danny, who's basically a case of the clap waiting to happen. I met my girlfriend dancing here. Saw her in the audience and just . . ." He shook his head. "Damn. So beautiful. So I pulled her up on stage, danced for her, flirted with her, got her number. We've been dating for like . . . three months now."

Sawyer's chest tightened with excitement as a plan to get closer to Brooke started to form. "Does she still come watch you dance?"

"All the time."

"He's so in love it's disgusting," said Hurley as he tapped a small amount of baby powder into his thong.

"You put pineapple on pizza," answered Jesse. "I don't trust your definition of disgusting."

"Pineapple on pizza is the shit." Hurley checked himself out in the mirror, flexed, and then started pulling tear-away clothes on.

"How long you been here, Hurley?" Sawyer asked, spreading his arms over the back of the couch, trying to look as relaxed and casual as possible.

"About a year." He shrugged. "It was supposed to be a . . . I guess a temporary solution. I used to be a firefighter, but that didn't work out, so here I am. Still trying to figure some shit out."

The front doors to the club must've opened, because music started playing and the buzz of excited female voices started to swell from the front of the club. Patrick came back through the beaded curtains, a bottle of whiskey in one hand, a collection of shot glasses in the other. He set the glasses down on one of the prop shelves and poured everyone a shot. The guys all gathered around and took one in what Sawyer gathered was a regular preshow routine.

"Make 'em wet so they make it rain," said Patrick, holding his glass up. The others all did the same and then tossed back the whiskey. It burned all the way down, adding to the acid churning in Sawyer's stomach. The music got louder, and so did the screaming women, and Patrick winked at him before heading back out on stage, wearing nothing but an open shirt and a pair of assless leather pants.

Showtime.

THE LIGHTS WENT down and a scream went up, and a feeling Brooke couldn't quite name took hold. It was sweaty but cold, nervous but excited, anxious but eager. A man wearing nothing but an open white shirt and leather pants stepped out onto the stage, mic in hand.

"Ladies of Atlanta, make some noise if you're ready to have fun tonight!"

The screams grew louder and Brooke joined in, taking a seat at the bar. The lights flashed, blue, pink, purple, illuminating the small space. Women sat in chairs lining the runway protruding from the stage and at tables spaced throughout the floor. More women sat around the bar, some dressed up, some dressed casually, and ranging in ages from early twenties all the way up to gray-haired grandmas. Brooke's lips twitched with a smile at the thought of bringing Nan here.

"I said—make some noise if you're ready to have some fun tonight!"

The screams somehow got even louder and Brooke started wondering if she should've worn ear protection.

The man on stage ran a hand down his chest. "Mmm. We got some fine lookin' ladies in here tonight. Look at you," he said, pointing at a woman near the stage. "You're beautiful." He made eye contact with several other women. "And so are you, and you, and damn, look at you, sweetheart. We got a house full of ladies in here who deserve a good show." He moved his body, a sexy sway as he toyed with the waistband of his leather pants. "A house full of ladies who deserve to be seduced." He ran his palm over the bulge in his pants. "Who deserve to be worshipped. Mmm." He thrust his hips and another round of screams erupted. "And we've got something special for you tonight."

In the background, the opening strains of "Like a Virgin" started playing.

"We've got someone new to introduce to you. I just saw him backstage, and ladies, I think you're gonna love him."

"You want something to drink, sweetheart?" The big guy behind the bar leaned toward her, a friendly smile on his face.

"Glass of white wine." She wouldn't really drink it, but she didn't want to stand out by sitting at a bar without a drink. He winked at her and turned away.

"So, ladies," said the man on stage, "if you're ready to have a good time, get ready to make it rain for the best-looking men in Atlanta. Give it up for the men of the Manhattan Ballroom!"

The lights flashed and went dark, and then the familiar opening chords of Nelly's "Hot in Herre" started blaring through the speakers. Four guys in black pants and white tank tops emerged onto the stage. Brooke turned away only long enough to pay for her drink, tipping generously, and then returned her attention to the show.

Sawyer wasn't one of the men on stage, but she knew he would be soon enough. The men danced in unison, thrusting and flexing, running their hands over their bodies before ripping their tank tops off and tossing them into the shrieking crowd. They took turns at center stage, each dancing on the runway, eyefucking the nearest women. Before the song was even half over, they'd all ripped their black pants off, leaving them each in nothing but a thong.

Brooke picked up her wine and took a healthy sip. She both wanted and didn't want to see Sawyer up on that stage, taking his clothes off for all these women. A cold pit settled in her stomach, and she recognized it as jealousy.

She took another big gulp of wine. Investigation. Focus. Figure other shit out later.

The music changed, Nelly fading out into a raunchier hip-hop song as the guys dropped down off the stage and into the crowd, each going in a different direction as they walked up to tables of screaming women and started giving impromptu lap dances. The music throbbed in time with her pulse as she watched eager fingers shove dollar bills into G-strings. Blood rushed to her cheeks and she crossed and then re-crossed her legs on her stool, suddenly feeling restless.

"First time here?" asked the bartender, wiping at the bar as he leaned toward her to be heard over the music.

She nodded. "Yeah. A friend told me about this place. Said it was great for stress relief, among other things."

"Oh yeah? What kind of other things?" The bartender leaned in a bit closer and so did Brooke.

Her heart pounded in her chest as she decided to just go for it. "She told me about the awesome time she and her boyfriend had using Tantrik. Said she picked some up here."

The bartender's face was blank for a second, and then he glanced around before leaning in even closer. "You looking to buy?"

She nodded, fighting to stay casual, as though she bought drugs in bars all the time.

The bartender glanced up at the stage and then back at Brooke. "I've got a guy. I can hook you up, sweetheart. Come back tomorrow night and we'll work something out. Bring cash."

She nodded and then tapped the bar. "Tomorrow night. Great."

He winked at her. "You're gonna love it."

She meant to say something back, but she was distracted by the reappearance of the MC. The other men had all disappeared, leaving him alone on stage.

"Now that you're nice and warmed up, who's ready to meet our newest dancer?" Screams erupted and Brooke's mouth went dry, her attention laser-focused on the stage. "Then please welcome to the stage, for his very first Manhattan Ballroom appearance, Lance . . . Silver!"

Brooke choked on her wine at the cheesy stage name he'd come up with. The opening guitar licks of Foreigner's "Feels Like the First Time" came through the speakers, and Sawyer strode out onto the stage, wearing a white tank top and jeans, an almost shy smile on his face. Screams echoed throughout the club as he took a few steps forward and then started to dance, keeping his moves simple as he made eye contact with various women, smiling and winking. He moved in time to the music, running his hands up his body and then pulling up his tank top and holding it for several seconds, giving everyone a good look at his abs. A few dollar bills fluttered onto the stage and he stepped up the dancing, dropping into the same graceful push-up-type move he'd practiced on her.

Rising to his knees, he ripped his tank top in half, making it look as though it was made of tissue paper. He tossed it into the crowd and, still on his knees, moved his hips in time to the music. More money flew up in the air, a few hands reaching up toward the stage and trying to touch him.

In a fluid motion, he rose back to his feet and moved down the runway, walking slowly and confidently as he toyed with the top button of his jeans, earning a loud round of screams from the audience. He turned, his back to the crowd of gleefully shrieking women, glancing over his shoulder and then ripping his jeans away, exposing his bare, muscular ass to the audience.

Screams accompanied the avalanche of dollar bills that tumbled down onto the stage, and he dropped back to his knees at the foot of the runway, the lights glinting off of the shiny fabric of his white thong. He rocked to the music as women reached up and ran their hands over his chest. He disappeared in a storm of dollar bills and grabbing hands, and Brooke realized she was gripping the edge of her barstool so tightly her hands were shaking.

Sawyer rose, his G-string flush with cash, and hopped down off the stage, targeting a stunning redhead sitting near the stage. Straddling her chair, he took her hands and laid them on his abs, his hips swiveling as he danced for her, his body just inches from hers.

Red tinged the edges of Brooke's vision, and it took everything she had to stay in her seat and not go over there and rip the woman's hands off of Sawyer. Her throat rumbled with a little growl as her jealousy burned right in the center of her chest, hot and cold at the same time. The woman grabbed Sawyer's ass and a wave of possessiveness so intense that it took Brooke's breath away rocked through her.

Shit shit shit.

The whirring disco ball lights blurred her vision as she watched Sawyer, her blood sour with jealousy. And yet, at the same time, she was on fire for him. Wet and throbbing. Achy and needy. A shiver ran through her as she remembered how crazy things had gotten between them in his apartment, and God, she wanted more. She was a mess over him, and as he left the stage to a loud round of screaming cheers, his G-string full of money, she slammed back the rest of her wine and ordered another.

Chapter Twelve

———————————————————

SAWYER HAD ALWAYS prided himself on his level of fitness. He could crank out a hundred push-ups followed by a hundred sit-ups no problem, could run two miles in thirteen minutes, could bench three hundred fifty pounds. Running was easy. Lifting weights was a piece of cake.

But dancing? Apparently dancing was kicking his ass. Muscles he hadn't even known he had were sore. After spending so much time practicing for his audition, followed by his first night at the club, and then a three-hour rehearsal with the guys this afternoon where he'd learned the group numbers, he was pretty sure his body hated him.

He reached into his locker and pulled out his bag, fumbling for the small bottle of Advil he'd thankfully had the foresight to chuck inside. After swallowing a couple of pills, he stripped down, wondering if he should wear the blue or the black thong tonight.

Once he'd decided on the black one, he started getting dressed, pulling on the cowboy hat, vest, and assless chaps for tonight's opening group number to "Save a Horse (Ride a Cowboy)." Thankfully, the group routines were all fairly simple and straightforward, and he'd be in the back, so if he messed up the choreography, it wouldn't be a huge deal. The last thing he needed to do was stand out; blending in was key. And so he joked around with the guys. Shot the shit. Learned about their lives. Worked hard to be friendly without being too friendly.

None of them had mentioned anything about Tantrik or the cartel. But if he was a betting man, he'd guess the dealer was either Danny, the cocky kid desperate to keep the fact he'd lost his scholarship from his parents, or Hurley, the tattooed guy who was rough around the edges and had already offered Sawyer both pot and coke. Shawn was too driven and clean-cut to really fit the profile, and Jesse even more so.

He pulled his burner phone out of his backpack, checking for any messages, but he hadn't heard anything from Brooke. Now that the op was on, he wasn't going in to the station, and beyond leaving her a voice mail asking her to check into the potential connection between Danny and Chase Anderson, he hadn't talked to her since she'd left his place three nights ago. He wasn't sure if he hadn't heard a word from her because she was keeping a low profile, keeping communication to a smart minimum, or because she was avoiding him.

Either way, it sucked. He was surprised at how much he missed her. Missed seeing her, being around her, missed her smart mouth and the way she didn't take his shit. He hadn't really wanted to date anyone in the traditional sense of the word since his divorce, but now he couldn't ignore the images flashing through his brain. Taking Brooke to dinner. Getting to know her. Waking up with her in his bed. Seeing if their intense chemistry could translate into something more, something deeper.

There was spark between them that wouldn't go away, and while he'd thought he wanted to extinguish it at first, he now found he wanted to feed it, see if it could grow into something bigger and brighter. Something hotter and slow-burning.

If only she wasn't completely off-limits.

He needed to see her. To touch her and be near her. And he had a plan for tonight that would allow him to do just that.

BROOKE WATCHED AS Sawyer ripped off his assless chaps, letting them drop to the floor as he swung his hips in a circle. The way he moved made his muscles ripple and flex in the flashing lights, and something hot pulsed between her legs. She'd have never guessed in a million years that watching him up on stage would've been such a crazy turn-on for her, but it was.

It really, really was.

Seeing all of these other women scream and lose their minds for him made her want to claim him. To walk up there, grab him, drag him away and not come up for air until the damn ache between her legs was finally extinguished.

She shook her head, almost laughing at herself. Fred, meet Wilma. Apparently she was just as bad as he was.

Damn. Not good. Not good at all.

He knelt at the edge of the stage wearing nothing but a cowboy hat and a black thong, moving his body in time to the music as a woman tucked money into his G-string. Brooke's eyes narrowed, and something about the jealousy rocketing through her only made her that much more aroused. Seeing how crazy he drove these other women made her want him more.

"Wasn't sure you were going to show," said a voice from behind her, and she turned to find the same bartender from last night smiling at her.

She returned his smile. "Here I am. You said you had a guy?"

He leaned in. "Yep. He's got the stuff. Meet him in the parking lot in five minutes."

"Great. Thanks for your help," she said, slipping him a twenty across the bar.

He took it and winked. "I got you, girl. Have fun."

She slid off her barstool and made her way to the exit, stepping out into the cool night air. As the door closed, the noise of the club dropped away, and she walked around the side of the building to the small parking lot in the back. Her eyes scanned from left to right in a constant sweep. She had no reason to think this was a trap or that things could go sideways, but she was on high alert all the same. She adjusted her purse on her shoulder, feeling for the reassuring weight of her Glock 26 in the concealed side compartment.

The parking lot was empty, so she went and stood by the metal door at the rear of the club, waiting. Time seemed to crawl by as she stood with her back against the stucco exterior of the club, the seconds stretching on interminably. She scanned the parking lot again, her eyes slowly moving from one parked car to the next, lingering on the shadows as she strained her ears, listening for anything suspicious.

She checked her watch, wondering how long she should wait before she called it a bust, when the metal door opened and a man stepped outside. She recognized him instantly as one of the dancers. Dark hair, perfect features. Maybe late twenties or early thirties. Model-worthy good looks, and she'd noticed that he had a friendly, relaxed presence onstage.

"Hey, sorry," he said as the door closed behind him. He wore a bathrobe and sandals, and probably very little else. "You looking for some Tantrik?"

Brooke nodded. "Yeah. How much?"

"Fifteen bucks each, or three for forty."

Brooke opened her purse and pulled out two twenties. "I'll take three."

The man smiled and reached into his pocket, pulling out a small plastic bag with three of the diamond-shaped colorful pills in it. He took her money and handed her the bag. "Enjoy. Come back to the club when you want more." He turned and disappeared inside.

Brooke dropped the bag of pills into her purse and headed around front, showing her hand stamp to the bouncer to get in. All of the seats at the bar were taken, so she settled for an empty chair at a table closer to the stage. Women threw dollar bills on the stage as a tattooed, muscle-bound guy who went by Jack Hammer stalked around the stage to Nine Inch Nails'"Closer."

She settled back in her seat, her eyes bouncing around the club. Hopefully now that they had undeniable proof of who the dealer was, they'd be able to wrap this up sooner rather than later. She saw Sawyer walking through the crowd, wearing jeans but no shirt, chatting up ladies, probably trying to convince them to buy the dances that would happen onstage later. One of them said something to him and he leaned in close. She ran her hand over his abs and he caught it, bringing it to his lips and kissing it. The woman giggled and pressed a hand to her cheek.

Brooke's nostrils flared as acid rose up in her chest.

Yeah. The sooner they could wrap up this torturous investigation, the better.

SAWYER ADJUSTED HIS hat and clip-on tie as he stood in the wings just offstage. Patrick had the mic and was waiting for the screams, elicited by Shawn's hot seat performance, to die down.

"All right, let's hear it one more time for Sebastian Steele!" he said, using Shawn's stage name. "Let me ask you something—do you fantasize about a man who can whisk you away?" Patrick paused for the cheers to fade before continuing. "A man who'll take you to all kinds of exotic places?" More cheers. "Then ladies, get ready to have your passports stamped—" At that he gave a thrust of his hips. "By Captain Lance Silver."

Jason DeRulo's "Talk Dirty" started playing and Sawyer emerged onto the stage, his eyes immediately going to the crowd. He'd been keeping track of where Brooke was, first at the bar, and then at a table not far from the stage. He tipped his hat low over his eyes as he danced, grabbing a chair from the wings and setting it in the center of the stage, earning a loud round of screams. Rolling his body to the music, he pulled his pilot's jacket off and hung it on the back of the chair, then yanked his tie off and let it drop.

Easing his hat up, he zeroed in on Brooke, whose eyes went wide when they locked with his. As he crossed the floor toward her, he pulled his shirt open and then held his hand out to her, cocking an eyebrow.

Say yes. Come on, Brooke. Please.

She hesitated for a second, but then stood and put her hand in his, letting him lead her up on stage. The feel of her palm against his sent an electric current charging through him, his heart pounding against his ribs. He led her to the chair and she sat down, smiling up at him. For a second, he almost forgot to keep dancing. There was something different about that smile. Something more . . . open.

He pulled his shirt all the way off and straddled the chair, rocking against her. The feel of her body against his was exactly what he'd needed. Goddamn, he'd missed her.

Without any prompting from him, she ran her hands up his stomach and over his chest, scraping her nails lightly over his skin. Swiveling his hips, he cupped her face, holding her eyes, wondering if she'd missed him the way he'd missed her. If she'd needed this fleeting contact as badly as he had.

"I know who the dealer is," she said, her lips brushing against his ear. "Damian St. Vincent."

Jesse. Sawyer didn't react to the information, just kept dancing. Brooke's fingers traced the ridges of his abs and he ripped his black pants off. Money fluttered down onto the stage as he ground against her. He dipped his head, whispering into her ear. "Put in for a warrant to bug his phone."

She met his eyes and nodded. Then, with an adorably cocky smile, she reached into her bra, pulled out a five and tucked it into his G-string, her eyes glittering with heat, with humor, with an open desire he hadn't seen since that night at the hotel.

He worked his hips against her, and he could tell that the energy between them had shifted. That she wasn't fighting against herself anymore, her defenses down. A thrill ran through him at what that might mean for them. Because, yeah, it was risky, but if anyone was worth the risk, it was Brooke. Gorgeous, smart, sarcastic Brooke, who turned him on while turning him inside out. Brooke, who felt perfect and right in a way no one ever had before.

The song ended and the lights went down. He planted a hard, fast kiss on her lips, satisfaction working its way through him at her gasp. "I miss you," he said, his voice coming out like a low rumble.

"I—I'll let you know about the warrant." She got up from the chair and stumbled off the stage on unsteady legs, leaving Sawyer wondering if he'd misplayed and misread the entire situation. He made his way back to his locker to get changed for the group number, and his phone buzzed from inside his bag. He fished it out, rubbing a hand over his mouth to hide his smile.

Brooke: I miss you too.

Chapter Thirteen

THE FOLLOWING NIGHT, Sawyer sat in his car—not his truck, but a Honda Civic belonging to the APD and temporarily registered to Ryan Williams—in the small parking lot behind the Manhattan Ballroom, waiting for Brooke's call. Earlier that day, she'd texted him with the info that she'd been able to secure a hearing late that afternoon to present the evidence they had justifying tapping Jesse's phone. Now he just had to wait to hear if the warrant had gone through and they could move forward with the plan.

He hadn't had a chance to talk to her about last night—the dance, the way he'd felt things shift between them, the kiss. The fact that she missed him too, and what all of that meant for them.

He knew what he wanted it to mean, but where

did she stand? And where did that leave the investigation? He needed answers to that almost as badly as he needed answers to all of his burning questions about Baracoa.

His phone started buzzing, and he swiped his finger across the screen, answering it.

"I've got the warrant," said Brooke by way of greeting. "We're good to go for tonight."

"I'll wait until Jesse's onstage and then grab his phone from his locker. Meet me in the hallway where the bathrooms are and I'll pass it off to you. You'll have about five minutes, maybe less, to get the software installed and the phone back to me so I can get it in Jesse's locker before he notices it's missing."

Brooke sighed. "Five minutes is tight, but yeah. It's our best shot. I'll see you in a bit." She hung up, and he immediately deleted the call log from his history. Excitement sped his pulse as he made his way into the club. They were getting closer. Once they had a tap on Jesse's phone, they'd be able to prove who his supplier was and could start wrapping up the investigation.

And then he'd never have to wear a thong again. The day couldn't come soon enough, as far as he was concerned.

He stepped into the dressing room, the usual pre-show banter bouncing back and forth between the guys. Scanning the room, he saw Jesse by the costumes, his head cocked thoughtfully as he slid the hangers along the rack. Sawyer never would've guessed Jesse was the guy, and maybe he wasn't the only one dealing, but he'd sold the drugs to Brooke, making him their target.

He opened his own locker and dawdled while chatting with the guys about nothing, lingering while he waited for Jesse to come back. Eventually he did, the marine costume slung over one arm. Sawyer quickly glanced around before leaning in as close as he dared to watch Jesse dial up his combination.

Twenty-six. Seven. Twelve. Sawyer repeated the numbers to himself over and over again, etching them into his brain.

"Hey man," said Jesse, who seemed completely unaware of the way Sawyer had just been lurking over his shoulder.

"Hey," said Sawyer, pulling his shirt up off over his head.

Jesse clapped him on the shoulder. "Everything okay? You seem tense."

Sawyer shrugged. "Yeah, fine." He glanced around the room before turning to Jesse. Hopefully confiding in him would bring them closer, building trust and camaraderie, and would make Jesse more likely to bring him into the fold once he found out about "Ryan's" money woes. "Remember that woman I pulled up on stage last night?"

Something in Jesse's eyes flickered. "The blonde? Oh yeah, I remember her."

"You know her?"

After a second, Jesse shook his head. "What about her?"

"I . . ." Sawyer rubbed a hand over the back of his neck. "Remember how you told me about the instant connection you felt when you first danced for your girl?"

Jesse nodded, the wariness in his eyes fading. "You felt it last night with the blonde?"

"Yeah. Big time. I asked her to come back tonight, but I don't know if she'll show."

An understanding smile spread across Jesse's face. "You're worried she won't."

"Yeah. And since that shitty breakup, this is the first time I've wanted . . . something."

Jesse clapped him on the shoulder again. "She'll show, man. You're hot, you turned her on, invited her back. And if she doesn't, maybe she'll come back tomorrow, or the night after that. You want some advice?"

Sawyer nodded, moving a bit closer to Jesse, wanting to give the impression that he was hanging on his every word.

"If she does show up again, just fucking go for it. Tell her she's gorgeous, kiss her. It means something that out of all the women here, you noticed *her*. Make sure she knows that."

"You think she'll go for that? If I just lay it all out?" And now he was seriously asking a stripper-slash-drug dealer for relationship advice. Because that was normal.

Jesse smirked. "Call it a hunch, but I have a feeling blondie is up for just about anything."

Right. Because he thought Brooke was a Tantrik user, since she'd bought the drugs off him yesterday.

"Thanks, man."

"No problem. You seem like a good guy, Ryan. We should grab a beer or something sometime."

"Sure, yeah. Sounds good."

Jesse smiled at him and moved away to change in front of the mirror.

Twenty-six. Seven. Twelve.

THE NIGHT SEEMED to drag on as Sawyer waited for Jesse's solo, but finally, it was his turn to take the stage and Sawyer hurried to Jesse's locker, angling his back so that anyone who looked in his direction would think he was at his own. His pulse hammered in his ears as he dialed the lock's combination, opened it and grabbed Jesse's phone from where it sat on the little shelf near the top. He wanted to snoop through it—read his texts and e-mails, see what else he could find—but there was no time. He slipped it into the pocket of his robe and quickly closed the locker, reengaging the lock. He glanced over his shoulder. Hurley sat on the couch smoking a joint and sharing it with Danny, while Shawn scrolled through his phone. No one was paying attention to him.

Sawyer hurried out to the hallway and spotted Brooke immediately. Slipping his hand in his pocket, he walked quickly in her direction and handed the phone off to her as they passed. It disappeared into her pocket and she practically ran into the ladies' room. Sawyer peeked around the corner, glancing up at the stage, where Jesse had his shirt off, but still wore pants, meaning they had three to four minutes.

And then Jesse bent and ripped his pants off. Shit.

More like two minutes.

BROOKE'S FINGERS TREMBLED slightly as she closed the stall door behind her and took Jesse's phone out of her pocket. The dull thump of the bass and the shrill treble of the audience's screams seeped through the walls. It sounded as though Jesse was still on stage, but she knew she had only a few minutes to get the software installed on his phone. If Jesse noticed his phone was missing, it'd compromise the op. If she wasn't able to get the software installed on his phone, it'd stall the investigation. So she had no other choice but to work with the time she had. Screwing this up wasn't an option.

She woke up the phone, surprised to see a picture of Jesse and a beautiful Latina woman set as the wallpaper. If she didn't know the dude was a drug dealer working for the most dangerous cartel in Atlanta, she'd almost think it was cute. She held down the home button.

"Hey Siri, what time is it?" she asked, trying to keep her voice as low as possible.

The clock popped up on the screen as Siri answered. "The time is 9:36 p.m."

Quickly she tapped the timer option at the bottom of the screen. From there, instead of selecting one of the preinstalled tones, she tapped Buy New Tones, and when the app store popped up, she pressed the home button again, which brought her to the home screen. She was in without having to waste precious time guessing his passcode.

"Thank you, Jack," she whispered, grateful that the trick he'd shown her worked. She opened Safari and navigated to the black APD site, typed in the password and tapped Install. With agonizing slowness, the invisible software that would allow HEAT to listen in to, record and track all of Jesse's phone calls started downloading. Every call Jesse made or received would generate a record, stored on a secure computer in the HEAT bullpen. Jack and Amelia would keep an eye on things, letting her know if anything interesting or noteworthy came through.

A loud scream rose up from outside, and she knew Jesse's performance must be wrapping up. "Come on, come on," she whispered, sweat gathering along her hairline as she stared at the little blue bar, willing it to move forward faster. Another loud scream and the blue bar seemed to come to a complete standstill.

"No, no, no," she chanted, staring at the phone. If she

couldn't get this to work, both the warrant and the risk they were taking right now would all be for nothing. In a desperate attempt to get things moving, she double clicked the home button to bring up the currently running apps and closed them all except for her download with a swipe of her finger.

The blue line started moving again, but the music had stopped. Finally, with a little chime, the download finished and Brooke closed out the site, erasing the history and locking the phone again. She practically sprinted out of the bathroom, almost running smack into Sawyer, who steadied her with his hands around her upper arms.

"Done," she whispered, slipping the phone into his robe's pocket. Without a word, Sawyer turned and disappeared into the dressing room. She stood stone-still, not leaving him on the chance that he'd be discovered and need backup. No way was she going to let anything happen to him. She couldn't hear anything from the dressing room, and fought the urge to cross the hall and press her ear to the door, knowing if she was caught, she'd likely get kicked out of the club. So she held her ground, pressed her fingers against the reassuring weight of the Glock in her bag, and strained her ears, listening. Hoping. Waiting.

Less than a minute later—a minute that felt like an hour—Sawyer came back out of the dressing room and gave her a covert thumbs-up. She sagged back against the wall, all of her tension dissolving and leaving her muscles limp. She sucked in a deep breath, trying to calm her still-racing heart.

She'd expected Sawyer to head back into the dressing room, but he didn't, instead making a beeline for her and caging her in against the wall, his big hands on either side of her. He dipped his head and kissed her, hot and slow, feeding the adrenaline still coursing through her. So much for slowing her heart rate down. With a soft moan, she slipped her arms around his waist, pulling him closer. Needing this. Needing him.

After a moment, he broke the kiss, cupping her face and pressing his forehead to hers. His voice was a low rumble when he spoke. "I can't stop thinking about you, Brooke, and I don't want to stop thinking about you. I want you in my bed. In my life. I was an asshole to you, and I'm so sorry. You . . . fuck, you make me crazy, and I can't—"

His words both ignited and soothed something inside her, setting her on fire while filling in the hollows she hadn't even been fully aware of. She cut him off with a kiss, sliding her tongue against his and earning a low, gruff moan from him. "I want you, Sawyer." Words that would've felt insane a week ago now felt good. Right. And yet she couldn't ignore the fear tugging at her either.

He made a strangled noise, a deep masculine sound filled with relief and happiness. "Come over tonight. After. I need you."

She kissed him again, nodding as she did, her body winning out over her brain. "I can't stay away from you."

Even though she knew she should. But maybe this was an itch they had to scratch, and once they had, they'd be able to move forward with clearer heads. After all, this was a sex thing. Just a sex thing.

He smiled, big and bright, the little lines around his eyes crinkling as he rubbed his thumb over her cheek. "Then don't."

The dressing room door opened and Sawyer moved away from her.

"I see you found your girl," Jesse said as he stepped out of the dressing room, wearing nothing but a purple G-string filled with dollar bills and an open robe, his chest glistening with sweat. Sawyer winked at Brooke before turning to face him, and something in her thrilled at the idea of being his girl. Thrilled her and scared her.

"Took your advice," he said, and Brooke had to admit that she was impressed with the way he was able to drop back into character like that. His body language was different, more relaxed, less alpha. Less intimidating. And his voice had lost the gruffness she liked so much. There wasn't an ounce of surliness or grumpiness. She missed it. Hell, maybe she even *liked* his grumpiness.

As if she needed more proof that there was probably something seriously wrong with her.

Brooke pressed a hand to her warm cheek, eyes bouncing between Jesse and Sawyer. "Uh, hi," she said.

Sawyer wove his fingers between hers. "This is Brooke. Brooke, this is Jesse."

Jesse gave her a knowing smile, but being the consummate drug-dealing professional he apparently was, he didn't let on that she'd bought from him yesterday. "Hey. Nice to meet you."

She nodded at him, but he'd already turned his attention back to Sawyer. "Group number's up next, man. Patrick was looking for you."

Sawyer grimaced. "Shit, yeah, okay. Be right in." He turned and gave Brooke a quick kiss on the lips. "I'll see you tonight." And then he disappeared back into the dressing room with Jesse.

As far as Brooke was concerned, the end of the night couldn't come fast enough.

As soon as he was done at the club, Sawyer headed straight for his car, eager to get home. All he could think about was the fact that Brooke had said yes, that she wanted him as much as he did her. He hadn't planned on just going for it like that, but he'd been riding high on the adrenaline rush of successfully bugging Jesse's phone and he hadn't been able to stop himself. She made him want things he hadn't even realized he'd been missing. Sleepy Sunday mornings in bed. Family dinners. Cuddling up on the couch to make out and watch movies.

She was different than any other woman he'd ever met before. She was as dedicated to the job as he was, and even though they'd gotten off to a rocky start, she made him feel understood in a way that he'd never experienced before. It made him want to get to know her better, both in and out of the bedroom.

He merged onto I-75, humming along with the radio as he risked a speeding ticket in his hurry to get home, and was only a block away when he remembered that he didn't have any condoms. He couldn't even remember the last time he'd had a woman at his place besides Brooke. As he made a quick detour to the twenty-four-hour Walgreens a couple miles from his condo, he realized it was because he hadn't since the divorce. His hookups had always been away from home—the woman's place, hotels. It felt . . . significant that he wanted Brooke in his bed. In his space.

Finally, after what felt like an eternity, he pulled into his parking spot, grabbed the box of Trojans from where he'd tossed them on the front seat and headed inside, his heart beating happily in his chest. Funny how things could shift in such a short amount of time. A week ago, he'd been struggling to keep his distance. To push her away. Now, he wanted her all kinds of close.

Hell, maybe he always had and just hadn't known what to do about it.

A smile spread across his face as he walked through the quiet parking lot. A car horn honked in the distance, the whirring hush of the freeway barely audible. Tonight had gone well. Really, really well. In the morning, he'd file an updated report with the captain. Normally he did it as soon as he got home, but tonight he had other priorities.

As he stepped inside his condo, his eyes did a quick sweep of the place. It was a bit messy—a few dirty dishes in the sink, laundry in a basket on the living room floor, waiting to be folded—but he didn't have time to care about that right now. He stripped his clothes off as he moved toward the bathroom, then cranked the shower on and stepped under the spray. Wanting to wash the club off before Brooke came over. He didn't want to smell like too much cologne and other women when she touched him. Just himself. Clean, and without the scent of the investigation on him. As though washing his night's work away would somehow make what he and Brooke were starting less wrong. Not wrong in a personal sense, but definitely in a professional sense. With a shake of his head, he shoved that away. Tomorrow. They'd figure everything out tomorrow.

He'd just yanked on a T-shirt and a pair of jeans, not bothering with boxers, not even bothering to button them, when there was a soft knock at the door. He opened it, his heart stuttering to a stop at the sight of Brooke, her cheeks pink, her lips slightly parted. As though she was just as excited and eager as he was. An intensity shone in her eyes and she launched herself at him. He let out a deep chuckle as her legs came around his waist, his palms supporting her ass. Their lips met, a sweet, slow, lingering kiss as he backed them inside and kicked the door closed.

She laid a palm against his cheek. "Hi," she whispered.

"Hi," he whispered back, claiming her mouth again with another kiss, unable to get enough of her. "You came." Despite what they'd said in the hallway at the club, a tiny part of him had been worried that she'd bail. That she'd run scared. Again.

An adorably naughty smile pulled at the corners of her lips. "Not yet."

God, he could fall for this woman. His attraction to her was almost overwhelming, but in a good way.

He kissed her again, and with his lips moving against hers, walked them into his bedroom.

Brooke pulled her mouth from his, looking around. "Not very cave-like."

He smiled and tossed her down on the bed, then pulled his shirt over his head, letting it fall to the floor. "Sorry to disappoint."

She stared up at him, part of the humor in her expression replaced with something more intense. "You never disappoint."

That tugged at something in his chest. A guilt. A fear, maybe. "No?" he said, taking a step closer to the bed. "Not even when I'm trying to fuck with your career?"

She rose to her knees and pulled her own shirt off,

tossing it down beside his. "Do you need me to tell you you're forgiven?"

Shit. Yeah, maybe he did. He had so much guilt over things for which he couldn't quite seem to forgive himself. Ryan's death, and all of its fallout. Being a dick to Brooke.

"Come here," she said, crooking her finger at him. When he made it to the edge of the bed, she took his hands in hers, weaving her slender fingers between his much larger ones. "I can't even imagine what you've gone through, but I can tell you that it's not your fault. I can tell you that grief makes us do stupid, thoughtless, selfish things. Out-of-character things." She traced her thumbs over the backs of his hands, and that small gesture contained so much warmth, so much comfort in it that he knew he never wanted to let her go. "I didn't realize it until just now, but I think I forgave you a while ago."

"Why?" he asked, his voice coming out strained.

"Because I know you're hurting. And because . . ." She paused, biting her lip. "I wanted to hate you, and I just couldn't." She met his eyes. She opened her mouth to say more, but then held herself back, closing her mouth and shaking her head slightly. Even though she was here, there was still a hesitation lingering in her eyes.

He dipped his head and kissed her, trying to pour everything he was feeling into the kiss. Relief. Happiness. Gratitude. All big and bright and intense. Hoping it'd be enough to chase away her uncertainty about being here with him.

Still kissing her, he eased her back onto the bed, careful not to crush her under his weight. Her legs wound around his waist and her nails scraped lightly down his back as she rocked her hips against him, making a deliciously needy sound. Taking his time, savoring her, he kissed his way from her mouth to her neck, her skin warm and soft against his lips.

She writhed against him again, but even though he was rock-hard and desperate to get inside her, he didn't want to hurry. The fact that she was here, in his bed, telling him she'd forgiven him meant something—meant a lot—and while words weren't his strength, he could show her what it meant. He could make her feel good, make her feel beautiful, make her feel adored. Make her understand the significance of her forgiveness.

He pinned her wrists above her head and kissed farther down her body, teasing her nipples through the lace of her bra. Scraping his teeth over her. Biting and licking until the fabric was wet and her back arched off the bed. Lifting his head, he blew a stream of air over one hard nipple, making her moan out his name as her legs tightened around his waist. He could feel the heat of her pussy even through her jeans, and his mouth watered at the thought of tasting her again.

He kissed his way down her body, lingering on her flat, toned stomach, all smooth, warm skin and lithe muscle. So beautiful. So perfect. He undid her jeans and worked them down her hips, moving off her briefly so she could wriggle out of them. As soon as they hit the floor, he settled himself between her legs, his shoulders nestled against the backs of her thighs. He inhaled deeply, tracing his fingers around the edges of her thong, toying with it, moving it against her.

"Please, Sawyer, I need you. Please," she panted, her voice higher and breathier than usual.

With a growl, he pushed her thong to the side and finally got his mouth on her again. Her taste flooded his tongue, and he groaned, licking a slow path through her folds. She wove her hands into his hair, tugging, encouraging him with her firm grip and breathy moans. He swept his tongue over her clit then sucked it into his mouth, kissing her deeply. Her hips jerked against the mattress and he tightened his grip on her to keep her in place.

"You taste so good," he said between licks and kisses. "I could do this all fucking night." He gently scraped his teeth over her swollen flesh and then closed his mouth over her again.

"And I . . . oh, God, do that again . . . fuck, *yes* . . . And I would let you, God," she panted out, her hips pushing against his grip as he worked her closer and closer to coming. He felt her muscles start to shake and then tighten as he kept up a steady rhythm of swirling licks and sucking kisses.

She suddenly went still and then let out a high

whimpering sound before screaming out his name, pulsing against his lips as she came. He kissed the insides of her thighs, giving her a minute to come back down before kissing his way back up her body, satisfaction curling through him.

Her hands were frenzied and desperate against his jeans, and she yanked the zipper down so roughly that she nearly took his dick off. She pushed at the denim, grabbing handfuls of his ass. "I need you inside me," she said before pulling his head down for a hot, deep kiss. Supporting his weight on one arm, he slid his other hand down her body, hooking his fingers into her thong and dragging it down her legs. She sent it to the edge of the bed with a graceful kick, and then opened her legs wider and moved against him, the head of his cock nudging at the impossibly hot, wet flesh between her legs.

"Shit, condoms," he said, sliding against her again. "In . . . in kitchen." He kissed her again, wanting more of her mouth.

She slapped his ass. "Hurry."

He lifted his head and winked at her. "Yes ma'am." He sprang up off the bed and ran for the kitchen like something was on fire, grabbed the box off the counter and then practically sprinted back to his bedroom.

Brooke lay on the bed, propped up on her elbows, her legs spread wide, the pretty pink between her legs glistening. Ready for him. His. An emotion he couldn't quite name rocked through him, making it hard to breathe.

He tossed the box on the bed and then stepped out of his jeans, and when his eyes met hers, she smiled. Not a coy, sexy smile, but a big, almost goofy one. And then realized she was probably smiling at him like that because of the dopey grin plastered to his own face.

She opened the box, pulling out a condom and tearing the wrapper. Rising to her knees, she reached for him and rolled it on, stroking him. He kissed her and eased down on top of her, a shudder coursing through him at the feeling of being skin to skin with her.

He notched the head of his cock at her entrance, working his hips and pressing in just the tiniest bit. "Will you stay tonight?" he asked, teasing just the tip in and out of her.

She let out a shaky moan. "Mmm, maybe . . . maybe if you go down on me again," she said, her eyes flashing with a teasing glint.

He chuckled and pushed all the way into her. "Deal." The truth was, he'd do whatever she wanted if it meant she'd stay.

He pulled almost all the way out and then slid back in, hitting deeper than before. Her legs locked around his slowly thrusting hips, and he kissed her, pinning her arms above her head and lacing his fingers with hers. Wanting to touch as many parts of her as possible. Taking her slow and deep until stars exploded behind his closed eyes and he lost himself in her. Until she clenched around him, moaning his name, flooding his cock. Until he'd poured everything he had into her and a bone-deep satisfaction took hold.

With Brooke nestled against his chest, his arms around her, he fell into a deep sleep, and for the first time since Ryan's death, he didn't wake up until morning.

Chapter Fourteen

BROOKE SLOWLY OPENED her eyes as she stretched her arms over her head, her body relaxed and satisfied. Sunlight streamed in through the slat blinds on Sawyer's bedroom window, bathing the room in a soft, golden glow. With a sleepy, sated yawn, she sat up. Sawyer's side of the bed was empty, but she could hear noise from the direction of the kitchen.

She looked around, wanting to see his bedroom in the daylight. Last night it had been dark, and she'd been too distracted to pay attention. It was simple and unfussy, just like the rest of his place. The king-size bed took up most of the room, with a little table on either side. A dresser faced the bed, with a couple of framed photographs on top. Smiling to herself, she swung her legs over the side of the bed and picked up Sawyer's discarded T-shirt from the night before, then pulled it on and inhaled deeply, loving that it smelled like him.

The first picture was Sawyer in his cadet blues with who she assumed were his parents at his graduation from the Academy. He looked a lot like his father. Same blue eyes, same smile, same build. Same brow. Same jawline. His mother was pretty, with shoulder-length blond hair, a slender build, and a warm smile. She ran her finger down the side of the frame, something wistful tugging at her. He looked so much younger. Fresh-faced and eager. Proud and happy. Less . . . hardened than he looked now. He'd become weathered during his decade behind the badge. The job had a way of making you old before your time. It was worth it, but a tough gig sometimes.

The second picture was more recent, showing Sawyer and who she assumed were his two brothers all on a boat, holding up a gigantic fish of some kind. What was it with dudes and fishing pictures? When she'd tried online dating, it had seemed as though every other guy had a picture just like this one. The three men all looked alike, bearing a strong family resemblance.

The third was of him and Ryan at a ballpark, both wearing Atlanta Braves T-shirts, each holding a beer and smiling. An ache flared up in her chest for what he'd lost, and she absently rubbed at it. She knew what it was like to lose someone and feel like your life would never be the same. And the truth was, after that loss, your life never *was* the same. Good, maybe, but forever quite name rocked through him, making it hard to breathe.

He tossed the box on the bed and then stepped out of his jeans, and when his eyes met hers, she smiled. Not a coy, sexy smile, but a big, almost goofy one. And then realized she was probably smiling at him like that because of the dopey grin plastered to his own face.

She opened the box, pulling out a condom and tearing the wrapper. Rising to her knees, she reached for him and rolled it on, stroking him. He kissed her and eased down on top of her, a shudder coursing through him at the feeling of being skin to skin with her.

He notched the head of his cock at her entrance, working his hips and pressing in just the tiniest bit. "Will you stay tonight?" he asked, teasing just the tip in and out of her.

She let out a shaky moan. "Mmm, maybe . . . maybe if you go down on me again," she said, her eyes flashing with a teasing glint.

He chuckled and pushed all the way into her. "Deal." The truth was, he'd do whatever she wanted if it meant she'd stay.

He pulled almost all the way out and then slid back in, hitting deeper than before. Her legs locked around his slowly thrusting hips, and he kissed her, pinning her arms above her head and lacing his fingers with hers. Wanting to touch as many parts of her as possible. Taking her slow and deep until stars exploded behind his closed eyes and he lost himself in her. Until she clenched around him, moaning his name, flooding his cock. Until he'd poured everything he had into her and a bone-deep satisfaction took hold.

With Brooke nestled against his chest, his arms around her, he fell into a deep sleep, and for the first time since Ryan's death, he didn't wake up until morning.

legs, she started touching herself, working her fingers against her swollen clit.

Sawyer let out an approving rumble as he fucked her. "Shit, that's hot."

"Oh yeah? You like watching me touch myself?" She nipped at his ear, earning a groan.

He slowed his thrusts and kissed her again. "I just like you. Period."

She met his eyes, a tentative smile spreading across her face. He mirrored it back to her, the skin around his eyes crinkling as he stroked his cock in and out of her. He kissed her again and pulled her closer.

It didn't take long before she started to tremble, a beautiful pressure throbbing between her legs as he drove her higher and higher. She stroked herself in tight little circles and then exploded, crying out as her orgasm crested over her, leaving her skin tingling. His grip on her hips tightened and he slammed into her with several hard, deep thrusts before he went still, his cock pulsing inside her.

With a contended sigh she sagged against him. He kissed her hair, wrapping his arms around her, stroking a hand up and down her back as they lingered in the afterglow.

And then the smoke alarm went off.

"Ah, shit," he said, pulling out of her and hurrying to deal with the alarm, almost tripping over his jeans around his ankles. She hopped down from the counter, shutting the burner off and waving a kitchen towel over the two pieces of bacon he'd left in the pan, charred to a crisp.

They looked at each other and started to laugh.

Sawyer took care of the condom and pulled his jeans back on, adding scrambled eggs—now cold—and toast to the plates with the unburned bacon. He poured her a cup of coffee, and she watched as he added a little sugar and a lot of milk to it before setting it down in front of her.

"You know how I take my coffee?"

He pulled his chair closer to the table, shrugging. "It's how you fix it at the station."

It was the tiniest thing, and yet it didn't feel tiny. It felt significant. Sweet, and special.

She took a small sip and then dug into her breakfast, suddenly famished. "Mmm," she said around a mouthful of scrambled eggs. "Really good."

He bit into a strip of bacon. "Thanks. It was important to my mom that her boys know how to cook."

"Where did you grow up?" He had the tiniest hint of a Southern twang sometimes, but it wasn't nearly enough to guess where he was from.

"Brunswick. It's about four hours southeast of here, on the coast. My parents still live there."

"What do they do?"

"My mom's a high school teacher—health and sex ed, so that was pretty fucking awkward—and my dad's a social worker with the local Department of Family and Children Services." He sat back and took a sip of his coffee. "Where did you grow up? You don't have much of an accent."

"I was born in Phoenix, and lived there until the accident. I came to Atlanta to live with my grandparents."

He reached out and laid a hand over hers, his features drawn. "I'm sorry."

"Thanks," she said, happy to take the comfort he was offering. "I still think about them a lot even though they've been gone for twenty years. Don't get me wrong, I love my grandparents, and they made sure I had a wonderful childhood. But sometimes I wonder what my life would be like if the accident hadn't happened." If she wouldn't be so afraid to be alone once Nan's time came.

He nodded slowly. "All the things that could've been."

"Exactly."

A comfortable silence fell between them, as though this wasn't their first breakfast together. As though they'd been doing this for months, years even. But they hadn't; they weren't even supposed to be doing this at all.

She pushed her eggs around on her plate. "So . . . so how's this going to work?"

"What do you mean?"

"We're breaking the rules. I'm not usually a rule-breaker."

At that, he slowly set his fork down and leaned back in his chair, an unreadable expression on his face. "So . . . what? You don't want to . . ." He swallowed, frowning.

She set her fork down, the movement careful and deliberate. "I didn't say that. I don't . . ." She trailed off and swallowed against the panic starting to claw its way up her throat. "I do want this. I think. But we could lose our jobs."

"We won't."

She shook her head, trying to organize her thoughts over the internal tug of war waging inside her. "You can't promise that."

Something in his eyes flashed. "You don't trust me."

"I didn't say that either."

"Well, help me out here, Brooke. I'm trying to fill in the gaps on my own and getting it all wrong, apparently." His mouth tightened in a frown. "Listen, if you don't want to do this, just say it."

She picked up her coffee and took a sip, stalling while she tried to figure out how she felt. "This is messy. I want this, but I don't want to lose my job. Maybe we should hit Pause until the case is over."

He arched a brow. "And then what? We trade partners? Leave everything on Pause?"

She shrugged and then blew out a long, slow breath through her nose. "So . . . where does that leave us?" She wanted to let him in—why was it so hard?

He leaned forward and laid a hand over hers. "We keep it on the DL. We'll figure everything out after we've wrapped the investigation."

"So, for now, this is just between us. An itch we're

scratching." Sex. Not love. For some reason, that made it a bit easier for Brooke to wrap her head around.

He nodded, although she saw something unidentifiable flicker in his eyes. "Right."

She wasn't convinced it was a good idea, but what other choice did they have? They couldn't seem to keep their hands off of each other, but she wasn't willing to risk her career—especially for a connection that was purely physical. They'd only known each other for a month if you counted back to their first night together; surely that wasn't long enough to develop any real feelings for someone. Keeping the fact that she was hooking up with her partner a secret—temporarily—was really the only option.

Hopefully it didn't blow up in their faces.

Chapter Fifteen

THE FOLLOWING MORNING, Brooke stirred in her bed. She opened her eyes slowly, Sawyer's big hand flexing against her hip. He slid his hand around to her stomach and pulled her against him, and with his solid, warm body behind her, she let her eyes drift closed again.

He'd worked at the club last night, and after his shift, he'd come over to her place. She'd had a harder time than usual watching him dance, but thankfully he hadn't had to do any hot seats or lap dances. She honestly wasn't sure if she'd be able to watch that and keep her cool. Now that they were doing this, she felt possessive of him, and didn't want to share any more than was absolutely necessary.

Her phone started buzzing from its spot on her nightstand, and she opened her eyes again, groping for it.

"Hello?"

"Is this Brooke Simmons?"

Brooke rubbed her eyes, stifling a yawn. "Yeah."

"My name's Ken. I'm calling from the Wellington Rock Retirement Community. It's about your grandmother, Miriam Woods."

The fog of sleep cleared immediately as Brooke sat up, her entire body going on high alert, pulse pounding, stomach clenching, sweat prickling along her hairline. "What happened?"

"She had a heart attack. She's been rushed to Emory."

Sawyer sat up beside her, laying a hand on her back. Brooke's hand shook. "So she's alive?"

"Yes, but she's in critical condition, as far as I know."

"Okay. I'm on my way. Thank you for calling," she said, her voice sounding numb and faraway. She disconnected the call and let her phone drop to the bed, her mind racing as the rest of her body seemed to turn to cement.

Sawyer rubbed her back. "What is it?" he asked quietly.

She managed to push her shock aside and flung back the covers. "It's Nan. She had a heart attack. I—I need to go to her." She opened the curtains and rifled through the pile of clothes on the floor beside her bed, then tugged on a pair of jeans and a T-shirt, not caring if they were clean.

Sawyer stood and quietly started pulling his clothes

on. "Which hospital?" he asked, slipping his phone into his back pocket.

She frowned as she scraped her hair into a messy ponytail. "You don't need to come with me."

"I know I don't need to. But can I?"

"You want to?"

"I don't want you to go alone." He took a step toward her, rubbing a thumb over her cheek. "You don't need to be alone, Brooke." *Not anymore.* His unspoken words hung between them, and after a second, she nodded.

"Okay. Thanks."

The trip to the hospital felt like the longest three miles she'd ever driven in her life, even though the Sunday morning traffic was light. Every song on the radio was jarring. The sunlight was too bright. Every single car was in her way.

She blew out an aggravated breath as she came to yet another red light. Sawyer laid a hand on her thigh, not saying anything. She took a deep breath, letting his touch anchor her. Letting it ground her against the onslaught of emotions pelting her like shards of ice. Worry, and fear for Nan, and anger that the only person she had left on this planet might be taken from her.

As they entered the Critical Care Center, the smell of antiseptic hit her, making her stomach turn. After checking in at the reception desk, they were directed to a room at the end of the hall.

"I'll wait out here," said Sawyer before pressing a kiss to her temple. Brooke nodded, steeling herself as she stepped inside the small hospital room.

Her heart clenched at the sight of Nan. She looked so small, so frail and weak, in the hospital bed. Tubes and wires surrounded her bed in an organized tangle, hooked up to various machines. Brooke's eyes stung and she blinked rapidly, pressing her fingers to her mouth to get her emotions under control. The last thing Nan needed right now was to see Brooke upset.

Brooke stepped farther into the room, forcing herself to approach the bed, and she carefully took one of Nan's hands in hers. At that, Nan's eyes fluttered open, a faint smile on her lips. "My Brooke," she said, squeezing Brooke's hand gently.

"Nan," said Brooke, her voice cracking. She cleared her throat and blinked furiously. "Do you know where you are?"

"I'm in the ICU at Emory. I had a heart attack, not an aneurism." A wry smile twisted her lips, and Brooke felt some of her panic start to recede. Even though her voice was thin and she looked pale and so very, very fragile, Nan was still Nan.

Brooke perched on the edge of the bed, still holding Nan's hand. "Have you seen the doctor?"

Nan nodded. "They're running tests to see how much damage was done to my heart."

"And then what?"

"Depends what the tests say. I might need to have heart surgery."

Oh, God. Brooke blinked, her eyes stinging again, and this time she couldn't hold the tears back. She sucked in a shuddering breath as they streaked down her cheeks.

Nan reached up and stroked Brooke's cheek. "It's okay, honey. Don't be scared."

Brooke nodded, feeling like a needy child. She should be the one comforting her grandmother, not the other way around. "I know. I'm sorry."

"It's okay. I'm okay." But something in her grandmother's expression faltered, and Brooke could see the fear there. "I love you so much, Brooke."

Her words only made Brooke cry even harder, and she wiped at her cheeks, nodding and unable to speak. Her throat felt clogged, with tears and worry and heartache.

"I'm so proud of the woman you've become. I'm so grateful for everything you've given me."

Brooke pressed her lips together, knowing her grandmother needed to say these things, and hating that they felt like goodbye. "I love you too, Nan, but please don't talk like this."

Nan smiled up at her. "Don't worry, I'm not giving up. I just . . ." Her own eyes grew misty. "I needed you to hear those things."

For a few minutes, neither of them spoke, just sitting together. But then Nan's eyes drifted over Brooke's shoulder and she smiled, her eyes twinkling. "You must be the man who tried to get my granddaughter kicked off your team," she said, her voice a bit stronger than it had been a few minutes ago. Brooke twisted to see Sawyer standing in the doorway. He'd gone pale, his mouth open slightly.

He rubbed a hand over the back of his neck, looking embarrassed and uncomfortable. "Uh, yes ma'am. I guess . . . uh, yeah."

Nan winked at Brooke. "I had a feeling I'd be meeting you. Why don't you come in? You're very attractive but you don't make a terribly good door."

Sawyer's eyes went wide, but to his credit, he stepped into the room and laid a hand on Brooke's shoulder. "It's nice to meet you ma'am, although I'm sorry for the circumstances." Well, well, well. Look who morphed into a sweet Southern boy around grandmothers.

Nan eyed him, her gaze appraising and shrewd. "As am I, but it's good to meet the man who managed to get so far under Brooke's skin."

Brooke's cheeks warmed, but she wasn't about to chastise her ninety-year-old ICU patient grandmother.

Sawyer chuckled and gave Brooke's shoulder a squeeze. Nan crooked a finger, beckoning him closer. He leaned down and Nan tapped his chest. "My, my. That is impressive." She shot Brooke a meaningful look, and Brooke smiled. "I want to ask you something." She motioned him even closer and he leaned down, his ear right by her mouth. Brooke couldn't hear what Nan whispered to him, but after a moment, Sawyer straightened, his eyes bright, a small smile on his face. He met Nan's eyes and nodded, once. Then he pressed a kiss to Brooke's cheek.

"I'll be outside," he said, giving them the room.

"What did you say to him?" Brooke asked, but Nan shook her head.

"My dear girl, I have loved you so much."

"Nan, come on. Don't talk like that. Enough."

"I'm ninety with a bad heart, Brooke. I'm going to try my best to stick around, but it might be out of my hands."

"No. No, because I'll miss you so much that I won't know how to handle it. I don't want to figure out how to keep going without you. I'm not ready for that." Brooke tried and failed to suppress the desperation in her voice.

Nan smiled. "You won't be alone. That man out there? He's in love with you. I can see it just from the way he looks at you. And that makes me glad, knowing you have him."

A prickling heat flushed over Brooke's body, panic and wonder and denial all fused together in one bundle that she didn't quite know what to do with. Surely it was *way* too early in her relationship with Sawyer—if you could even call it a relationship—to talk about love, right? She'd just figured out that she didn't hate him a few days ago.

Nan's eyes started to droop, and Brooke rose and kissed her on the cheek. "Get some rest. I'm going to go rustle up some coffee. I'll be back in a bit."

Nan nodded and Brooke left the room, her heart feeling heavy.

Chapter Sixteen

MUSIC THROBBED THROUGH the Manhattan Ballroom's speakers, echoing with rhythmic dull thuds through the cinderblock walls backstage. Sawyer flipped through the costume rack, ultimately deciding on a pair of tear-away jeans, white tank top, tool belt, fake sledgehammer made out of foam, work gloves, and a construction helmet for his upcoming solo. Checking the time, he started pulling the costume on.

It was surprising how many of the costumes he'd managed to wear since he'd started working at the club a week ago. He'd have to start cycling back through them soon. Hopefully by the time that happened, they'd be close to wrapping the investigation up.

They'd gathered more intel from Jesse's phone, confirming that he was in contact with the Sheriff as well as two key Desperado members. The meet with the supplier was going down tomorrow at noon, so now that they had a date, time and location, he and Brooke planned to observe from a distance to see what more they could learn.

He hadn't had as much luck actually infiltrating the dealers, though. He and Jesse had gone out for beers on Monday, two nights ago, but so far he hadn't made any progress. Jesse had never mentioned Tantrik to him, despite having sold some to Brooke, who he now thought Sawyer was dating.

A loud screaming cheer rose up from the audience, and Sawyer gave himself a final once-over in the mirror, knowing he was up next. Shawn gave him a high-five as he came offstage, his thong stuffed with ones and fives. Patrick poked his head backstage to see what costume Sawyer had chosen, then winked at him before heading back out.

The lights went down and a spotlight came on, landing on Patrick. "Ladies, make some noise if you like a man who's good with his hands." A loud cheer rose up and Patrick chuckled, his voice echoing through the speakers. "If you like a man who knows how to handle his tool." Another round of shrieks and Sawyer smiled and shook his head. Patrick only danced sometimes— his favorite role was teasing the crowd and getting them all riled up. "A man who knows how to use heavy, over-sized equipment." More screams, but Patrick cupped his hand to his ear and leaned forward. "What's that? I couldn't hear you." The screams got louder and Patrick finally introduced him. The spotlight disappeared as the famous opening electronic chords of Ginuwine's "Pony" blared across the stage.

He did all of his usual moves: rolling his body, running his hands over his chest and pulling his tank top up, dropping down and thrusting his hips against the floor. He worked the sledgehammer between his legs and then let it pop straight up, the symbolism not lost on anyone if the piercing shrieks were any indication.

With a roll of his hips, he let the tool belt fall to the stage, and then ripped his tank top off and tossed it into the audience. A woman sitting maybe three or four feet from Brooke caught it and waved it in the air excitedly. He caught Brooke's eye and winked at her, wanting to let her know that he saw her. That even though all these other women were screaming for him to get naked, it didn't mean anything. Only she meant something. Not just something. A lot.

She smiled up at him, but the sadness and worry lingered around her eyes. Her grandmother was still in the hospital, and he knew that the investigation was wearing on her. That she was trying to be tough and brave, but keeping it all together was taking its toll.

He unbuttoned his jeans and then hopped down off the stage, making a beeline for her. Her cheeks went pink and he swung a leg over her chair, taking her hands and guiding them to his abs. Abs that she'd kissed that morning before taking his cock into her mouth. He let his arms fall over the back of her chair and leaned in close as he ground against her in time to the music.

"Hey sexy, come here often?" he said, his lips scraping against her ear.

She laughed, humor dancing in her eyes, and the fact that he'd been able to cheer her up, just for a minute, felt like a prize. He winked and moved back to the stage, hopping back up and ripping his pants off. Money cascaded onto the stage as he dropped to his knees and thrust his hips, a few women from the front row reaching out and slipping money directly into his thong.

He glanced up and Brooke's smile had disappeared again. The song faded out and he tossed a wave over his shoulder as he went backstage, worry clawing at his chest.

Brooke meant a lot to him. A hell of a fucking lot. But what if they couldn't make this work because of the investigation and the secrecy and the way she wasn't fully letting him in? What if he'd found the perfect woman only to let her slip through his fingers because life really sucked sometimes? He blew out a frustrated breath as he made his way to his locker. He needed to find a way to move this investigation along.

"Hey man, you okay? You look tense." Jesse shot him a concerned look. He stood in front of the mirror, leaning in close as he tweezed a few stray hairs from between his eyebrows.

Sawyer pulled on his bathrobe and sank down onto

the couch, shaking his head slowly. "I don't know. Just frustrated."

Jesse nodded. "What's going on? Problems with your girl?"

"Nah, it's not that. Brooke's great. I just . . . shit, I just can't seem to make it work."

"Make what work?"

"Even though I'm working here four nights a week and I've got a bunch of personal training clients, I can't seem to scrape enough money together to get my business going. I want to have my own gym, with equipment and other people working for me. Plus money for advertising and marketing shit. Just can't seem to get up the fucking hill." He pushed a hand through his hair.

Jesse had gone still at the mirror. "Do you know how much you'd need?"

"I've got about ten grand saved up now, but I think I need another twenty to actually get anything going. And because of some stupid shit in my past, my credit's garbage, so I'd probably get laughed out of the bank if I tried to get a loan."

Jesse glanced around the room and, apparently satisfied that everyone was wrapped up in something else, came and sat down on the couch beside him. "I might have a way you can make some extra cash."

Sawyer arched an eyebrow. "Oh yeah? What?"

Jesse glanced around again. "You ever hear of Tantrik?"

Sawyer smiled. Jackpot. "The little rainbow-colored pills?" Jesse nodded. "Uh, yeah. I've heard of it."

"I sell a little, on the side, for the extra cash."

Sawyer frowned. "How much extra?"

"I have a guy who gives me the pills. I sell them for fifteen a pop or three for forty. I keep thirty percent, give the rest back to my guy. It's easy money, man. If you want, I can cut you in. I'll give you some of my stash, see if you can move it. If not, no big deal, just give the pills back."

"What in it for you?"

Jesse smiled as though it was obvious. "I'd get a cut of your sales. My fee for hooking you up."

"How much you make doing this?"

Jesse shrugged. "It varies. Few thousand a month, anyway."

"Jesus. And all I have to do is sell the pills you give me and give you a cut?"

"That's right."

"How much of a cut?"

"We'll split the thirty percent take 50/50. You do well, we can renegotiate."

"Shit, man. How'd you get into this?"

"My girlfriend's dad. He hooked me up."

Sawyer so badly wanted to ask who his girlfriend's father was, but this wasn't an interrogation. He rubbed a hand over his mouth, pretending to think it over. "Yeah, okay," he said after a minute.

Jesse slapped him on the back, rose from the couch

and crossed to his locker. He rummaged around inside and then came back, handing Sawyer a small plastic bag with about fifteen Tantrik pills inside. "Consider this your test run. See if you can move them—here at the club, wherever. Remember, fifteen each or three for forty. Since this is my supply, I either need cash for the pills, or the pills back. Think you can move them within the next few days?"

Sawyer glanced down at the little baggie in his hand. "I can try." He stood and clapped Jesse on the shoulder. "Thanks man. I appreciate the opportunity."

"No sweat. A couple of ground rules, though. First, anyone finds these on you, you didn't get them from me. And second, you still have to pay for any you use yourself. Third, don't steal my customers. Clear?"

Sawyer nodded.

"Good luck, and let me know if you have questions."

Sawyer tucked the pills away in his locker. He'd get Brooke to submit them to Evidence tomorrow, trading them in for the cash he'd need to hand in to Jesse.

They were close, and they were getting closer.

Brooke stared up at the stage, her stomach churning.

Fucking hot seats. She'd been dreading this day. Last week, Sawyer hadn't been at the club long enough to have any real, dedicated fans, but Brooke had noticed that there were women who seemed to come once or twice a week, and one of those regulars had noticed Sawyer.

She couldn't decide if the fact that he was dressed up like a cop—hat, aviators, tight uniform—made it better or worse. A wave of jealous nausea coursed through her stomach as Sawyer handcuffed the woman's hands behind her back and then bent her over the chair, dancing as he pretended to pat her down. He dipped low, his hands sliding down the woman's leg, and Brooke shifted in her seat, a restless, helpless anger taking hold.

She forced herself to take a breath. She was on edge because of Nan. Worried about the fact that her ninety-year-old grandmother was likely going to have open heart surgery in a couple of days. Angry at the world that she might lose her only remaining family member. She couldn't fault Sawyer for doing his job. This, while not fun to watch, didn't mean anything, and she'd be an idiot to take it personally and let it get to her.

Sawyer gripped the woman's hips and thrust against her from behind. To Brooke's horror, her eyes stung, her throat constricting as the jealousy and anger swirled together, making it hard to breathe. She couldn't watch him pretend to fuck another woman. It made her want to scream, to hit something, to walk up there and make him stop. Make him promise that he'd only ever touch her, which was completely insane. Her heart throbbed in her chest, sweat coating her palms, and for a second, she thought she might actually be sick.

Sawyer smacked the woman's ass and Brooke grabbed her purse, rushing outside for some fresh air. She'd only meant to step outside, but her feet kept moving until she was nearly half a block away, her hands trembling, tears pricking at her eyes. She forced herself to stop and leaned against the outside of a sushi restaurant, sucking in a deep breath that hitched into a sob as it caught in her chest.

What the fuck? What had just happened? Typically she wasn't a jealous, insecure person. And yet the reaction she'd had in there had been visceral. Almost painful. As though she was coming apart at the seams and couldn't do a damn thing about it.

She pressed a hand to her mouth, taking several deep breaths through her nose, trying to calm down. A few stars hung in the night sky, but there was too much light pollution to see any but the brightest ones. Around her, the city lights twinkled, the street lamps casting a warm glow onto the sidewalk. A couple walked past, chatting and holding hands. Cars slid by on the street. The door of a pub opened, laughter and music spilling out as a few men left. The air smelled like pizza and autumn.

She glanced back in the direction of the club, feeling a bit calmer. That, in there, wasn't real life. It was the job, and she couldn't let it mess with her like that. She just needed to find a way to get through everything. Nan's surgery. The investigation. It was a lot to deal with, but it was what she'd signed on for.

Granted, being with Sawyer made everything that much more complicated. He'd come back to visit Nan with her more than once. He'd told her that he liked working with her, that she was a good detective. He made her feel good in ways she hadn't even known she'd needed.

Maybe watching him perform the hot seat routine bothered her because what was supposed to be just sex was turning into something more. Something deeper, more significant.

She started walking back toward the club, wondering if her freak-out had nothing to do with Sawyer himself and everything to do with the fact that she could actually fall for him, if she let herself.

Chapter Seventeen

THE MUSTANG'S ENGINE purred as Sawyer navigated through the late morning traffic, adjusting his sunglasses on his face. It was warm for October, and he fiddled with the temperature dial, trying to get the AC going to compensate for the fact that he was wearing a hooded sweatshirt.

"Let me know if you're too cold," he said to Brooke, who stared out the passenger window, her hands laced together in front of her. She nodded, not saying anything. She'd been quiet last night after the show, too, and he couldn't help but feel as though there was a tension between them, even though nothing had changed. At least, as far as he knew. Which, frankly, when it came to women, wasn't always a whole hell of a lot. "You okay?" he asked. God, what a dumb question. She was worried about her grandmother. Of course she wasn't okay.

She turned and smiled at him. "Yeah. Just thinking about Nan." She nibbled on her thumbnail. "Still waiting to hear if they can go ahead with the surgery tomorrow or not." She'd picked up an infection, and they were waiting for her to recover before moving ahead with the surgery.

He reached over and laid a hand on her thigh, knowing there was nothing he could say or do to make her worry less. To make her feel less shitty. But he could be here, with her. By her side while she faced losing someone important to her.

He slowed as he turned onto Northside Drive, looking for the overpass where the meet-up was supposed to happen. It was about a mile ahead, marked by several concrete pillars supporting the I-20 as it passed above. He scanned the area, his eyes moving from left to right, but there was no sign of Jesse or anyone from the cartel. He swung the car around to the very far end of the overpass, pulling in beside a few other vehicles, and then cut the engine and pulled his hood up over his head.

Brooke reached into the back seat, grabbed the camera and screwed the telephoto lens into place. "If it is Baracoa who Jesse's dealing with, do you think Hernandez will show?"

He shrugged. "Don't know, but it would make my day if he did. Then we'd actually have a line on that weasel."

Less than a minute later, a dark blue BMW rolled up and Jesse got out, looking around nervously. He paced around his car, his hands in his pockets, scuffing at the dirt with his toe.

"Someone's on edge," Brooke murmured, snapping a few pics of Jesse.

She was right. Jesse was normally laid back, relaxed. But right now, he looked about ready to jump out of his skin.

A black Mercedes pulled up and stopped, facing Jesse's car, a few feet away. The camera clicked as Brooke took pictures of the Sheriff stepping out of the driver's seat. Another man stepped out of the passenger side, and Sawyer recognized him instantly as Domingo Da Silva, another known cartel member. The doors of the Mercedes were still open when three leather-bound bikers wearing Desperado patches pulled in behind it, their rumbling Harleys echoing against the concrete overpass.

Three Desperados, two cartel members, and one male stripper turned drug dealer, but no sign of Hernandez.

Jesse popped the trunk of his car and pulled out a backpack. Sawyer took the camera from Brooke and adjusted the lens, zooming in farther. He couldn't be sure, but if he had to guess, he'd bet that was the same backpack he and Brooke had witnessed the Sheriff dropping off at the club a couple of weeks ago. His heart rate picked up, his muscles going tense as he watched Jesse toss the backpack to the Sheriff, who opened it and looked inside, most likely at wads of cash from sales.

The Sheriff rifled around in the backpack and then

nodded, saying something to Jesse. Then he pointed at the Mercedes, and Domingo opened the back seat. He emerged with a giant teddy bear. Then he strode toward Jesse, shoving the bear in his arms.

Jesse stared down at the bear with a frown, saying something. The Sheriff said something in return, his body language shifting from confident and in control to tense and agitated. After maybe thirty seconds of arguing, the Sheriff got in Jesse's face, jabbing him in the chest as he spoke. For a few seconds, they just stared at each other, but then Jesse nodded and put the bear in the trunk of his car.

"What the fuck was that about?" asked Brooke.

"I'm guessing that bear's full of drugs. That's a lot more to sell than just a backpack's worth. They're pulling him in deeper."

Jesse slipped back behind the wheel of his car and peeled off. Sawyer and Brooke slunk low in their seats. A few seconds later, the rumble of the bikes peaked and then faded.

Brooke inched up a bit. "Just the Baracoa guys. Should we follow?"

Sawyer paused, rubbing a hand over his mouth. It was risky, but it also might lead them right to Hernandez. After a second, he nodded. "Yeah. Okay."

They waited for the Mercedes to pull out and then started following at a safe distance as it headed north. But they'd made it less than a mile from the overpass when Brooke let out a quiet "shit."

"What?" he asked, his eyes darting to the rearview mirror. "Ah, shit." The three Desperados were behind them, and getting closer. "Goddammit," Sawyer said, his grip tightening on the wheel. "I should've guessed they'd circle back."

"Don't panic yet. They might not have made us and might just be keeping tabs on the Mercedes. Let's ditch the Sheriff."

Sawyer nodded, merged into the right lane, and headed for the closed on-ramp to the I-85, weaving through the pylons blocking the road.

So did the three bikers.

"Shit," he said, punching the gas. "They're gonna make us." Adrenaline coursed through his veins as he focused on the road, his foot heavy on the gas. The Mustang's engine roared as he fought to lose them.

A gunshot cracked through the air, sending both him and Brooke ducking. The shot had missed their Mustang, but not by much.

"Motherfuckers," Brooke ground out, unholstering her own gun and then pulling her shirt up over the bottom half of her face. "Just keep driving," she barked at him, and then rolled down the window and angled the top half of her body out of it. She got off a couple of shots before dropping back inside. "They're still gaining," she said, her voice tight with tension.

The gas was already kissing the floor. "I can't lose them. They're faster."

"Then keep us on the road and I'll take care of them."

Two shots pinged off the Mustang and Brooke maneuvered her head and shoulders out the window again, returning fire. This time, he heard the satisfying squeal of tires followed by the sound of metal scraping on pavement.

"Two down," she said, dropping back into her seat. "I lost sight of the third one." His palms grew sweaty on the wheel, his chest tightening, his lungs heaving as he focused on keeping them alive.

The unmistakable sound of a motorcycle engine grew closer, and then suddenly the third biker had pulled even with them, opening fire on the Mustang. The back driver's side window shattered.

"Keep us straight," called Brooke, leaning over him, powering down his window about two inches and pumping three shots off. The sound exploded inside the car, leaving his ears ringing, but not so badly that he couldn't hear the sound of one of the bike's tires blowing. Brooke fell back into her seat, her chest heaving.

"*Holy shit*," he said, his heart trying to jackhammer its way out of his chest. "Holy fucking shit."

"Uh-huh," said Brooke, pulling her shirt back down and sliding her gun back into its holster. "Holy shit."

"I had no idea you were such a fucking badass," he said, turning off the closed section of highway and starting on an indirect route that would take them back to the station. His eyes darted back and forth between the road and his rearview mirror, but there were no signs that anyone was still following them.

"Wouldn't have been able to pull those shots off if you hadn't kept us steady."

He glanced over at her, and he knew it was because of the adrenaline, but he couldn't stop the laugh that burst out of him. She laughed too, eventually wiping her eyes with the back of her hand.

Once she'd settled down, she turned to look at him. "So . . . do you think you're burned?"

He shook his head. "No. I don't think anyone got a clear look at us, and they have no reason to connect this to me, but I guess we'll see what happens when I go into the club." She nodded, and they fell into a relieved silence until he pulled into the station's underground parking garage. Before he'd even shut the car off, he hauled her against him and kissed her, hard and deep. "I'm glad you're okay," he said, kissing her again. She returned the kiss, her mouth hungry and urgent against his, her hands weaving into his hair, but then her phone rang, breaking the moment. Which was definitely for the best.

"Hello?" she answered, one of her hands still in his hair. She went very still. "When?" she asked, her voice suddenly sounding much different. "I . . . are you sure?" Her face crumpled and she nodded rapidly. "Okay. I'll . . . I'll be right there. Thanks for calling."

He had a sinking feeling he knew what was coming, but needed to ask anyway. "What happened?"

She stared straight ahead through the windshield, her eyes fixed on the concrete wall in front of them. "Nan just died."

With a sob, she fell into his arms.

Chapter Eighteen

BROOKE SAT ON the edge of the gigantic octagonal fountain in the fancy walled-in courtyard of the Buckhead Grill. It had been Nan's favorite restaurant and where she'd wanted her wake to be held. She'd prearranged everything—the funeral, being buried next to her husband, the boozy party—so really Brooke hadn't had to do anything except white-knuckle her way through the past few days. Collecting Nan's things from the hospital. Choosing an outfit for her to be buried in. Calling a couple of real estate agents to inquire about listing Nan's condo. She hadn't gone through any of her things yet. She hadn't had the strength.

It didn't feel real. She kept expecting to wake up in her bed, drenched in sweat and ready to cry with relief that it all had been a nightmare. But it wasn't a nightmare, it was reality, and she needed to somehow accept that Nan was gone. That she was alone on the planet. No family to speak of.

She could hear the sounds of the wake still spilling out of the restaurant, mingling with the soothing trickle of the fountain behind her. It was touching how many people had come out for Nan. She'd had so many friends, had touched so many lives. Had been such a presence.

Brooke felt numb and heavy, and forced herself to take a deep breath, pulling the fresh air into her lungs. She'd cried so much over the past few days that she felt wrung out. Lost and empty. Taking each second as it came and just trying to bear it without falling apart.

Last night, she'd woken up sobbing, and Sawyer had been right there, his arms around her, his hand stroking her hair. Not telling her not to cry. Not telling her everything would be okay. No platitudes, only comfort. He somehow seemed to have a sixth sense for what she needed, and she was grateful for it.

She bit her lip and tapped her fingers on her thigh, glancing down at her purse, which sat on the ground at her feet. With a sigh, she pulled out the sealed envelope, labeled "Brooke" in Nan's spindly handwriting. She'd given it to one of the nurses to give to Brooke "should anything happen." The letter had been sitting in her purse for days now. She hadn't wanted to read it. Hadn't wanted to face the final goodbye she knew it held.

But it was time.

With trembling fingers, she carefully opened the envelope and pulled out the single sheet of paper.

My Darling Brooke,

I have a feeling that my time left is short, and while I know you don't go in for sappy, mushy stuff, there are a few things I need to say to you—things that I need you to hear and take to heart so that you may carry them with you.

I have loved you to the ends of the earth. I have loved you unconditionally. I'm so proud of you, and I feel blessed to have been here long enough to watch you grow into the amazing woman you are. You've come so far from the sad, lost girl who became mine when you were nine years old. You can accomplish anything you set your mind to, and I know you'll thrive after I'm gone. Your strength and resilience gives me peace.

Don't be afraid to let people in. I know you've been hurt, and those hurts can leave scars. But don't close yourself off to the point where you're not living your life. I don't want that for you. You have so much good to offer—your strength, your intelligence, your work ethic, your sense of humor. Trust yourself to choose the right people. The right man, whether or not that man is Sawyer or someone else.

You still have so much ahead of you, I know. Career successes, happiness, love. Marriage and

motherhood if those are things you want for
yourself (and I think you do). It breaks my heart
that I won't be here to see it, but know that I'll
always be with you.

Love big. Live loud. Take risks. Be happy.
Remember me with laughter and smiles, not tears
and sadness.

I will always love you with all of my heart,
Nan

Brooke's eyes stung as they filled with tears, her throat clogging almost painfully. For several seconds, she stared down at the letter, the words fuzzy through her tears, letting herself feel it all. The pain, the sadness, the loneliness, the loss. Letting herself hurt. Letting herself feel angry and miserable that the person she'd loved most was gone. There were no words for any of it. Just a gaping hole right in the center of her chest.

She pulled a crumpled tissue out of her purse and wiped at her eyes, then carefully tucked the letter back in its envelope and slid it into her purse. After fishing out another tissue, she blew her nose, a loud honking noise that felt out of place in the peaceful courtyard.

The door to the restaurant opened and Sawyer emerged, a bottle of beer in each hand. He looked so handsome in his navy-blue suit and white shirt, open at the collar. He'd ditched the tie pretty much the second they'd left the church.

He handed her one of the bottles of beer and sat down beside her on the edge of the fountain, his leg brushing hers. She scooted a tiny bit closer and he slipped his arm behind her, his hand rubbing soothing circles on her lower back. Although he'd been nearby for most of the day, they'd kept physical contact to a bare minimum, but right now, she needed his touch.

"Thanks," she said, her voice hoarse with tears, and then tipped the bottle to her lips. The cool liquid was soothing on her parched throat.

He nodded, peering up at the sky. "Amelia said she's sorry she couldn't come. I think it just would've been too much for her. Too soon."

"It's okay. I get it."

"So, listen . . . do you want to take some time off? From work, I mean. I know it's tricky because we're getting close, but if you need some time, you should take some time."

She frowned. "Did you take time off after Ryan died?"

"No."

"I don't want time off. Work's keeping me going." The last thing she wanted was more time to sit around and wallow. Staying busy and focused was the only way she'd get through it.

"I'm just saying to think about it. A few days off might be good."

She bristled at that. "Would you be saying this to

me if I was just another detective? If I was just your partner?"

He shrugged. "I'm just trying to help."

For some reason, this conversation was making her irrationally angry. "Don't treat me with kid gloves just because we fuck, Sawyer."

He exhaled a long, slow breath and held up his hands. "That's not what I'm doing."

She rubbed a hand over her face and then laid a hand on his thigh. "Shit. I know. I'm sorry. That was . . . uncalled for. I know you're coming from a good place, but just let me do my thing, okay?"

"Okay. Do your thing. But I was going to suggest that we get out of town for a couple of days. I've got a cabin up at Carters Lake, and it's where I go when I need to think. It's peaceful. We can go together, or you can just use it by yourself. Either way."

"Ugh, I'm such a bitch."

He set his beer down and pulled her against him. "You're not a bitch. You're hurting."

Don't be afraid to let people in.

She nodded, snuggling into him. "Okay. Let's get away for a couple of days."

"We can leave tonight."

"Do you think anyone on the team will notice?" she asked, warming to the idea of spending a few days alone with him in a lakefront cabin.

"Nah. I have a few days off from the club, and we

should both be lying low anyway after getting shot at by the Desperados."

God, how had that only been a few days ago? It felt as though a lifetime had passed.

Hell, in a way, it had.

Chapter Nineteen

CLOUDS COVERED THE sky over Carters Lake, the green of the pine trees on the rocky shore the only break in the gray-blue of sky and water. Waves lapped peacefully against the side of the fishing boat, rocking it gently. The winds were low, but without the sunshine, the morning air was cool. Sawyer reached into the bag of supplies and pulled out the Thermos full of coffee and two sturdy plastic cups, filling them and handing one to Brooke.

They'd arrived at the cabin last night, and not long after they'd settled in, Brooke had fallen into a deep sleep. She'd been running on empty for days now, emotionally, mentally and physically, so he hadn't been surprised when she'd conked out almost immediately. He hoped that the peaceful setting and fresh air would help her through some of her grief. That maybe *he* could help her through the worst of it. He hated knowing that she was in pain.

Brooke took the cup of coffee with a grateful smile, blowing away the steam rising up over the rim. After taking a sip, she sat back in her seat and stared out over the lake, looking more relaxed and calm than she had in days. Maybe even longer.

"Isn't it too cold to catch anything?" she asked, eyeing his fishing rod skeptically. He'd set it in one of the holders, and he watched the line as it bobbed gently in the water.

"Now's a good time to catch walleye and spotted bass. They've been sticking to the deep waters of the lake because they like the cool, so you won't see much of them if the temperature's above seventy. But now that it's cooler, they're coming closer to the surface to look for food." He stood and pointed over the side of the boat. "See the schools of minnows? There, and there?" She nodded. "That's what the walleye and bass are looking for."

She fiddled with her own rod. He'd had to bait it and cast it for her—she was no fisherwoman, that was for sure—but she seemed to be enjoying herself. "I didn't realize you were such an expert fisherman."

He smiled. "One of my favorite pastimes. Been doing it since I was a kid."

She poked at her rod again, staring down at the shimmering school of minnows and frowning. "How come I'm not getting any bites?" She picked up her rod and started reeling her line in.

He chuckled. "Give it time. Don't fish your lure too fast."

"Maybe I need a different lure."

"You're fine. Be patient. We're in the right spot." He got up and cast her line back in, then handed her the rod.

She pursed her lips, looking a bit skeptical, but then settled back, her gaze once again drifting out over the lake and the tension easing out of her body. After a few minutes, she returned her attention to him. "Tell me something I don't know about you."

He thought for a moment. "Don't think I ever told you that I'm divorced."

Her eyebrows rose slightly. "No, you didn't."

"Does it bother you?"

She shook her head. "How long were you married?"

"About three years. Together for a couple before that."

"So what happened with you and . . . ?"

"Krista."

"Yeah."

He rubbed a hand over his mouth and took a sip of coffee, taking his time. Wanting to get the words right. "She'd really liked the badge and the uniform—at least at first. Then it started to become clear that she only liked the idea of them, not the reality."

She tilted her head, studying him. "It's hard when you're with someone who doesn't get the long hours and the dedication."

He nodded. "The stress, too. She had a difficult time

understanding that I couldn't just switch shit off some-times."

"Things get to you. Take up space in your brain."

"Yeah." He slowly shook his head. "It caused a lot of tension between us, and we started fighting. Eventually, she asked me to choose, her or the job."

Brooke licked her lips, her gaze intent on him. "Not much of a choice as far as I'm concerned. A lot of civilians just . . ." She shook her head. "They can't understand what the job's like. What it takes. How it's not just a job, but a part of your identity." She met his eyes and something passed between them. An unspoken understanding.

Her eyes held his, full of warmth and maybe some-thing else. Something that would've scared him not that long ago, but now made him feel alive. Maybe because he knew that Brooke understood who he was, and what was important to him.

"Do you see yourself ever getting married again?" she asked softly. Her eyes widened immediately, as though she hadn't meant to ask the question out loud.

He smiled, unable to stop himself from teasing her. "Why Detective Simmons, are you proposing to me?"

She smiled and flipped him off.

He laughed and then shrugged. "Someday, if it's right." She nodded, once again looking out over the lake. "Is getting married something you want?" he asked. His heart jumped around in his chest.

She shrugged, a faraway look in her eyes. "Maybe."

He leaned in, needing to kiss her, to chase away the fear and hesitation he saw lingering on her face, but at the same moment, her rod bent. She jumped up. "Oh my God! What do I do?"

Chuckling, he picked up the rod, handed it to her and moved around behind her, guiding her movements, showing her how to reel her catch in. An impressive spotted bass dangled from the line, three, maybe four pounds.

"Well, well, guess we're having bass for dinner tonight," he said as he worked to unhook the lure.

Brooke's happy laugh echoed out over the lake, filling the air and his heart at the same time.

BROOKE'S HIKING BOOTS crunched against the dirt beneath her, in unison with Sawyer's. Late afternoon sun streamed through the trees, an assortment of pine, maple, birch, oak and hickory. The loamy scent of the forest filled her nostrils, and she took a deep breath. Birdsong floated in the air, and in the distance, the lake lapped softly against the shore.

Her legs were tired, her feet maybe a little sore, but the hike had been worth it. For the exercise and the fresh air, but also for the gorgeous waterfall Sawyer had taken her to see. Without him, it never would've occurred to her to get out of the city for a few days, but she had to admit, he'd been right. She still felt sad, but after a few days up here with him, she felt more at peace with the sadness. As though she were walking alongside it, not getting swallowed up by it.

There was something special about this place, the way it grounded her with its peaceful seclusion. Or maybe the place wasn't special. Maybe it was Sawyer.

They emerged from the trees and the cabin came back into view. She slipped her hand into his, wanting to remember this moment. The beauty of nature surrounding her. Sawyer at her side. Nan gone, but not erased. The feeling that maybe she'd be okay. That she'd figure out a way to be okay.

When they were back inside the cabin, she changed out of her hiking gear and into yoga pants and a T-shirt, and then picked up Sawyer's discarded flannel shirt and pulled it on too. Smiling to herself as she walked back toward the kitchen, she pulled the collar up to her nose, inhaling deeply. It smelled like his skin and pine and woodsmoke. It smelled like peace in a way she hadn't known would be appealing to her, but it was.

She picked up the kettle and filled it with water, setting it on the stove to boil. From the living room, she heard the groaning creek of the door to the wood-burning stove opening, the soft shuffle of logs as Sawyer built a fire. The window over the sink looked out over the lake, the water painted with golden-pink streaks as the sun sank behind the horizon. The sky was a fiery orange, the underbellies of the few clouds a glowing lilac.

From behind her, Sawyer slid his arms around her

waist and dropped his head to the crook of her neck, kissing the skin there.

"Thank you for bringing me here," she said, her gaze still on the beauty out the window. "Thank you for sharing this place with me."

"I came up here after Ryan was killed. It helped, a little."

"I can't even imagine how difficult that must've been for you."

Sawyer stayed quiet for a minute, his arms still around her. He cleared his throat softly. "He was such an awesome guy, and I was lucky to call him my friend. I . . . I wish I'd told him that."

Brooke laid her hands over his, tracing her fingers over his knuckles. "Why didn't you?"

"I took for granted that he knew. That we had so much more time."

She turned in his arms and reached up, pressing her palm to his cheek. "Wherever he is now, I think he knows." A sudden rush of gratitude for Nan's letter hit her. A tiny part of her had resented that letter at first because of how much it hurt to read, but she knew she'd treasure it forever. Nan had done her the service of not leaving anything unsaid. Not leaving any regrets or doubts.

"I hope you're right." He looked down at her, the light in his eyes warm and intense. "You mean so much to me, Brooke. I need you to know that."

She arched up onto her toes and kissed him, soft

and gentle, wanting to show him that she understood. And that she cared about him too, felt deep, significant things for him that she wasn't quite ready to give voice to yet. But that didn't mean they weren't there.

He deepened the kiss and slid his hands to her ass, lifting her. She wound her legs around his waist, and with his mouth still on hers, he carried her into the living room, where he'd laid a pile of blankets and pillows on the floor in front of the fire. The logs popped and crackled as he eased her down to the floor, lying beside her.

He took his time with her, every kiss, every touch tender and meaningful. His mouth hot and sweet on hers, his hands slow and gentle on her breasts. She shrugged out of his flannel shirt and then he started inching her T-shirt up. He dipped his head and kissed a path from one breast to the other, sending liquid heat pooling between her legs. She wove a hand into his hair, the other caressing the hard muscles of his broad back, wanting to memorize every inch of him.

He pulled her T-shirt up over her head and then kissed his way back up from her breasts to her neck. He closed his mouth over hers again, his tongue stroking against hers and making her writhe beneath him. He smiled against her mouth. "Always so eager. I love that about you."

Something in her stilled at his words, but before she could decide how she felt about them, he slipped a hand into her yoga pants and her brain turned off. She let her legs fall open, and he kissed her again as he circled his fingers over her clit. Her hips came up off the floor and she moaned softly as deliciously warm pressure started to gather in her belly. She closed her eyes and gave herself over to how good he made her feel with just his mouth and the tips of his fingers. Kissing. Stroking. Her eyes fluttered open when he pulled his hand out of her pants. His gaze was dark with lust as he sucked his fingers into his mouth. "Fuck," he groaned, and then moved over her and hooked his fingers into her pants, working them down over her hips and stripping her bare.

He settled himself between her legs and kissed her clit, a soft, slow movement that had her insides going crazy. "I fucking love eating your pussy," he said just before he closed his mouth over her. God, she loved the way he could be dirty and sweet at the same time. It was perfect. He was perfect.

One of his hands settled on her thigh, urging her to open wider, while the other slid up her body, caressing her breast, the skin of his palm rough against her nipple. He licked and sucked at her, her hips working in a slow, writhing movement. There was no teasing, no torment this time as he built her up without interruption. Her moans grew louder and her legs started to shake as hot pleasure curled tight inside her. He slid one, and then a second finger inside her, massaging her from the inside while he devoured her from the outside. It didn't take long before she couldn't hold on anymore and came hard against his mouth, her clit throbbing, her body clenching at his fingers.

He rose to his knees and pulled his shirt off, toss-ing it aside. In that moment, the firelight bathing his gorgeously muscled body in a soft, warm glow, her body still humming from his mouth and fingers, she felt so lost in him. As though she could dive into this thing between them and never come up for air. It was exciting and terrifying at the same time.

She rose to her knees too, and kissed him, tasting her-self on his tongue, tracing her hands over the muscles in his arms. Then she planted a hand in the center of his chest and urged him back down to the floor, straddling his hips and kissing her way down his chest, savoring the chiseled planes and masculine dips of his body. Just as he'd done with her, she took her time, teasing and tasting, scraping her teeth over his nipples, nipping at his skin. She opened his cargo pants and urged them down his hips, freeing his hard, thick cock.

Meeting his eyes, she licked up the shaft, wanting to make him feel good. As she took the head into her mouth, he moaned and gathered her hair in his fist. Wrapping a hand around him, she took him deeper into her mouth, sucking and licking as a restless heat began to build between her own legs. She worked her mouth up and down his shaft, his hips shifting beneath her, his breathing becoming more and more labored. His grip tightened in her hair and he pulled her away, the expression on his face a heady mix of adoration and hunger.

"I won't last if you keep that up. Come here," he said,

his voice husky. He sat up and pulled her toward him, laying her down so she was facing the fire. She heard the crinkle of a condom wrapper and then he was behind her, spooning her as he slowly worked his cock into her. She twisted and wrapped an arm around his neck, pulling him down for a kiss. He tugged her closer and began to thrust his hips in a slow, steady rhythm, stroking that spot deep inside her that always made her lose her mind.

As he slowly made love to her, he kissed her—her mouth, her neck, her shoulders—making her entire body feel golden and glowing.

"God, Brooke," he said. "You're so beautiful. God." He extended the arm running underneath her neck and caught her hand, intertwining their fingers.

"You feel incredible," she said, her voice caught somewhere between a moan and a sigh. "So good. So perfect. It's so amazing with you."

The speed of his thrusts picked up and she clenched around him. Throbbing pleasure pounded through her core and she let out a long, loud moan as she came again.

He groaned and slammed into her once, twice more before going still. He kissed her neck, soft, gentle kisses up and down her skin, his body jerking inside hers one final time.

She toyed with his fingers, still laced with hers. She didn't have any words for what she was feeling, and she loved that with Sawyer, she didn't need them. He understood. But that didn't make opening herself up to him any less scary.

From the direction of the bedrooms, a phone started to ring, bringing her back to the present.

"Ah, shit, that's my burner," he said, giving her shoulder one more kiss before pulling out of her and disappearing into the bedroom. He answered it on speaker, bringing it back into the living room with him and sitting down beside her.

"Ryan, hey man, it's Jesse." His voice sounded strained, almost breathless.

"Hey, what's up?"

A silence hung for a few seconds before Jesse spoke. "I . . . shit, I'm worried."

"About what?"

"I had a meeting with my supplier—our supplier—last week, and some shit went down after. They think cops might've followed me. I just got my ass reamed by the supplier. I thought he was going to kill me."

Brooke and Sawyer exchanged a look. "Really? That's crazy, man. Are you serious?"

Jesse made a strained sounding noise. "Yeah. They're pressuring me to move more product. I just . . . shit's going sideways. I can't . . . fuck, I can't go to jail for this."

Sawyer didn't say anything and Jesse let out a long, slow breath.

"Listen, I'm calling you now because there's a deal going down with the supplier this week, and I need you to come with me. I need someone I can trust there in case shit gets fucked up."

"Jesus."

"I know it's a lot to ask, but I have a bad feeling. I need someone in my corner to back me up."

Sawyer paused. "Fuck, all right man. I'll be your guy."

"The deal's going down at some charity gala on Friday night. I don't know if he's going to try to fuck me over or what, but as long as you have my back, everything will be fine." He let out a freaked-out-sounding laugh. "Totally, completely fine."

"What's the deal, Jesse?"

"I don't know. All I know is I have to show up to talk to the big guns about new opportunities."

"Okay. I've got your back. Text me all the details and I'll be there."

"I can't go to jail," he said and then hung up.

Sawyer looked at Brooke. "Big guns could mean Hernandez."

She nodded.

It was time to get back to reality.

Chapter Twenty

BROOKE DRAPED HER hand over Sawyer's arm as they walked into the gala on Friday night. Back at the station, Jack and Amelia had done a little digging and discovered that the charity, the Saint Damian Foundation, was actually a shell corporation and extremely difficult to trace. If Sawyer was a betting man, he'd put it all on it having ties to Baracoa, which explained why the deal was going down here. They were probably conducting all kinds of business tonight.

A restlessness seethed just beneath his skin, and he forced himself to stand still as he and Brooke waited for any sign of Jesse. They were so close—so goddamn close—to Hernandez. They had enough to take Jesse, even the Sheriff down, but he wasn't interested in that, and neither was the captain. Hernandez was the goal. Hernandez was the end game.

"Audio test," came Jack's voice in his ear.

"Copy," said Sawyer softly.

"Copy," said Brooke. They'd both been fitted with tiny two-way earpieces that would connect them back to Amelia, Jack, and the captain via audio. In addition, Brooke's necklace contained a small, state-of-the-art hidden camera. If Hernandez was here, and they were able to capture him conducting illegal activity on camera, he'd be done. Sawyer would finally be able to slap cuffs on him and start moving on with his life.

"You clean up pretty nice, Simmons," he said, giving Brooke a kiss on the cheek. She wore a stunning red gown with a deep V, the sleeveless cut showing off her toned arms. The fabric knotted just below her breasts and then flowed gently away from her body, easily hiding the leg holster she wore underneath it. He bit his lip, willing himself not to get distracted by the memory of Brooke getting ready for the gala in nothing but a pair of lace panties, stockings, and a thigh holster.

Damn.

"You don't look so bad yourself," she said, sending him a wry smile. He scanned the room as he tugged on his tuxedo jacket, hoping the concealed shoulder holster wasn't bulging.

Jazz music floated through the air as hoity-toity guests mingled, eating caviar and smoked salmon on little triangle crackers. White-jacketed waiters circulated the room with silver trays of bubbling champagne. Above them, a massive chandelier twinkled, casting a warm light on the intricate wainscoting. The entire place reeked of money, privilege, and underneath it all, corruption. How many of these people knew what Saint Damian's actually was? How many of these people had criminal ties? He scanned the room again, wondering if he could pick them out.

"Guys," said Amelia in their ears. "Two o'clock. That's Maria Hernandez. Hernandez's daughter and alleged cartel lieutenant." Sawyer's gaze swung in that direction.

"Purple dress?" asked Brooke, sipping casually at the glass of water she'd picked up from a passing waiter's tray.

"That's her. Never been able to tie her to cartel activity with anything but circumstantial evidence before."

"Shit, you know who that is?" said Brooke, peering up at him. "That's Jesse's girlfriend."

"Wait, what? How do you know that?" he asked.

"Because when I bugged his phone, there was a coupled up picture of the two of them as his wallpaper."

Dread settled like a lead weight in Sawyer's stomach. "What the hell are we walking into?"

"Do you think Jesse made you?" Brooke's fingers tightened on his arm ever so slightly. "Or me?"

"I fucking hope not. Otherwise shit's about to get really ugly."

Sure enough, at that moment Jesse walked up to Maria and pulled her in for a kiss. When he looked up, he saw Sawyer and Brooke standing across the room and his eyes narrowed. He said something to Maria, who turned and headed for the elevators, while Jesse quickly crossed the floor to them.

Sawyer's pulse kicked up a notch. Something was different. Off.

"What's she doing here?" he said, pointing at Brooke with his champagne flute.

Sawyer scratched the back of his head, playing dumb. "She's my date."

Jesse let out an exasperated sigh. "I didn't tell you to bring a date."

Sawyer took a step closer to him. "You didn't tell me much of anything. Just to back you up. What's this all about, man?"

Jesse smiled. Nothing about his attitude meshed with how panicked and frightened he'd sounded on the phone a few days ago. Acid burned in Sawyer's stomach. "You'll see. Come on. Supplier's waiting."

Without checking to see if they were following, he started weaving through the crowd, leading them toward the elevator bank. He hit the call button, standing in front of them and rocking on his heels as he waited. Sawyer glanced over at Brooke, and he could see that she'd noticed the change in Jesse too.

They followed him into the elevator and stuck close behind him when he exited the car, taking them to one of the corner suites. Jesse knocked once and the door opened immediately.

"He's watching TV," said the armed cartel guard,

his assault rifle slung casually over his shoulder. Jesse nodded and continued into the suite.

The Sheriff sat on a couch, watching *Adventure Time*. He took a sip of his drink and then cracked up at a joke on the show. Sawyer scanned the room, noting a few Desperados hanging around the back, drinking and talking.

"Oh, man. The Ice King gets me every time." He laughed again and turned to look at them. "What a loser, am I right?" He stood, all the humor vanishing from his face. "Who is this?" he asked Jesse.

"This is Ryan Williams, the guy from the club I told you about. And his girlfriend. Don't remember her name. Britney, or something. She's not important."

"Well, she is now, since you fucking brought her up here," said the Sheriff, talking as though Jesse was five and not understanding something very, very simple. He moved forward, stepping up to Sawyer and giving him a once-over. "I guess you'll do."

"You guess I'll do what?" asked Sawyer, stifling the urge to move in front of Brooke. Sweat broke out on the back of his neck.

The Sheriff turned and looked at Jesse, an expression of glee on his face. "You didn't tell him? Oh, fun. I love surprises." He clapped his hands together once before moving toward a closet. He hauled out two suitcases and dumped them on the adjacent love seat, then opened one. Hundreds of baggies of Tantrik were visible inside. He picked up a handful of them and held them up. "Do you know what this is?"

"Sure. It's Tantrik."

"And you know that how?"

"Because Jesse gave me some to sell."

"And did you?"

"Yeah."

"So here's the deal, kids. We're taking Tantrik wide. Beyond the MBR. Beyond Atlanta even. And to do that, we need more bodies. We need to bring new blood into the fold to move the product." He walked over and clapped Jesse on the shoulder. "Jesse here is one of our top recruiters." Then he frowned as if reconsidering his words. "Although *recruiter* maybe isn't the right word. *Scout*, maybe? Hmm, no still not quite right. Oh, I know! *Head hunter*." He mimed slitting his own throat and then laughed at his own joke.

Holy shit, this guy was unhinged.

"What does this have to do with me? Why am I here?" asked Sawyer.

"Because Jesse recruited you, and you work for us now. Remember the whole spiel about going wide, needing new bodies, yada yada? That's why you're here. Try to keep up."

"What if I don't want to work for you?"

He held up a finger and pulled his phone out of his pocket, hitting a number on speed dial. Whoever was on the other end answered immediately. "Hi, it's me. Yeah. Listen, you're gonna have to come talk to him . . . That's right, the new guy that Jesse brought in . . . No, I didn't shoot him. Wait, can I shoot him?" He sighed.

"Ugh. Fine." He ended his call and folded his hands behind his back, waiting patiently.

Less than ten seconds later, Ernesto Hernandez walked in, surrounded by cartel security. Sawyer's blood ran hot and he clenched his fists, his jaw aching with tension. If only it was as simple as pulling his gun out and shooting Hernandez dead between the eyes. But it wasn't, and he couldn't risk doing anything to give himself away. Not when they'd come this far.

Hernandez started fixing himself a drink, not even looking up. "You deal Tantrik for Baracoa now. We own you. If you don't like it, I'll let him shoot you. Those are your options."

"Fine," Sawyer ground out between clenched teeth. Hernandez looked up at him and nodded, as though that was exactly what he'd expected.

Something flickered across his face as he looked at Sawyer. "You can go. We'll be in touch with further instructions."

Sawyer turned to leave, but then Hernandez's voice stopped him. "Wait. Leave the woman. Consider it . . ." His eyes crawled over Brooke's body in a way that made Sawyer want to break him in half. "Collateral."

"No." He stepped in front of Brooke, which brought him closer to Hernandez. Hernandez took a few steps toward him, peered up at him and then his eyes widened, an expression of delight on his face.

"Detective Matthews. I thought I recognized you."

"You're a fucking cop?" Jesse's outraged shout

echoed through the room as he pulled a gun out from under his jacket, alerting all the other cartel members and Desperados.

Brooke stepped out from behind him and for the briefest second, their eyes met. In sync. This was it.

In unison, they pulled their guns. "Atlanta Police, everyone get down on the ground!" he shouted. But no one obeyed, only pulling out their own weapons and leveling them at Brooke and Sawyer.

"Drop your weapons," commanded Brooke, her gun trained on Jesse. "Now!" But no one complied, the room filling with tension as the standoff wore on. Sawyer could hear his blood rushing through his ears. His stomach lurched sickly.

"Don't you fucking point your gun at him, bitch," said Maria, who'd snuck up behind Brooke and grabbed her. She held her gun to Brooke's temple. "Gun on the floor. Now." Brooke inhaled a shaky breath and dropped her weapon. Maria smiled, an eerie, perverse smile, as she looked at Sawyer. "You too." He hesitated and she jerked Brooke. "Do it!"

Very slowly, with his gun extended in front of him, he lowered it to the floor, wondering how the fuck they were going to make it out of this alive.

The door exploded inward and the SWAT team poured in. Using the distraction to her advantage, Brooke grabbed Maria and threw her over her shoulder, wrestling her gun away from her. Jesse fired at Brooke, missing, but that one shot set everyone else off. Gunfire erupted in the suite, bullets flying from every direction.

Sawyer grabbed Brooke and they dove behind the couch. It wouldn't offer much protection from the bullets, but at least it would keep them out of sight. Out of the corner of his eye, he saw the Sheriff run by and—miracle of miracles—he accidentally kicked Sawyer's gun back toward him. He picked it up, lying low on the floor with his back to the sofa. Bullets hit the couch, sending stuffing and feathers from pillows flying.

Brooke rose to a crouch, peering over the top of the sofa and returning fire. She got a few shots off before ducking back down. Adrenaline coursed through his veins, and he did the same, covering the other side of the room. Bodies lay on the floor, SWAT members and Desperados alike. Sawyer prayed that the SWAT guys had enough armor on to prevent any life-threatening injuries.

More bullets hit the couch, and they both crouched above the edge to return fire again. Just as Brooke came back down, another bullet shot right through the couch, missing her by an inch, maybe less. Her eyes met his and he pulled her toward him.

"If we don't make it out of here, I want you to know that I love you." The lamp on the coffee table to his left exploded in shards, gun fire still echoing through the room.

She leaned forward and kissed him, hard and fierce. "I—I know."

"Go on three?" he asked.

She nodded.

"One, two, three!" he counted, and they sprang up from behind the couch in unison, firing at the remaining cartel members and Desperados. There was no sign of Hernandez or the Sheriff.

He'd just fired his last bullet when a dozen more SWAT guys swarmed into the room.

The fight was over, but Hernandez was gone, leaving the investigation in tatters.

Chapter Twenty-One

THE FOLLOWING MORNING, Brooke and Sawyer sat in the captain's office, in the same chairs they'd sat in the last time they'd been called on the carpet for screwing up. Except this time, the situation was much, much worse. Everything had gone sideways, and they weren't blameless in it. She glanced over at Sawyer, whose hands were folded between his legs, his jaw tight as he stared at a spot on the floor.

The captain came in, the door snapping shut behind him, and sat down at his desk, meeting first Sawyer's eyes and then hers. She felt sick at the anger and disappointment she saw there. It didn't matter that they'd managed to arrest Jesse, Maria Hernandez and a few other cartel members. The main focus of their investigation had fled, they'd blown their cover, and everyone on the comms had heard Sawyer tell her he loved her.

She hadn't said it back, and even though it probably made her a grade-A bitch, she was glad. She didn't know how she felt about him right now—it was impossible to untangle it from the stress of everything else that had happened over the past week. The stress of being undercover, of sneaking around, of losing Nan, of nearly getting killed in a shootout with a drug cartel.

The captain waited a moment before speaking. "I could sit here and yell at you. I could scream myself hoarse. I could slam doors and throw things. But I'm not going to do that because I'm too damn angry to let myself go down that road. If I start, I won't stop, and I need to be at Headquarters in less than an hour to explain how and why my detectives—my allegedly elite detectives—fucked up so monumentally." He blew out a sharp breath, his nostrils flaring, and shook his head. Brooke's entire body felt heavy, weighed down with nervous apprehension. She clenched her teeth together against the wave of nausea working its way through her stomach. "So here's what's going to happen. I'm going to talk. You're going to listen. And then you're going to get the hell out of my office."

She and Sawyer both nodded. Brooke inhaled a shaky breath, wiping her sweaty palms on her pants.

"There's a reason we don't allow partners to date. It's distracting. You don't think clearly. You make compromised choices. You risk lives—both your own and those around you."

"Sir, if I may—" said Sawyer, but the captain cut him off with a stern glare.

"You may not." He folded his hands in front of him on the desk. "Not only were you openly insubordinate, becoming romantically involved behind my back, but your relationship caused you to blow your cover and sent four SWAT members to the hospital. You should've left Simmons behind and we would've found a way to extract her. But you didn't do that. You got in Hernandez's face and now you're forever burned when it comes to the cartel. If that was Ward in there with you, things would've gone down very, very differently." His eyes bored into Sawyer. "Agree or disagree?"

Sawyer sighed and closed his eyes for a moment. "Agree," he ground out.

The captain nodded in a *you're damn right you agree* way. "There is *no* excuse for your unprofessional, dangerous behavior. You risked not only your own lives but the lives of others because you weren't thinking clearly. You broke the rules, and you *knew* you were breaking the rules. Your selfish recklessness is unbecoming of a member of HEAT and an Atlanta Police officer," he finished, his voice much louder than when he'd started.

Brooke thought she might be sick. She had no defense. No excuses. Everything the captain was saying was 100 percent true, no questions asked.

"You are both hereby suspended until further notice and subject to additional disciplinary measures should the police board see fit. Guns and badges on my desk, and then I want you out of my sight."

Oh, God. Oh God oh God oh God. Everything she'd worked for, everything she'd ever wanted was slipping through her fingers. Her hands shook as she stood and placed her gun and badge on the captain's desk. Sawyer did the same. Black teased at the edges of her vision as she fought back what felt a hell of a lot like a panic attack.

"Dismissed."

She turned and wrenched the door open, grabbing her purse from her desk and then making a beeline for the parking garage. Needing to get the hell out of here. Humiliation burned across her skin as she jabbed at the elevator button, everyone's eyes on her. They all knew. They all knew what she'd done, the lives she'd risked, the mistakes she'd made. They all knew that she'd been stripped of her badge and her service weapon. That she'd decided sex with her partner was more important than her career.

"Brooke, wait," said Sawyer from behind her, but she turned and pushed open the door to the stairwell, taking the steps two at a time. She heard the door hit the concrete wall as he followed her into the stairwell.

But she didn't want to talk to him. Didn't even want to look at him, not right now when she felt naked. Stripped raw.

A surge of anger burned through her. He'd tried to get her kicked off the team, and when that hadn't worked, he'd come on to her. And now she desperately wanted to believe that it was his fault she'd been suspended. His fault the mission had gone sideways. His fault her world had been turned upside down.

But as much as she wanted to blame him, she'd known better. Known better and gotten involved with him anyway and now look where she was. Professional reputation ruined, suspended from the job she'd worked so hard for. The job that meant everything to her. She'd foolishly let her guard down. It was a mistake she wouldn't make again. If she had any chance—even a remotely small one—to get her career back on track, she needed to get straight with herself and start cleaning up her mistakes.

"Brooke, just talk to me," said Sawyer from several feet behind her, his voice echoing off the concrete walls of the parking garage. "I'm sorry. I fucked up."

Steeling herself, she turned to face him. "Yeah. You did. We both did." She jammed her hands on her hips, shaking her head. She couldn't seem to string two coherent thoughts together, and when she tried, she thought she might scream from the pressure building inside her.

He took a step toward her and reached for her, but she twisted away from him. Pain flashed across his face, but he didn't reach for her again. "I'm sorry," he repeated. "I know what this job meant to you."

She let out a bitter laugh. "Do you? Do you really? Is that why you tried to get me kicked off your team? Or pursued me when you knew what the consequences could be? You've always put yourself first, Sawyer. Always." Even to her own ears, the words sounded unfair, but she needed someone to blame besides herself, and it felt good to cling to that anger. To convince herself that she didn't need him.

He frowned. "I sure as fuck didn't put myself first yesterday. Do you have any idea what Hernandez would've done to you if I'd left you there?"

She scoffed. "I would've been able to handle it. I'm a big girl."

He shook his head. "No, I—"

"You don't get it, Sawyer. This job was everything to me. I'm alone in the world, and it's all I have. It's who I am. And now it's *gone*. Because I was stupid, and got caught up in something I shouldn't have."

He took another step toward her. "So being with me is stupid? Why? Because you're scared to let me in? Because you're afraid to get hurt?"

She crossed her arms over her chest. "Yeah, well, too late for that, because having my professional reputation in tatters *does* hurt." He scowled at her and she blew out a long breath. "That's not what this is about. This is about my career and the fact that if I have a hope in hell of getting it back on track, I need to start playing by the rules."

His features tightened in pain. "What does that mean?"

She bit her lip and then ripped the metaphorical

Band-Aid off, leaning into the fear swirling through her. Embracing it. Feeling justified in it. "I can't do this with you, Sawyer."

"Can't do this?" Then his eyes widened as though something had just dawned on him. "You didn't say it back," he said quietly, almost to himself.

"Because I can't." She hadn't been able to say it back, and now she wondered if she'd been protecting herself from the fallout the entire time. If deep down, she'd known exactly where they'd been headed. Because that's what loving someone was: pain and hurt and loss.

"Can't? Or won't?"

She shook her head, not answering his question. "There can't be an us. Not if I want to save my job."

His brows drew together, his face a chiseled, masculine mask of hurt and frustration. "For what it's worth, Brooke, I do love you. I don't think I can be any clearer than that. I regret what happened, and I'm sorry, but I don't regret us. You can pretend I'm wrong for you too, just like all the other losers you date, but what we have is different. And I know you know that. I can't . . ." He held his hands out at his sides. "I can't give you more than I have."

"This isn't about you being right or wrong for me. This is about me protecting my career and figuring my shit out and I can't do that with you!"

He pointed at her. "You're running scared, just like she warned me you would."

"Who warned you?"

"Your grandmother. She told me you'd run, that you get scared when it comes to letting people in. That's what you're doing right now. Everything that happened—the investigation coming off the rails, the suspension—it's a convenient excuse for you to push me away."

Anger charged through her like lightning. "Don't you dare try to manipulate me with her!" Her voice shook as she jabbed a finger in his direction. She narrowed her eyes at him, calling on reserves of strength she hadn't even realized she had. "Let me clear something up for you, Sawyer. You didn't know her. You don't know me. And I don't love you. We're done."

Hurt flashed across his face, quickly replaced with anger. His jaw clenched as he shook his head. "You're being fucking ridiculous. Don't put your shit on me."

"I've lost everything because of you. Everything. I don't think I'm being ridiculous."

He opened and closed his mouth, once, twice. "Then I guess there's nothing left to say." He turned and headed back toward the stairwell. She watched him disappear through the doorway, flinching as the metal door slammed behind him.

"Fine. That's fine," she whispered, her fists clenching and unclenching.

She got in her car and drove home, needing to have a good, long cry.

Chapter Twenty-Two

SAWYER OPENED THE door of The Speakeasy, stepping aside and holding it for a young couple on their way out. The man slipped his arm around the woman's waist, pulling her close as they headed toward the parking lot. She looked up at him and said something, making him laugh.

He'd never gotten to do any of that with Brooke. Never been able to do something as normal and natural as taking her out for a drink after going to the movies. Never got to put his arm around her in public and let the world know she was his.

And now she wasn't his anymore. Maybe she never had been. He'd offered her the best of himself and it hadn't been enough. He'd chosen her over the job, risked what mattered most to him for a shot at something real with her, and she'd still run. Facing possible death, he'd needed her to know that he loved her, no matter the consequences, and he didn't regret the choice he'd made. But she'd pushed him away anyway. Maybe he couldn't win. He'd finally chosen someone over the job, and he'd still wound up alone. Maybe there was something fundamentally wrong with him, and he'd never be able to have both the career and the personal life he wanted. He couldn't help but wonder if the badge was more of a shield—against happiness, against a full life. And he hated that he wondered that at all.

He rubbed a hand over his chest as he watched the couple round the corner.

"Hey, you in or out, man?" asked a guy heading into the bar.

"Sorry," he bit out, gesturing the man in ahead of him with a wave of his hand.

He hadn't felt like coming out tonight and being around people. Being around people meant talking. It meant showering and putting on clean clothes. It meant having to pretend he wasn't walking around with a gaping hole in his chest. He'd planned on spending tonight as he had the previous two nights: eating pizza, drinking too much beer, and watching ESPN until he fell asleep on the couch. But no, Jack and Amelia just couldn't leave well enough alone and had made him promise he'd come for a drink tonight.

Bastard friends.

He spotted them at their usual table, a plate of nachos and a pitcher of beer already waiting. He wove his way through the crowd and then dropped down into his seat.

"Jesus, you look like shit," said Jack as he poured Sawyer a glass of beer.

"And hello to you too, sunshine."

"Hey, lay off," said Amelia, punching Jack in the arm. "How would you feel if you'd been suspended?"

"I wouldn't look like I was panhandling on a street corner, that's for sure." He slid a full glass across the table to Sawyer.

He picked it up and took a long drink, then set it down with a loud *clack*. "What about if you'd been suspended *and* dumped?" He shot Jack a look.

Jack scratched the back of his head. "Shit, man. Sorry."

Amelia squinted at him. "So you guys really were together? I heard what you said on the comms, but I thought—"

"I don't want to talk about it, and if you try to make me, I'll leave."

Amelia held her hands up in front of her. "Okay, jeez. You're the one that brought it up, is all." She shrugged and crunched down on a nacho.

Jack leaned back in his chair. "You know that once this all blows over, you'll get reinstated, right? Shit rolls downhill. The captain had to answer to Headquarters. Once they're happy you've been punished, you'll be back at work. Just give it time to settle."

Sawyer blew out a breath. "Yeah, but I'm burned

with Baracoa, and Hernandez is still out there." His jaw tightened and he clenched his fist, wanting to slam it against the table. "I needed to do this for Ryan, and I fucking blew it." He drained the rest of his beer. "*Fuck*." He said it loudly enough that several heads swiveled in his direction. He forced several deep breaths into his lungs, trying to calm down.

This was who he was now, an empty shell whose only two emotions were seething anger and mopey despair. It was disgusting.

"So . . . I'm guessing you haven't heard from Brooke." Amelia took the discarded black olives from Jack's plate and added them to her nachos.

"Ames," said Sawyer, turning her name into a low warning.

"Hey, she's a member of the team. None of us have heard from her. I hope she's doing okay." She shrugged. "I mean, since you *love* her and all."

He pointed a finger at her. "Don't even start," he bit out, his skin feeling tight and itchy. "If you're just gonna tell me all the ways I fucked up, I don't need you for that, okay? It's on a constant loop up here." He pointed at his temple.

Jack and Amelia both just looked at him. Sawyer shook his head and started to stand, but then Jack grabbed his arm and tugged him back down. "Sit." He refilled Sawyer's glass and pushed it back toward him. "Drink, and let's figure shit out."

Sawyer eyed him warily as he brought the glass to his lips.

Jack tapped the table, leaning forward. "Here's what's gonna happen. You're going to keep a low profile until the dust settles, and then you'll be reinstated. You didn't break any laws, and you did the best you could in a shitty situation. And as for Brooke . . ." He trailed off.

"What about Brooke?"

Amelia cut in. "What happened, exactly, with you guys?"

Sawyer drummed his fingers on the table, trying to figure out the quickest way possible to tell the story. "We . . . connected. Got involved. I fell for her, and she didn't fall for me. Basically told me to fuck off after the suspension." The ache in his chest flared up as he remembered just how much that rejection had hurt.

Jack sighed. "Look, I like Brooke, but if she wants to go, let her go. It's not like you guys have any kind of future, anyway. It sucks, man, but you'll get through it."

Sawyer nodded slowly, staring down into his beer. A silence fell over the table and Sawyer swallowed thickly, trying to contain the pain churning through him at the idea of not having a future with Brooke.

"Holy shit," said Amelia softly, and he glanced up at her. "You really do love her, don't you?"

"Yeah."

"Then give her some space. She's been through a lot. She lost her grandmother. Got shot at and then suspended less than a month into the job, all while putting up with your grumpy ass. Give it all time. If it's meant to work out, you'll find a way." She bit her lip, toying with the ring on her necklace. "Love—real, true love—is rare and special, and if that's what you guys have, that's worth fighting for. Give her space, but if you love her, don't give up."

"Oh my God, barf," said Jack, before making loud gagging noises like he was going to throw up.

Amelia ignored him and pointed at Sawyer with a nacho, salsa dripping onto the table. "Do you want to give up on a future with Brooke, yes or no?"

"No."

She smiled. "Then you'll figure it out. You're smarter than you look."

"DO YOU THINK Ben and Jerry are actually two recently single women who enjoy eating their feelings as opposed to being hippies from Vermont?" Brooke asked around a mouthful of Cherry Garcia.

Dani nodded, pointing at her with her spoon. "Solid theory. Entirely possible."

Hey, at least her theories were still solid even if nothing else in her life was. Setting the half-eaten pint of ice cream down on the coffee table in front of her couch, she leaned forward, reaching for both the remote and her glass of wine.

On her way home from the gym—where she'd spent hours over the past few days trying to sweat out her troubles—she'd grabbed a bottle of wine, but the idea of drinking it by herself had been too depressing, so she'd finally taken Dani up on her offer to come over. The TV played quietly in the background, some stupid horror movie where teenagers got chased through the woods before getting hacked to pieces by a psychopath.

It fit Brooke's current mood perfectly.

Readjusting the blanket on her lap, she took a sip of her wine. It felt odd to sit still. She'd been trying hard to keep busy so that her brain wouldn't pull her down a rabbit hole she was scared she wouldn't emerge from. She'd been working out. Her apartment was spotless. She'd walked around the city, not wanting to be alone in her apartment once it was clean. She'd checked out a stack of thick books from the library. She'd even treated herself to a mani-pedi.

And temporarily, it had worked, and for little pockets of time she'd been able to forget how much she missed Sawyer. How much she missed Nan. How worried she was she'd never get her job back, that she'd be demoted, even fired. That her life as she knew it was over, everything good gone. In the past.

Something broke open inside her, the pressure of everything too much to hold, and she started to cry.

"Oh shit," said Dani, hastily setting her own ice cream down. She waved her hands in front of her in a panicked motion. "Uh . . ." She moved closer and rubbed Brooke's back. "Blink twice if you want me to hunt the bastard down and kill him."

That was enough for Brooke to choke out a laugh, and she grabbed some Kleenex from the half-used box on the floor. "No, but I appreciate the offer."

"I hate seeing you like this, Brooke. This isn't you."

Brooke frowned. "Yeah, well, this is me right now."

Dani studied her for several seconds and then sighed. "Listen, you want some tough love?"

"No," Brooke said, her voice sounding maybe a little pitiful.

"Too bad."

Brooke pulled her knees up to her chest and laid her head on them, looking at Dani, waiting. Dani reached forward and pushed Brooke's hair out of her eyes.

"I'm not gonna lie. There are several things that really, really suck right now. I'm sorry that you lost Nan. I'm sorry your cover got blown. I'm sorry you got suspended. All of that really fucking blows. And yes, Sawyer screwed up. But what you did, pushing him away like that, just ending it, was kinda the emotional equivalent of burning your house down because there's a spider in it. I'm not saying that you don't have shit—some heavy shit—that you're justifiably upset and pissed and worried about. All I'm saying is that maybe—just maybe—throwing your relationship with Sawyer into the garbage disposal because of it wasn't the best move."

"You think I overreacted."

Dani smiled sympathetically and held her thumb and forefinger about half an inch apart. "Maybe a little, yeah."

Brooke pursed her lips, thinking. "Maybe, but I think the way you're summing it up is overly simplistic." She sat up, worrying the blanket between her fingers. "I can't change Nan being gone. It hurts, but I know with time it'll hurt less. I can't take back how the mission went sideways. So the only problem I can really address is the suspension, and I just don't see how I have a hope in hell of being reinstated if I'm still in the relationship that got me suspended in the first place. I can't get my career back on track *and* be with Sawyer. End of story."

Dani frowned, staring at the carpet. After a second, she rubbed a hand over her mouth and shook her head. "Yeah, no, I call bullshit."

"You call bullshit on my logic?"

"I do. Because it's not logic. You're scared and looking for an excuse to run."

Brooke clenched the blanket in her fists and let out a frustrated groan. "Why does everyone keep telling me that?"

Dani shrugged. "Because that's what you do. You love Sawyer, and that so obviously scares the shit out of you."

"No, I don't," she lied, not wanting to admit that Dani was right and face what she'd done.

"Yeah, you do. And guess what, B? Not everyone you love will die or leave you. Sometimes, love really does mean forever and always."

And in that moment, it hit her. Everything became crystal clear, and she felt like an idiot for not realizing it sooner. The reason she'd always dated loser guys, the reason her relationship with Sawyer scared her so much, was because she was afraid to love. Because loving meant excruciating pain when you lost that person. She'd loved her parents, and they were gone. She'd loved her grandfather, and he was gone. She'd loved Nan, and now she was gone too. And so while insisting that she didn't want to end up alone, she'd dated guy after guy who she couldn't possibly fall for, because when it ended, she'd walk away with her heart intact.

"You sound like a diamond commercial."

"If you keep running scared, you'll stay closed off to ever finding diamond commercial love. It could be Sawyer. But you'll never know if you don't give him the chance to try. And I get it. Giving him the chance means being vulnerable. It means trusting. And those are hard things."

Dani's words hit home and it felt as though someone had ripped Brooke's chest in two. With a gasping sob, she started to cry again. She'd found a man who loved her for exactly who she was, and she'd thrown it away because she was scared to let him in. After her years of complaining about ending up alone and never finding anyone, she'd found someone, maybe even *the one*, and she'd gotten in her own way and torn it to pieces.

"I broke it. I broke us and he probably hates me now," she said between sobs. For a minute or two, Dani let her cry before tucking her fingers under Brooke's chin and forcing her to look up.

"So get him back."

"You don't understand. I was so angry about every-thing, and so scared, and I was really shitty to him." Her stomach turned as she remembered the hurt he'd tried to hide. The way he'd told her he loved her. The tender way he'd looked after her when she was a mess over Nan.

"What would Nan tell you if she was here?"

Brooke forced herself to take a deep breath, wiping at her eyes. Remembering her letter, and the way she'd known what Brooke would need to hear before she'd even known it herself. "She'd tell me not to be afraid to let him in. That sometimes love is messy, but you can't make an omelet without a few broken eggs along the way. That if it's worth fighting for, I should put on my big girl panties and fight."

"Damn right she would."

Brooke took a healthy gulp of her wine. Maybe by morning she'd have figured out a way to unbreak what she'd broken.

SAWYER STEPPED OUT of his truck into the cool eve-ning air, his sweaty workout clothes sticking to his skin. Jack was a member at the Buckhead Fight Club and had invited him to come hit stuff with him, and he had to admit, hitting stuff had felt really freaking good. Hadn't made him hurt any less, but the temporary catharsis had been a nice distraction from the fact that his heart felt like it had gone through a meat grinder.

The past few days had seemed to stretch on interminably as Sawyer had tried to lift himself out of his funk. With nothing to distract him—no work, no Brooke—every minute felt like an hour. He'd wanted to head up to the cabin, but had thought the recent memories of Brooke there might make it suck, and he wanted to give them a chance to fade before going back. He'd been following Amelia's advice, giving Brooke space. He knew they'd walked away angry, but he wasn't angry anymore. He just missed her, and hoped she was okay. More than once he'd been tempted to call her or text her, but that wasn't exactly giving her space. So he waited and checked his phone obsessively. Hoping that maybe she missed him too and they could figure their shit out. She'd told him that she didn't love him, but he knew that was bullshit. She did. She wouldn't have freaked the hell out if she didn't.

He slowed his steps as he strode through the parking lot, keys jingling in his hand. Pausing, he did a slow visual sweep of the area. Something had made the hair on the back of his neck stand up. A creeping sensation, almost as though he was being watched.

Which was stupid. The parking lot was empty. It was just the chill in the night air and his overactive cop brain. Shaking his head at himself, he pulled his phone out of his pocket and headed toward his building.

Nothing new from Brooke. He'd have to ask Amelia how much longer he was expected to give her space, because *damn* did he want to call her just to hear her voice.

Sawyer felt something hit his back, and then his entire body went stiff as pain shot through him. He dropped his phone and even though he tried to move, tried to prevent himself from falling to the ground, he couldn't make his body obey.

He knew this sensation. He was being Tased.

Pain thundered through him as the shock continued and he hit the ground, hard. A black cloth sack came over his head just as the amps stopped tormenting him. He yelled as he kicked out and swung, but he couldn't see anything, and he only connected with empty air. He felt the pinch of a needle in his arm and wooziness hit almost immediately.

"Get him in the van," he heard someone say just before he passed out.

Chapter Twenty-Three

BROOKE YAWNED, FLIPPING through the channel guide and looking for something to watch besides lame sitcoms, trashy reality TV, or unrealistic cop dramas. She shut the TV off. It was no use. She was out of distractions, and needed to figure out a plan to get both Sawyer and her job back.

She opened up the note-taking app on her phone and typed in the words "Step 1" and then stared at the screen. As she stared, her phone started to ring with a call from an unknown number.

She swiped her finger across the screen. If this was her cell provider trying to get her to upgrade her plan again, so help her God . . .

"Hello?"

"Hiya Brooke."

Her blood ran cold as everything inside her went

very, very still. She recognized that voice. That smooth, sarcastic baritone. The Sheriff.

"How'd you get this number?" she asked, her fingers gripping her phone tightly.

"It was in Matthews's phone."

Her heart beat with a heavy, sick thudding in her chest. "Why do you have Sawyer's phone?"

"Because he's here, hanging out with us. Say hi, Sawyer!"

A pain-filled scream came from somewhere in the distance and then the Sheriff came on the line. "Sorry, he's a little busy right now. Being tortured."

"Why did you call me? What do you want?" she asked, shooting to her feet. She moved around her apartment, tugging on her shoes and unlocking the safe in her bedroom to remove her Beretta M9. Just because she'd handed in her service weapon didn't mean she was defenseless.

Another scream from Sawyer in the background, unmistakably his voice. Her stomach lurched.

"I called you because it's fun to gloat. I don't want a damn thing from you, sweetheart. Just wanted to make it clear what happens when you try to fuck us." He laughed. "We fuck you right back, and our dick's *so* much bigger, so it might hurt a little." Sawyer screamed again. "Or a lot. Toodles." The line went dead.

Panic started to rise, but she shoved it down, forcing herself to detach the way she would on the job. Immediately, a checklist formed. Grab an extra clip for the M9.

Call both Jack and Amelia on her way to the station. Do whatever it took to trace the call, find Sawyer and get him the hell out of there. Open a can of whoop ass on the cartel. Beg forgiveness for it all after.

Having a plan and a purpose for the first time in almost a week made her eerily calm, despite the danger of the situation. Despite the fact that she'd just heard the man she loved being tortured. She shoved the extra ammo in her back pocket, slipped her gun into her waistband and sprinted for her car, phone in hand.

As she ran, two things occurred to her. One: there was a high probability that this was a trap. Why else would someone as savvy as the Sheriff contact her? He probably wanted her to trace the call in order lure HEAT into a dangerous situation where the cartel would have the upper hand. But trap or not, Sawyer needed them and she sure as hell wasn't going to leave him in Baracoa's hands. Two: how had he known her name? Jesse had introduced her as Britney in the hotel suite.

Clearly, the cartel knew more than they'd let on. Maybe a lot more.

Brooke pulled out of the parking lot, her tires squealing as she turned onto the street. As she wove through traffic, she dialed Jack, who answered after a couple of rings.

"Hey, I was wondering when I'd hear from you."

"Baracoa has Sawyer. I need your help."

"What? What are you talking about?"

"The Sheriff just called me, taunting me, saying

that they have him. I could hear him screaming in the background." Bile rose in her throat at the memory of Sawyer's anguished shouts.

"Jesus fuck. I just saw him like . . . like less than two hours ago."

"Where?"

"We went to a boxing gym together."

"Did he say he was going anywhere after?"

"No, I think he was just going home."

"Okay. We need to try to trace the call so we can find him. Also, see if there are security cameras in and around his condo complex. If we can't trace the call, maybe we can trace plates or something. Shit."

"Why would he have called you?"

"I don't know. He said it was to gloat, and to warn us. I think it might be a trap."

"Yeah. That was my thought too." She heard the roar of an engine in the background. "I'll meet you at the station. I assume you're on your way?"

"Yeah, I'll be there in ten minutes."

There was a pause. "You know showing up at the station while suspended breaks the code of ethics, right?"

"I don't give a shit. Sawyer needs us. And besides, I already broke it when I started dating my partner."

"I'll call Ames. I think she's still at the station."

"Good. Trap or not, we need to figure out a way to get him back."

"We will, Simmons. I promise."

A few minutes later, she pulled into the parking lot, threw her car into Park and ran toward the building. Just as she realized she wouldn't be getting far without her keycard, the door opened. Amelia waved her inside.

"What the fuck's going on?" she said as they headed for the stairs, not wasting time on the elevator.

"The Sheriff called me. I think it's a trap, but it doesn't matter. They have Sawyer."

Amelia nodded, a grim expression on her face. "Not for long, they fucking don't."

The bullpen was only about half-full, many of the detectives either on assignment or gone for the day. As they moved toward Amelia's desk, the captain came out of his office.

"Simmons! Want to explain what you're doing here?"

Jack stepped out of the elevator. "Baracoa has Sawyer. We need to trace the call they made to Brooke's cell phone so we can get him back."

The captain rubbed a hand over his head, his eyes bouncing back and forth between them as Brooke silently prayed he wouldn't fight them on this.

"You're sure?" he asked, leveling his gaze at her.

She extended her phone toward him. "I heard him screaming in the background. I know it was him. If we don't move on this, he's dead." A piece of her heart shriveled up and turned to ash just thinking of it.

"Goddammit," said the captain as he took her phone from her. "Who's your provider?"

She told him and the captain nodded. "Let me make

a call. Ward, call the SWAT sergeant and have them on standby."

Jack nodded and picked up his desk phone, his features tight.

"If we can't get a location from that, we can get an emergency warrant to trace Sawyer's phone, and for any security camera footage from around where we think he was taken," said Amelia.

The captain started back toward his office. "Go home, Simmons. You can't be here."

She ignored him and sat down in her desk chair, drumming her fingers on the desk. Feeling helpless and useless as they waited to see if they could ping the location of the cell that made the call. The sounds of Sawyer's screams echoed through her brain and made her want to hurt someone. Not just punish them. Not just put them in jail. Hurt them.

The minutes stretched on as they waited, and finally, after maybe ten minutes, the captain emerged from his office, a piece of paper in his hands. "We've got the location. Notify SWAT. It's a warehouse off Fulton. We're going in."

Brooke rose from her seat and the captain shook his head. "Not you. You shouldn't even be here."

She opened her mouth and spoke to her commanding officer in a way that would've surprised her if she'd had room to feel anything besides fear and determination. "You wouldn't even have this intel without me, so suspended or not, I'm a part of this. There's no way in hell I'm letting you go in without me, so if you want me to stay here, you're gonna have to cuff me and lock me up. I'm a part of this team. I'm damn good at what I do and leaving me behind would be a mistake." She ground her teeth together, clinging to the anger flaring through her. "Fucking no one kidnaps *my boyfriend* and gets away with it." She stared at the captain, who gave her a once-over and then turned and walked back into his office. When he reemerged a few seconds later, he tossed something to her. She caught it, staring down at her badge.

He nodded at her. "Let's go."

Sawyer came to with a gasp as ice cold water hit his face. Blinking rapidly, he tried to wipe his eyes, but couldn't move his hands from behind his back. The cold, concrete floor bit into his skin. His head throbbed and a shiver wracked him as he struggled to sit up. The room came into focus around him as rough hands hauled him to his knees.

He must've passed out. They hadn't even told him what they wanted from him. They'd hauled his ass into this freezing warehouse, stripped his shirt off and taken turns shocking him with a car battery and holding his head underwater. Pain and panic all twisted together, and the only thing that had kept him from begging them to shoot him, to end it all and take the pain away, was the thought that if he gave in, he'd never see Brooke again.

"Make sure he suffers." Hernandez's voice, moving away. The room was dark with a stark white light shining down on the small space where Sawyer knelt. He blinked again and looked around, catching sight of a small metal table covered in tools and weapons.

Shit. Apparently it was time for round two.

Domingo Da Silva crouched in front of him. "Welcome back, pig." He backhanded Sawyer across the face, causing his vision to fade out as pain exploded across his cheek and jaw. Unstable, he fell back and the same rough hands as before lifted him back into place. "Now that you've had a taste, you're going to talk. Then maybe I'll let you die quickly."

Sawyer sneered at him, his face throbbing. "I'm not telling you shit."

Domingo laughed. "That's what they all say." He rose and pulled a thick knife with serrated edges from the table. "That's what they all say. All these little birdies who think they don't want to sing." He pressed the tip of the knife against Sawyer's chest and then walked around him in a slow circle, dragging the point of the knife across his skin, leaving a scorching hot trail behind him. A warm trickle of blood ran down his skin, and Sawyer gritted his teeth, refusing to react. Refusing to scream the way he had with the car battery's volts charging through his body, leaving him feeling charred from the inside out.

Domingo laughed again. "But you just have to find the right song, and they all make such beautiful . . . *music.*" On the last word, he slid the blade into Sawyer's shoulder, leaving it in place. Sawyer grunted, trying to breathe through the searing hot pain coursing through him.

"Who's the girl?"

Sawyer glared up at him, his jaw working against the pain-filled groan threatening to break free. His entire arm felt like it was on fire. Blood dripped down from his wound and onto the floor. "What girl?"

"The girl who was with you the other night at the hotel. The other cop."

Sawyer just stared at the floor, not answering. He closed his eyes and conjured up images of everyone he cared about. His parents. His brothers. Jack and Amelia. Brooke. Silently saying goodbye to each of them, because this was it. They were going to kill him, because no fucking way was he telling them a goddamn thing about Brooke. If his last act was to keep her safe, so be it.

Domingo threw another bucket of ice water on him, making him shiver and sending pain coursing through his shoulder and down his arm. "Talk. Now. The girl. Her name. Her address."

Sawyer spit on the floor. "What girl?"

Domingo reached forward and yanked the knife out, making Sawyer cry out through gritted teeth. Blood rushed down his arm and chest, pulsing from the wound. "Don't be stupid. Tell us who she is. That's the only way to make the pain stop." He thrust a finger into Sawyer's wound, twisting and scraping. He screamed, needing to let out the pain. The room dimmed around him and he swayed on his knees.

"Just fucking kill me. I'm not telling you anything about her. I'll die before I talk."

At least he'd see Ryan again soon. The thought was enough to bring a smile to his face just as Domingo's fist connected with his temple. Two thoughts ran through his mind before he slipped back into the darkness.

Brooke, I love you. Ryan, I'm coming, man.

Chapter Twenty-Four

Brooke hopped out of the van before it had come to a complete stop, adjusting her Kevlar vest and unholstering her Glock. Damn, but it felt good to have her service weapon back in her hands, loaded and ready to go. But even though the captain had given it back to her, her Beretta was still tucked into her waistband. It never hurt to have backup.

At the thought, her eyes darted around the warehouse's parking lot. Jack, Amelia and the captain were all there, all clad in matching Kevlar, as well as two vans full of SWAT guys. Granted, the SWAT guys were all giving her the cold shoulder, but she'd expected that, and frankly, she didn't care. All she cared about was getting Sawyer out of there.

If this was a trap, it was a very poorly guarded one. There were floodlights on in the parking lot, no visible security around the small building. It wasn't like Baracoa to be sloppy, and she had to wonder what the hell was going on. Why had the Sheriff called her? How had he known her name?

The SWAT sergeant waved everyone over and they huddled around in a tense circle. The city's night sounds filled the air around them. The whirring rush of nearby traffic. The roar of a semi truck's engine. The distant clanging of a railroad crossing. Brooke wiped her sweaty palms on her thighs as she eyed the building behind them. Sawyer was in there. In pain. Alone.

Please don't let us be too late.

If they weren't too late, she'd do whatever it took to fix things between them. Anything to know that she had a shot at a future with him. Because in a situation like this, the truth became obvious. Simple. She loved him, and the idea of losing him was a million times scarier than loving him.

The SWAT leader was a grizzled-looking man in his early forties, tall and lean with thick brown hair falling around his shoulders, his temples and beard streaked with gray. "Here's what we know. One of our own, Detective Sawyer Matthews, is being held in that warehouse. We don't know how many cartel members are in there, or if, given the circumstances of how we were able to locate Matthews, we're walking into a trap. Recon of the building indicates two entrances, one on the east side of the building, another on the west side. We're going to divide up. Alpha team and HEAT will take the west entrance. Omega team will take the east entrance. The objective is to get Matthews out. You see cartel members, you have clearance to shoot to kill, but this isn't a hunting trip. This is a snatch-and-grab.

"Once we breach, move in, move fast. We don't know what the layout is inside. If there are separate rooms, clear in teams of two and move on. The faster we move, the better chance we have of getting Matthews out of there alive. Move in."

Half of the SWAT members went around to the far side of the building. Brooke moved forward with her team, laser-focused on the building ahead of her. Not letting herself feel guilty or afraid. Not letting herself feel anything but pissed off and determined. They'd rescue Sawyer and she'd make things right. That was the only way this could end.

One of the SWAT guys fired what looked like a cannon at the door, the explosion shattering the quiet of the night.

"Atlanta Police! Everyone get down on the ground!" the captain shouted, his gun trained ahead of him as he moved swiftly into the building. Brooke was only a half step behind him, blinking as her eyes adjusted to the semidarkness of the warehouse. She did a visual sweep of the space, her heart vaulting into her throat when she spotted Sawyer.

"There, far corner!" she called, thrusting her chin in the direction of where Sawyer's very, very still frame lay on the floor. She started to run toward him, and gunfire erupted from the far side of the warehouse, right around where Omega team would've breached.

A metal door just to her right slid back and several armed cartel members spilled out. From somewhere to her left, Jack fired, dropping a few of them. "Go," he called to her. "Go get him. We've got this."

Amelia tossed a smoke bomb toward the cartel members and then nodded at Brooke. "We'll cover you. Go!"

Glancing once over her shoulder, Brooke sprinted across the warehouse, gunfire echoing out in staccato bursts. She was less than ten feet away from Sawyer when her feet went out from under her and a hand yanked her hair back. She felt the biting press of a knife against her throat. "You move, he dies," said a voice she didn't recognize.

Sawyer stirred on the floor, the light catching on the pool of blood around his shirtless body.

"You picked the wrong crew to fuck with," she said, and he laughed, pressing the knife in a bit harder.

"I should've known you'd come. We tried and tried to get him to tell us your name, where to find you, but he wouldn't. You should've heard him scream."

In a series of rapid movements, Brooke stomped on her assailant's foot and twisted his wrist, causing him to drop the knife. He grabbed at her, but she chucked her weight forward, sending her attacker off balance, and then kicked backward, catching him in the leg. He grabbed for her again, and the knife scraped against her skin, a sharp, rasping sting that she barely felt as she whirled and, with a steady hand, pumped two shots into Domingo Da Silva's chest. He crumpled to the floor and she ran to Sawyer. Shouts and gunfire bounced across the room.

Dropping to her knees, she pressed a shaking hand to his throat, relief flooding her when she felt his pulse. His chest rose and fell, and she left her hand on him as she took stock of his injuries. His eye was black, his lip split and swollen. Dried blood trickled from his ear. Angry red burn marks marred his chest. His hair was soaked, not with sweat, but water. Worst of all was the stab wound in his shoulder. She shook him, trying to rouse him.

"Sawyer. Sawyer! Come on, Sawyer. We've gotta get you out of here."

He moaned but didn't open his eyes. He wasn't responding, and she needed to wake him if she had a hope of getting him out of here. She didn't want to, but she'd have to try a painful sternal rub.

"I'm sorry," she whispered as she made a fist and pressed her knuckles against his sternum, then rubbed up and down, applying pressure.

He grunted and then grabbed her fist, his eyes flying open.

"It's me. It's me," she said, not trying to pull her fist away.

A nearby wooden crate splintered as flying bullets chewed through it.

"Brooke," he said, his voice raw.

She nodded. "Can you get up? We gotta get out of here."

"You think I'm going to just let you walk out of here?" She spun to see Ernesto Hernandez standing a few feet away, a gun trained directly at her head.

Behind her, she felt Sawyer slip her Beretta out of her waistband. She smiled. "No. I think he's going to fucking kill you."

Sawyer sat up and pumped three shots into Hernandez. With an anguished cry, he dropped to the floor. "Fuck you," Sawyer ground out, and then spat on the floor.

With quick movements, Brooke stripped off her vest and slipped it on over Sawyer's head, adjusting the Velcro straps gingerly around his injuries as fast as she could.

"No, Simmons," he protested, shaking his head woozily. "Keep your vest on."

"I'll be fine. I'm not half-unconscious. You are. Come on," she said, slipping Sawyer's arm over her shoulders. "Let's go."

Her legs shook with the effort it took to help him off the ground. She was strong, but Sawyer was over two hundred pounds and was having trouble supporting himself. The gunfire started to die off and Jack ran over, taking Sawyer's other arm and laying it over his shoulder.

Sawyer's head swiveled in Jack's direction. "Hey, Posh," he said.

Jack let out a grim laugh. "Shut up and walk, Matthews."

With a groan, Sawyer started putting one foot in front of the other, his breath coming in sharp pants from between clenched teeth. They stuck close to the wall as they moved him toward the entrance, sweat cascading down Brooke's back.

Behind them, she could hear the SWAT team corralling the remaining cartel members. Sirens wailed in the distance, more reinforcements arriving. They stumbled out through the same door she'd come in, and Brooke gulped down several deep breaths of the cool night air. Her heart was beating so hard in her chest she thought it might break her ribs.

Amelia came running over, a huge, relieved smile lighting up her face. "Thank Christ," she said, her eyes dancing over Sawyer's injured body.

"I shot Hernandez," said Sawyer, lurching against her, and then Jack. "I did it, Ryan."

Amelia frantically waved the paramedics over, who ran up with a stretcher. Brooke's arms shook with the exertion of helping Jack load him onto the stretcher. She didn't get a chance to say anything to him before they rolled him into the waiting ambulance and tore off, sirens screaming.

"Any sign of the Sheriff?" she asked Amelia.

"I shot him in the ass, but he seems to have slithered away." Someone called to her, and she jogged away from Brooke, leaving her alone.

She suddenly felt as though she couldn't catch her breath and dropped her hands to her knees, hanging her head between her legs. A hand gently touched her back. She glanced up to see the captain.

"You did good in there, Simmons."

She nodded rapidly, trying to breathe through the adrenaline overload. "Thank you, sir." She looked over at the road, watching the fading lights of the ambulance as it turned a corner and disappeared. A set of keys appeared in her line of sight.

"They're taking him to Grady. Take one of the patrol cars and go."

She stood and took the keys, her entire body coursing with electricity. "Yeah?"

He nodded. "Yeah. Go."

She started running in the direction of the cruisers, glancing down at the keys in her hand to check the car number. "Thank you, sir!" she called over her shoulder.

She drove with her lights and sirens on the entire way.

EVERYTHING HURT. SAWYER'S face. His chest. His shoulder and arm. Pain covered him like a blanket, heavy and oppressive, and for a minute he lay still with his eyes closed, letting it swallow him up.

Flashes of memory came back to him. The sensation of the Taser coursing through his body. Water. No air. Drowning. Panic. Fear. Searing hot pain on his chest. His shoulder being ripped open.

Shooting Hernandez in the chest.

He managed to pull his heavy eyelids open. Hospital. He was in the hospital. He blinked a few times, trying to clear the fog.

Brooke stood at the window, her arms wrapped around herself, her back to him. She'd come for him. He didn't know how they'd found him, but she'd come. And now she was here, and that had to mean something.

His mind lurched back to her putting her vest on him. An intense emotion filled him and then overflowed, warming him from the inside out. Giving him more hope than he'd felt in days.

He cleared his throat and sat up a little, his shoulder throbbing. "Hey, Wilma."

She spun, her eyes wide and bright, her face pale, and then she ate up the distance between them in a few long strides. "Hey, Fred," she said softly, perching on the edge of his bed and taking one of his hands between both of hers.

For a minute, maybe longer, they just stared at each other, Brooke's fingers tracing over his knuckles.

"Thanks. For saving my ass," he said, swallowing thickly. "How did you find me?"

"The Sheriff called me to gloat that they'd taken you. We traced his location."

Sawyer frowned. Something wasn't adding up here. "He called you? But they were beating the shit out of me trying to find out who you were."

Brooke's confused frown mirrored his own. "Then why did he call me?"

Sawyer shook his head slowly, something else coming back to him. "Why did he kick my gun back toward me at the shoot-out at the hotel?"

Brooke's eyebrows rose. "Was he . . . was he helping us? That makes no sense."

"You're right. It doesn't." She shook her head. "We'll unpack it all later, with Jack and Amelia and the captain." He nodded and a silence fell between them. Brooke bit her lip, a nervousness he wasn't used to seeing flickering across her features.

"Sawyer, I . . . I'm so sorry."

He opened his mouth to tell her that he got it, that she had nothing to be sorry for, but she pressed a finger to his lips.

"Just let me say this, okay?"

He leaned back against his pillows, studying her. She was so beautiful. So strong and brave. Amazing, in every single way. The beeps on his heart monitor picked up.

"I've never been good at letting people in. Losing my parents was hard, and I think because of it, I walked around with these invisible shields up. I mean, I didn't even know I had them up a lot of the time. But I was protecting myself, because I knew how much it hurt to lose people you loved. I was scared to open myself up to someone." She paused and then shrugged. "And then you came along, and you challenged me on every level, and I didn't know what to do with that, because it was like . . . like my shields wouldn't hold. And I panicked. I thought maybe if I just held on long enough, I'd figure something out. But then I lost Nan, and everything just got so hard."

"Brooke, I—"

"I'm not done." She took a deep breath. "I liked being with you, from the moment I met you. Even when I wanted to strangle you, I liked being with you. And then things got more intense between us, and it freaked me out. So when we got caught, and got suspended, I didn't know what else to do besides push you away." She looked down and shook her head. "But that was a mistake. A huge mistake. Because I love you, Sawyer. I love you so damn much."

She looked at him with glistening eyes, and even though she'd said a lot, he could see all the things she wasn't saying, too. She'd been scared to lose him, and hated that that's what it had taken to wake her up.

He reached out to tuck a strand of hair behind her ear, grimacing. "I know."

"Are we . . . I mean . . . can you forgive me? I'm so sorry. I love you." She let out a small laugh. "Now I can't seem to stop saying it."

"Yeah, Brooke. I forgive you. Because that's what you do when you love someone." He tipped her chin up, forcing her to meet his eyes. "I've fucked up. You've fucked up. We're human. It'll probably happen again. But here's the thing. You, Brooke Simmons, are it for me. And I think I've known that since the night I met you. So I'll be an asshole caveman, and you can try to cut and run, but we're in this together. I'm not going anywhere, and I'm not giving up on you." He tugged her close, brushing a kiss over her lips. "I don't know if I believe in fate, but I sure as fuck believe in us."

She kissed him back, her lips warm and gentle against his. He pulled her against him, not caring that it hurt. He was willing to put up with a lot on what had turned out to be the best-worst day of his life.

DETECTIVE SAWYER MATTHEWS stood stiffly at attention as sweat trickled between his shoulder blades. The spotlight shone down on the stage, blinding him so he could see only the first few rows of people seated in the main hall of the Georgia Congress Center. Captain Hill stood at the podium on the far end of the stage, his voice booming as he spoke into the microphone.

"Today, we pay tribute to two members of our own who risked their lives to make our city a safer place. We are all inordinately proud of Detectives Sawyer Matthews and Brooke Simmons."

Sawyer glanced over at Brooke, wondering if she found this moment as surreal as he did. She stared straight ahead, her throat working as she swallowed. They'd both been reinstated shortly after the rescue, but had been told they'd need to switch partners. In the future, Brooke would work with Jack, while Sawyer would work with Amelia. So far, the new pairings were going well.

"These detectives exhibited bravery in the face of extreme danger and loyalty to fellow officers, going above and beyond the call of duty. They also did so while defying orders. Apparently, the key to getting the best out of your team is to tell them they can't do something."

Laughter rippled through the crowd and Sawyer glanced down, hiding his smile.

"Because of their bravery, one of the most dangerous drug cartels in Atlanta's history has been crippled. Because of their honor, our city is now a safer place. Because of their commitment, they've shown others what it means to be part of a team. And so, I invite you all to stand as we recognize Detective Sawyer Matthews and Detective Brooke Simmons as recipients of the Atlanta Police Medal of Honor."

Being awarded the medal while standing beside Brooke was one of the happiest, proudest moments of Sawyer's life. Even though he wasn't done with his grief over Ryan, he was working through it. Slowly, with Brooke by his side, he was learning to live again.

After the ceremony and shaking hands with the brass, he grabbed Brooke's hand and led her through the crowd, excited to introduce her to his family—his parents and his brothers, who'd all come up in support.

They only had time for brief introductions before he and Brooke were called away for pictures. But it didn't matter. He was willing to bet his shiny new medal that they'd be seeing a lot more of Brooke in the months and years to come.

After he'd been released from the hospital, he'd asked Brooke if he could stay with her. The cartel had known where to find him, leaving him feeling unsafe, and some of the key members, including the Sheriff, were still out there, so he wasn't willing to take any chances. It had been a month, and he was still healing from his last run-in with them.

"Let me know when you're ready to get out of here," Brooke said once they'd finished posing for photographs with the chief and members of the police board. "I have a surprise waiting for you at home."

That was all it took to start the round of good-byes—to his family, to Jack and Amelia, to the captain—before he was practically dragging Brooke back to his truck. In the recent past, her surprises had included a massage—which had ended in sex. Cooking a meal for him wearing nothing but an apron—that had also ended in sex. Giving him an up-close-and-personal demonstration of her vibrator—you'd better believe that had ended in sex.

Yeah, it was a safe bet that Brooke only had to say the word *surprise* and he was half-hard.

When they arrived back at her place, she tossed

her keys on the little table by her front door and then pointed at him. "Strip down to your boxers and sit on the couch." She disappeared into her bedroom.

He didn't know what she had planned, but he liked where this was going. As he tossed his clothes on the floor, a wide grin spread across his face. If someone had told him a couple of months ago that life could be this good, he wouldn't have believed them. Wouldn't have believed that he'd be in a better place with his grief over Ryan. Not over it, necessarily, but finally in a healthy enough space to start processing it. He wouldn't have believed that he'd be awarded the Medal of Honor for killing the man responsible for Ryan's death. And he *definitely* wouldn't have believed that he'd found the love of his life.

Yeah. Life was pretty fucking great.

He sat down on the couch, spreading his arms out over the back of it. His shoulder still ached, but he'd made good progress with his physical therapy. Within a week or two, it probably wouldn't hurt nearly as much anymore.

Music started playing from the little Bluetooth speaker on Brooke's coffee table, and he recognized the song instantly as "Bad Girls." And then Brooke appeared in the doorway, wearing her police hat, her old uniform shirt, a corset, and black lace panties.

She cocked her hip and smiled at him, a coy, sexy smile that promised everything good. "I figured it was about time I return the favor and give you a show," she said, taking a few slow, sexy steps toward him.

"Yeah? You want some pointers?"

She stepped up in front of him and turned in a slow circle, running her hands up her body and into her hair, tossing her hat aside and letting her hair fall around her shoulders. Her shirt slipped down her shoulder, exposing her creamy skin. "Do I look like I need some pointers?"

He made a low rumbling sound and reached for her, needing to touch her. He pulled her into his lap, his cock twitching to life at the feel of her pressed against him.

"No," he said as she worked her hips against him, popping open the first few clasps on her corset in time with the music. "I think you're perfect."

She leaned forward and kissed him, a hot, lingering kiss that promised all kinds of filthy things. "I should get that in writing."

"You're not supposed to kiss the clients," he teased, his eyes raking over her. Savoring this insanely gorgeous woman he'd somehow earned.

"What can I say, Matthews? You bring out the rule-breaker in me."

She tossed her police shirt to the floor and ground against him. "Was it worth it?" he asked, tugging her earlobe between his teeth.

She stilled and cupped his cheek, meeting his eyes. "Yeah, Sawyer. You were worth it. Every maddening second. Now help me get this corset off."

Don't miss the next suspenseful, sexy romance in the Blue HEAT series!

SCHOOLED

Coming soon!

Jack Ward is one of Atlanta's most successful detectives, and he's on a mission: bring an end to the drug cartel responsible for the death of his friend and colleague. While tracking the financials of several shell corporations believed to be tied to the operation, Jack spots an anomaly, with funds being diverted to an elite private preschool. The best way to get the information he needs is to go undercover as a teacher at the school. For designer-suit-wearing Jack, a preschool is the last place he wants to be, but he'll do anything for intel, including getting close to the gorgeous assistant principal . . .

DETECTIVE JACK WARD slowly stretched his arms above his head without opening his eyes, basking in the last few seconds of the warm, hazy space between sleep and wakefulness. As he lowered his hands back down, his fingers brushed the bare skin of a naked female back, warm and smooth. He felt Simone stir and he opened his eyes, turning his head on the pillow to look at her. She shot him a sleepy, sated smile.

"Morning," she whispered, snuggling deeper into her pillow. Her big brown eyes drifted closed again, the silhouetted feminine planes of her face just visible in the shadowy light spilling in through the edges of the blinds covering the floor-to-ceiling windows. Just then, the automatic shades began to open with a soft whir, and Jack sat up with a sighing groan, pushing a hand through his hair as he squinted at his watch. It was already 7:30.

"Damn," he whispered, both at the fact that it was time to get up and that Simone had just stretched, causing the white sheet to fall below her full breasts topped with delectable light brown nipples. Despite all the fun they'd had the previous evening, his cock twitched at the sight. At the thought of last night, he glanced to his right, trying to remember the name of the stunning redhead Simone had brought over with her. Carla? Carly?

Carmen? Something with a "car"—he was about ninety percent sure. He stared at the sheet of red hair spilling over the white pillow, wondering if it should bother him a lot more than it did that he couldn't. Shit.

With careful movements, he crawled to the edge of the bed, stepping around the piles of discarded clothes and condom wrappers, leaving the two naked women sleeping in his California king, sheets rumpled around them. The corner of his mouth kicked up, a self-satisfied smile breaking through his morning fogginess. Even though there were two of them and only one of him, he was the one who'd worn them out, not the other way around. He quickly picked up the condom wrappers, not wanting to leave them for Mildred to deal with later. He stepped into the bathroom, closing the door with a quiet snick behind him.

After tossing the wrappers, he opened the large glass shower door and reached inside, turning the water on. It flowed from the massive waterfall showerhead, the water pattering softly against the marble. A tendril of steam curled up over the glass and Jack stepped under the spray, washing away last night's debauchery.

Jack stretched as the hot water worked its magic on his tired muscles, turning over the word debauchery in his head. Some people—maybe even most people—would associate the word with something dirty. Something wrong, and taboo. Something excessive. But he didn't see it that way. Debauchery, as far as he was concerned, was just another word for fun, and as long as that fun was consensual and wasn't hurting anyone, he didn't have any issues with it. It was immensely satisfying, living life to its fullest, experiencing all the pleasures it had to offer. Debauchery was freedom, and that freedom was everything. The key to happiness. Shackling himself to some woman—only one woman, God, he shuddered at the thought—because it was what society (and worse, his family) expected of him was a one-way ticket to misery. He'd seen that scenario play out first hand, more than once, and just like he'd turned his back on the family business, his refusal to settle down was both a declaration of freedom and act of pure rebellion.

He snorted and shook his head as he shut off the shower and stepped out, wondering how many other people walked away from running a multimillion dollar corporation in order to become a beat cop. But he'd never regretted his choice, not even for a single day. Thanks to his trust fund, he'd never have to worry about money for the rest of his life, and thanks to his job as an elite undercover detective, he got to spend his time cleaning up the streets of Atlanta. And because he'd refused to entertain his family's expectations, he got to wake up with not one, but two beautiful women in his bed.

His life, as far as Jack was concerned, was perfect. Complete. Not lacking in a single damn thing.

He dried off and wrapped a towel around his waist, then rubbed a bit of pomade between his palms and then ran his hands through his thick hair. He stepped out of the bathroom, happiness washing over him at the view.

The empty bottles of Moet & Chandon. The gorgeously sated women still sleeping in his bed. The sunshine streaming in through the windows of his penthouse apartment. He strode to them, taking in the impressive view of the Atlanta skyline. His city, the one he'd sworn to protect. A sense of pride and duty filled him, and he took a deep breath, soaking it in.

He heard a soft rustling noise from behind him and turned. Simone sat with the sheet twisted around her, her knees pulled up to her chest and her head resting on them. Her halo of messy curls fanned out around her pretty face.

"Enjoying the view?" she asked, her voice rusty with sleep. He nodded and she bit her lip. "Me too." A playful glint flickered in her eyes, and Jack shook his head and moved toward the walk-in closet on the far side of the room. He caught Simone's pout out of the corner of his eye and smiled.

He grabbed a black V-neck T-shirt and tugged it on over his head, and then pulled on boxers and a pair of jeans. As he zipped up, he glanced wistfully at his row of suits, knowing he'd catch endless amounts of shit from his team if he showed up to the station in Armani.

"Are you sure you have to go?" asked Simone, smiling ruefully at him. He gathered up his phone, wallet and keys and then slipped his badge into his pocket. He walked over to the bed and kissed her forehead.

"Bad guys aren't going to arrest themselves." And

while he didn't *need* this job, it needed him. What he did made a difference, and to him, that mattered.

"You mind if I hang out here for a bit? You know I love that bathtub." She pointed toward his master bath, which held a massive freestanding tub nestled against windows that provided a bird's eye view of the Buckhead neighborhood.

"Sure. You and . . ." His eyes darted to the redhead, who was still snoring softly. He winced slightly. "Your friend can stay as long as you like. Help yourself to whatever. Mildred will be here around noon, I think."

Simone smiled up at him, a challenge in her eyes. She pointed at her friend. "What's her name?"

Jack glanced at his watch. "Shit, look at the time. I'm gonna be late for work. Gotta run." He started to beat a hasty retreat, and a pillow hit him square in the back, followed by Simone's laughter.

"You, Jack Ward, are the fucking worst. Don't ever change."

RACHEL NOVAK YAWNED sleepily and snuggled deeper into her pillow. Her alarm hadn't gone off yet and she sighed contentedly, letting the tingling allure of sleep dance over her skin and start to pull her back under. But before she could fall back asleep, something deep in the recesses of her brain tugged at her. She stretched, her eyes opening, just a little. White light shone through the drapes over her window, bathing the room in a soft gray light.

Wait, light?

She bolted upright, fumbling for her phone, which had gone dead overnight, the charger not quite connected. Almost, but not fully inserted.

"Shit shit shit," she hissed, throwing the covers back and practically sprinting for the kitchen. 7:05. She'd overslept by thirty-five minutes on the first day of her promotion. Of course.

She did a panicked little dance in the center of her kitchen, her eyes darting to the fridge. No time to make a lunch—she'd have to make do with cafeteria food today. Mentally, she started running down her to-do list for the day as she ran for the shower, almost overshooting the door. She skidded and stubbed her toe against the door jamb.

"Motherfucker," she ground out between clenched teeth as she clutched at her foot and hopped awkwardly toward the shower, thrusting her arm in behind the shower curtain and cranking it on.

Right then, in that moment, Rachel faced what she knew was a crucial choice: wait for the water to heat up—wasting another five minutes given the plumbing in her 1930's bungalow—or stop by Starbucks for a Venti Blonde Roast to help fuel her through what was sure to be a tough morning.

Choice made, she whipped off her T-shirt and pajama shorts and stepped under the still freezing spray, letting out a series of incoherent yips and shrieks. Bobbing her head and moving her legs up and down, she went through her shower routine—shampoo, conditioner, body wash—as fast as humanly possible, shivering as the cool water slid over her skin. Just as she was rinsing the last of the soap away, the water started to warm, and while it was tempting to linger, the prospect of coffee was too alluring to ignore.

She pulled her hair up into a high, elegant ponytail and then threw on the clothes she'd set out the night before—black blazer, black blouse, and white pants. Thank God Sunday Rachel had been so much more organized and with it than Monday Rachel. Hurriedly, she applied a tiny bit of makeup, grabbed her bag and headed out the door, her pulse beating a frantic tempo in her ears. She glanced at the clock as she started her car. If traffic was on her side, she'd *just* have enough time for a Starbucks run without being more than a few minutes late. She sent up a silent prayer to the traffic gods as she merged onto I-20, heading first east and then north toward the swanky Buckhead area, where the prestigious Bowman School was located—the elite private preschool of which she was now, finally, after years of hard work, the newly minted assistant principal.

The running-late-woefully-undercaffeinated assistant principal. But thankfully, traffic wasn't only on her side, but lighter than usual, probably thanks to people still being on Christmas vacation. She pulled into the Starbucks parking lot only three minutes behind her normal schedule.

Almost of their own volition, her eyes scanned the parking lot, her stomach doing a little flip when she spotted the vintage red Ferrari in the next row over. She pulled into an empty space and parked her car, grabbing her purse and hurrying inside.

For coffee. Not because she was hoping to catch a glimpse of *him*. He of the blond hair, blue eyes, gorgeous body and dangerous smile. Sometimes, while she waited in line and stared covertly at him, she made up stories about him. His name, his job, the different ways he'd approach her and sweep her off her feet. That was the point where the daydream verged into fantasy territory, given that if a man actually asked Rachel out, she wouldn't have the first clue what to say. Was she lonely? Without a doubt. Did that mean she was ready to get back on the horse? Reply hazy, try again. And besides, as far as her Starbucks crush was concerned, it didn't matter, because she was pretty sure he'd never noticed her. Probably because any time he looked in her direction, she did her best to blend in with the furniture.

The little chime over the door rang as she was enveloped by the warm air and scent of freshly brewed coffee. Her mouth watered at the heavenly aroma, and her morning fog started to clear. Standing in line, she surreptitiously scanned the interior of the coffee shop, but didn't see Mr. Ferrari. Without her usual eye candy to keep her occupied while she waited, she took the opportunity to check her email and start to organize her day—orientation, paperwork, followed by the first step in their teacher complement evaluation. The school was growing, which meant new teachers would have to be added, and the sooner the better.

"Hi, can I take your order?" asked the smiling girl behind the counter.

"Can I please get a Venti Blonde Roast with room for dairy?"

The barista nodded as she grabbed a paper cup. "Anything else?"

Rachel shook her head and opened her large purse.

"That'll be $5.15."

"Yeah, sorry, hang on," she said as she rummaged with increasing franticness through her purse. Phone, keys, pens, tampons, an old parking ticket, a notebook, five lipsticks, crumpled up receipts, her school ID, sunglasses, an empty Tic-Tac container . . . but no wallet. She glanced longingly at the steaming cup of coffee waiting for her on the counter, letting out a pained little whimper, and started to take out items and set them on the counter, hoping against hope that if she cleared enough stuff out, her wallet would magically appear.

And then an image flashed suddenly through her head: her wallet sitting on her little computer desk at home, left there after a bit of online shopping yesterday.

Great. She'd have to forego her morning caffeine fix because of the new vibrator she'd ordered. It had *better* be worth it.

"Shit," she said, dumping her stuff back into her

purse, her cheeks hot. "I'm really sorry, but I left my wallet at home. I don't—"

"I'll get it," said a pleasant male voice from behind her. She spun, and there he was. Mr. Ferrari. Holding up his credit card. All the blood rushed out of Rachel's head, making her feel slightly dizzy.

"Oh, uh, you don't have to do that," she said, moving to tuck a strand of hair behind her ear before she remembered she'd put it up in a ponytail. She dropped her hand awkwardly to her side before deciding to cross her arms, and then just as quickly deciding to uncross them.

He shrugged, and her mouth watered slightly at the way his black T-shirt clung to his athletic frame. "I don't mind. Happens to the best of us." He smiled, and there was a kindness in his eyes that warmed her from the inside out. He leaned in a bit closer, extending his credit card to the barista. "Seems like you need it bad," he said, dropping his voice. It had a slight husky quality to it. A hint of expensive cologne hit her, making her legs feel wobbly beneath her. Up close, he was even better looking. Thick, dark blond hair. Startlingly bright blue eyes. Full lips, perfect teeth. Big, strong hands. Like a fantasy come to life.

He waved a hand in front of her. "Hellooo? You okay?"

"Seems . . . seems like I need what bad?" She licked her lips, blood rushing to her face as she spoke. This wasn't how any of her fantasies about finally speaking to him had gone. Maybe it was the fact that she'd left her wallet at home, or maybe it was the fact that he was actually talking to her, looking at her, but she felt off-kilter. As though a small breeze could send her toppling right over.

"Your coffee," he said, plucking it off the counter and handing it to her. "Monday morning and all that." The corner of his mouth tipped up, and the little lines around his eyes crinkled. Her stomach bottomed out somewhere around her ankles.

She took it, their fingers brushing. A shock jolted through her at the contact and she let go of the cup with a soft gasp.

It should've fallen to the floor, splattering over her pants, her shoes, making a mess. It should've but it didn't. Because Starbucks Ferrari Crush Man had cat-like reflexes, and as though it was nothing, dipped and shot out a hand, catching the cup before it could come to any harm.

He placed it back in her hand, this time wrapping her fingers securely around it. Their eyes met, and something passed between them. A spark. A flicker of awareness. A sensation that she hadn't felt in a long time unfurled in her belly, warm and sweet.

It was terrifying.

With a strained "thank you" tossed over her shoulder, Rachel bolted for the door and the safety of her car. Once inside, she slipped the cup into the holder and then gently beat her forehead against the steering wheel.

"Smooth, Rach. Real freaking smooth."

TARA WYATT is a contemporary romance and romantic suspense author. Known for her humor and steamy love scenes, Tara's writing has won several awards, including the Golden Quill Award and the Booksellers' Best Award, and has been nominated for the prestigious RITA® Award.

When she's not hanging out with your next book boyfriend, she can be found reading, watching movies, and drinking wine. A librarian by day and a romance writer by night, Tara lives in Hamilton, Ontario with the world's cutest dog and a husband who makes all her of her heroes look like chumps.

Discover great offers, exclusive offers, and more at hc.com.